Big London Dreams

by Clare Lydon

custard
books

First Edition July 2021
Published by Custard Books
Copyright © 2021 Clare Lydon
ISBN: 978-1-912019-20-5

Cover Design: Kevin Pruitt
Editor: Kelli Collins
Typesetting: Adrian McLaughlin

Find out more at: www.clarelydon.co.uk
Follow me on Twitter: @clarelydon
Follow me on Instagram: @clarefic

This is a work of fiction. All characters and happenings
in this publication are fictitious and any resemblance
to real persons (living or dead), locales or events
is purely coincidental.

Also by Clare Lydon

London Romance Series
London Calling (Book One)
This London Love (Book Two)
A Girl Called London (Book Three)
The London Of Us (Book Four)
London, Actually (Book Five)
Made In London (Book Six)
Hot London Nights (Book Seven)

Other Novels
A Taste Of Love
Before You Say I Do
Christmas In Mistletoe
Nothing To Lose: A Lesbian Romance
Once Upon A Princess
One Golden Summer
The Long Weekend
Twice In A Lifetime
You're My Kind

All I Want Series
All I Want For Christmas (Book One)
All I Want For Valentine's (Book Two)
All I Want For Spring (Book Three)
All I Want For Summer (Book Four)
All I Want For Autumn (Book Five)
All I Want Forever (Book Six)

Acknowledgements

I hope you enjoyed my first foray into historical romance — I know I did! Yes, it was challenging, but I loved discovering a world before my time. Plus, despite claiming to dislike history, my natural nosiness meant I loved finding out how people used to live. Particularly queer people. I'm grateful to be alive today, but I also have a huge debt of gratitude for everyone who went before me.

In prepping for this book, I learned a lot from talking to my parents, Kitty and Tom, who courted and married in 1950s London. Particular thanks to my mum who lived in the White City and was a machinist in a factory. The similarities to Eunice stop there, but she was the original inspiration. Thanks also to Margaret Price for talking to me about her experience working in a factory in the 50s too.

Thanks to Angela for her first read and encouraging comments. Also to my fantastic advanced reading team for their eagle eyes. You're all ace.

As usual, thanks to my cohort of talented professionals who make sure my books look and read the best they can. To Kevin Pruitt for the stylish cover. To Kelli Collins for the editing and cheerleading. To Claire Jarrett for the final proof. And to Adrian McLaughlin for his typesetting prowess.

Thanks also to my wife for putting up with me throughout.

Last but definitely not least, thanks to you for buying this book and supporting this independent author. I hope you enjoyed journeying back to 1950s London, and that you'll stick with the London Romance series for its final stop next year, starring Eunice's granddaughter Cordy.

If you fancy getting in touch, you can do so using one of the methods below. I'm most active on Instagram.

Twitter: @ClareLydon
Facebook: www.facebook.com/clare.lydon
Instagram: @clarefic
Find out more at: www.clarelydon.co.uk
Contact: mail@clarelydon.co.uk

Thank you so much for reading!

To all those who came before.
Thanks for paving the way.

Chapter One

Present Day

The door to the hotel conference room opened and India Contelli walked in.

Joan glanced up, then frowned. India seemed spooked. Joan had no idea what had happened to her since they'd last seen each other a couple of hours earlier, but whatever it was, it didn't suit her. Joan stood up, her attention for the first time since she'd arrived not wholly focused on Eunice.

"Are you okay?"

India looked startled by the question. She put down her bag, her knuckles white around its handle. Her nod was far too vigorous for it to be genuine. "Absolutely. Just ran into an old flame and it's thrown me somewhat." India blinked, then exhaled, trying to shake off whatever it was bothering her. "Although, who I am to talk? You two haven't seen each other for 60 years." She walked around the oval-shaped table and sat down opposite Joan and Eunice.

"Are you sure? Because you look like you could do with a black coffee. Or perhaps something stronger?"

India's eyes were puffy, her makeup freshly reapplied. Her frame was tall, but her spirit sagged. She shook her head.

1

"That's kind of you, but I'll be fine. Today is all about you and your story. Then we'll let you go and it'll be just the two of you, I promise." She checked her watch. "Give me, say, an hour of your time and then we'll see how we're all feeling?"

Joan glanced at Eunice, and they both nodded.

India clasped her hands in her lap and beamed. Her professional face slipped back on. The one Joan knew from the TV. India took a deep breath before she spoke again.

"So, tell me ladies. You haven't seen each other since 1959. You met and fell in love in 1958. We're now well into the 21st century, 60 years on. We have the internet. We have imminent space travel. We have smartphones. But what intrigued me was when you saw each other for the first time a few hours ago, you recognised each other right away." She turned to Joan. "Tell me, have the years not changed Eunice at all?"

Joan glanced at her first love. How to adequately explain it? "They have, of course. Neither one of us is Peter Pan." Her mind flew to the statue of JM Barrie's fictional boy, nestled by the Long Water in London's Kensington Gardens. She and Eunice used to meet there in the summer months, and plan their future on the lush green grass.

"I was worried we might have nothing to say to each other, that I might not recognise her. That our politics would be at odds. That I would feel nothing." Her face creased into a smile. "But the opposite was true. When I walked into the foyer of The Savoy and saw the back of her, I recognised her shape immediately. The very essence of her. It was instinct. When she turned, I wanted to embrace her. I wanted everything to be okay. I've no idea if it will be, but that was my thought."

Eunice nodded as she spoke. "I was about to go and hide

in my room when Joan walked in. I've lain awake at night dreaming of this moment, but also dreading it." She paused. "But then, when it happened, it was perfect. Almost scripted. Just like one of the shows we used to love to watch, that Joan's brother Jimmy used to get us into for free." Eunice paused, her eyes flickering over Joan's face. "I don't suppose Jimmy's still here?"

Joan shook her head. "He's not, but his son is. What's more, Vincent is gay and still lives at our Southwark flat."

Eunice's jaw dropped. "How wonderful! I'd love to go back there."

Joan's grin spread right across her face. "It can be arranged for you, my love." At her own words, Joan jolted. She put a hand over her mouth, sat upright and drew in a breath.

"Are you okay?" India asked.

Eventually, Joan nodded. "I am, but this is just strange." Her heart pounded in her chest. Sweat broke out on her top lip. "I just called Eunice 'my love'. It's how I always thought about her. She was always 'my love'. That's never changed. And now, here she is."

"You're going to make me cry," India told Joan.

"You're not the only one," Eunice added. She picked up Joan's hand and gave it a gentle squeeze.

Glitter lit up Joan's veins. She'd thought this sort of feeling was long gone. That it had left first with Eunice, and then when Sandra, her wife, had died.

But now, here it was again. Eunice had flicked a switch.

India's voice brought her back to the moment.

"But before we talk about how you're feeling now, which I promise we'll come back to, I'd love to know a little bit of history," India said. "I've read your heartbreaking letters, Eunice, of course. But I'd love to know how you met, how you came to fall in love, and what happened that drove you apart. We can take our time because I know this will be emotional." She reached across the table and pulled over a box of tissues to within reach of the couple. "Just know, we can stop whenever you want, take a break or get a drink. If you could cast your mind back to 1958 and tell us about the young lovers, that would be brilliant. We just need some meat on the bones of your story."

Eunice cleared her throat. "We already had this conversation upstairs. We might cry, because although it's a love story, it's also sad. But ultimately, we both had good lives, and we're both happy to be here. So we're going to tell our story, because it needs to be heard."

Joan took a deep breath before she spoke. "We're going to tell it as a thank you for bringing us back together again."

India dabbed her eye with a tissue. "Look at me, I've already gone." She turned to Heidi, working the camera and lights. "Are you good to go?"

"I'm rolling, so whenever you're ready."

Joan nodded. "Okay, then. Julie Andrews once sang that the beginning was a very good place to start. Shall we try that?"

"That sounds perfect," India replied. "Who wants to go first?"

Eunice sat up straight, holding on to her chunky beads. She pushed her royal-blue glasses up her nose, looked into the camera, and then at Joan.

"I'll start," she said.

Chapter Two

1958

Eunice hurried down the cracked pavements of the White City Estate, a maze of concrete flat blocks shivering in the March gloom. Naked trees rocked in the late-afternoon breeze, and a group of younger boys played football in the internal grassed courtyard, their jumpers laid down as goalposts. One of the boys, Colin, took a shot that sailed just wide. The ball slammed into the orange front door of a ground-floor flat, and the door rattled in its frame. A barrage of expletives filled the air.

"Don't let your mother hear you talk like that, Colin. She'll come and wash your mouth out with soap!" Eunice told him as she walked past.

In reply, Colin stuck out his tongue.

Eunice laughed, shifted her faux-leather brown bag up her arm, then turned right onto the external concrete stairs. She climbed the three floors to her family's flat, before deciding she couldn't quite face her mum after yet another failed date. She carried on up to the fourth and final floor.

David was already there, leaning on the concrete wall that came up to his hip, staring at the boys playing below. David was her neighbour and the only boy she'd ever really got on with. They'd known each other since they were babies, born a month apart. Eunice slotted her body against the wall next to him.

David turned his head, then smiled. He took the Woodbine from his lips. "From the look on your face, I'm guessing the date did not go well." They'd discussed it the night before in this exact spot. It had been a set-up with one of her mum's friend's sons.

Eunice snorted, then rolled her eyes. "How did you know?"

"The deep sigh, the look I know well." David paused, pushing his already slicked-back hair to one side. He wore turned-up jeans and a chequered shirt, but didn't seem cold.

Unlike Eunice, who still wore her thick winter coat. She hoped there was enough water for a hot bath when she got in.

"What was wrong with this one?"

Eunice frowned, trying to conjure the words without being too harsh. "He had bad hair."

David laughed, his grey eyes dancing as he did. "Bad hair is new. The last one you told me had breath like a horse. The one before that was too short." He took a drag on his cigarette before he continued. "You know you can change physical attributes. He could get a new hairstyle or grow it. You could buy the other one some mouthwash."

"Next you'll be telling me I could put the other one on a stretching rack."

"Nah, Mr Shorty is a no-go." David's cockney accent made her smile. Somehow, Eunice had an accent her family thought of as 'posh'. They had no idea where she came from. Often, Eunice wondered how she wound up here, too.

David straightened and walked behind her. He put his hands on her shoulders, then began to knead them. "Tense," he said. "I'm guessing this fella today didn't make you relaxed, so I'll have a go." David dug his fingers into Eunice's tight muscles.

Eunice leaned into his touch. If David ever tired of being a plumber, he could certainly work as a masseur.

"What was his name?"

"Reggie."

"You could never go out with a Reggie. You'd always be thinking of our Reggie." David's older brother, Reggie, worked for the same plumbing firm he did. "Did this Reggie always have food in his teeth, too?" David let go of Eunice and leaned his bum on the balcony wall, his back to the open air.

Eunice glanced up at him. "I don't know, we only met for coffee. That was enough. The coffee and cake were good, at least." She paused. "And free."

"You women. Leading us on, making us pay in more ways than one."

She shook her head. "I didn't want to lead him on. I wanted to like him. I wanted him to sweep me off my feet. But Reggie wouldn't know how to do that. He's a trainee electrician, but there was no spark."

"Fatal," David smirked.

Eunice stood upright. She stretched her neck, then put her bag on the ground.

David stuck his hands in his jean pockets. The turn-ups were new, although David swore he wasn't a Teddy Boy. His gaze dropped to the floor before bouncing back up to Eunice. "For what it's worth, he's an idiot. You look lovely."

Eunice gulped. David had started to say this sort of thing

more and more of late. She was never sure what to do with his compliments, so she ignored them. Still, they hung around afterwards, like a persistent stone in her shoe. She leaned back over on the balcony, as much as to escape the heat of David's gaze as anything else. "Do you think we'll meet someone eventually and get married?" They were both 17 now, both had been in full-time jobs for two years.

David drew in a long breath. "Isn't that the law? It's either that or become like my Uncle Billy. I don't fancy that. He just drinks cider all day. My mum says he may as well be dead."

Eunice squeezed her toes in her shoes. The looming deadline had begun to make her feel uneasy. "But don't you ever think you might want to do something different? Be somewhere different?"

"Not really. I love London."

That was the problem. Eunice wasn't happy with her lot. Whereas David had been born content.

"But there are different places to live. If you moved out of London, you might be able to afford a house." A light bulb flicked on in her head. "Imagine not living in a flat. Having your own garden. Not having to share a bedroom with your two sisters."

David didn't take his eyes off her. "So long as I have somewhere to live and someone to live with, that'll do me." He paused. "Did you see those houses they're building by the river? They're massive. I bet they have more than one bathroom. Maybe even heating in every room."

Eunice glanced down the concrete-sided corridor balcony that ran the length of the block of flats. David's dad had described them as ocean-liner style. He'd seen an ocean liner in real life, so he knew.

However, Eunice was sure there was something more to life than concrete. That beyond this block of flats, even beyond White City and West London, something bigger and better was waiting for her. She wanted to see an ocean liner, even sail on one. She wanted to do something creative. She longed for a world of glamour. She wasn't going to get it living here.

She turned back to David. "I wake up at night burning with something. I don't know what it is, but I can feel it in my feet. They're itchy. They want to travel." She stroked an arm through the cool spring air. "I want to see the world. I want to go to Europe, to America. I want film stars to be dressed in my clothes, my designs. My new job tomorrow is the start of my journey."

David blinked. It wasn't the first time he'd heard this. "And you'll do it all." He gave her an adoring smile. "How's your dress coming along?"

Eunice had been working on a new design for the past few weeks. "It's nearly ready. Now I just need a suitable date and dance to wear it to."

"The start of your journey. The world's not going to know what hit it." He tilted his head to the evening sky. "Whereas I'll be a plumber with Reggie, and with any luck, some girl might have me."

Eunice pressed herself next to him and threaded her arm through his. "Any girl would be lucky to have you. If I come back from my travels single and you're still available, I'll pick you, David."

He perked up at that, turning his face to her. "I'll hold you to that, Eunice Humphries." He paused. "Or as you might be, Eunice Cranks."

"I'm not changing my name for you."

"A feminist, too?" David raised an eyebrow.

Eunice smiled as she stared across the courtyard. The six boys were collecting up their jumpers and heading home for dinner. "Mum says I have to marry rich, otherwise my life will be like hers." She spread her arms wide. "But why does life have to be about who you marry? Can't it be about my career? The people I meet? The places I go?"

"You've always been too good for the White City."

Eunice caught his gaze. "So have you. You're going to make someone a fabulous plumber. They're going to be in high demand with so many extra bathrooms everywhere."

He smiled, showing off the gap in his front teeth. "Maybe I'll make my fortune by staying here."

"Maybe you will." She put a thumb to her chest. "But me? I'm getting out. I'm going to travel the world and make sure everyone knows my name. Whoever I marry will have to be okay with that."

David gazed at her. "Here's to a world beyond the White City. If anyone can conquer it, you can."

* * *

"Have you got everything ready? All set for tomorrow? Lay out your clothes, because otherwise you'll be fretting and your sisters will get narky with you for waking them up."

Eunice's mum, Valerie, cracked another egg into the frying pan as she spoke. It was for her dad, who'd just got in from the pub. He'd missed dinner, which was standard practice. Grease coated the kitchen air. It grated on Eunice that her dad couldn't eat with everyone else, meaning only one clear-up. Her mum, though, never moaned. She had endless patience. She told Eunice it came with having six children.

"It's all done." Eunice leaned against the chrome sink and draining board. The handle of the mint-green kitchen drawer below dug into her bum, but she ignored it. "My clothes are hung on the door. Now I just hope Rose doesn't keep me awake all night with her snoring." Eunice shared a room with her younger sisters, Mabel and Rose. She at least had her own bed; the other two slept in bunks.

Her mum twisted the thick knob on the cream cooker and lifted the frying pan. She slipped the fried eggs onto a plate that already had two slices of thickly buttered Mother's Pride, some chips and a slice of black pudding. The latter turned Eunice's stomach. She'd liked it until she was told what it actually was.

Her ten-year-old brother, Graeme, ran in, shooting imaginary bullets from his fingertips. Their dad was hot on his heels, chasing him with bullets of his own. His dark stubble contrasted with his flushed skin, and his braces sagged on top of his white shirt. The pair ran out of the kitchen, Graeme squealing. Dad winked as he ran past. The smell of stale beer followed him out.

"Your dinner's ready, Eddie!" Mum shouted.

Dad reappeared at the door, out of breath. He licked his lips, then grabbed cutlery from the drawer, along with his plate. "I'll take it through to the other room. Leave you girls to chat."

Eunice and her mum sat at their small, white Formica table. It sat four comfortably, six at a push. Family dinners for eight always involved a couple of kids on stools balancing plates on their knees.

"Do you want a cup of tea? I was going to put the kettle on."

Eunice nodded, and her mum filled the shiny blue kettle, twisted a cooker knob, lit a match and set it to heat. In a few minutes, the kettle would whistle, and her mum would marvel. Her dad had brought it home two weeks earlier, and the speed and noise were still a novelty. Up above, the suspended wooden drying rack held an assortment of the family's smalls. Mum dried bigger clothes in the designated drying room, but never underwear. Hence Eunice's bras and pants always smelled of fried eggs.

"Has Mrs Higgins been again?" The telltale cake tin sat temptingly on the side, so Eunice already knew the answer. Beryl Higgins lived three doors along in their block of flats, and seemed to spend her whole life baking. She was widowed, and her son had moved to America in search of a new, better life, so Mrs Higgins' baking often ended up in their kitchen. She also had a sewing machine and space, so Eunice was often there using both. Her designs would be nowhere without Mrs Higgins' help. She'd never create anything in their overcrowded flat.

"This morning," her mum replied. She still wore her pink apron, and her tights had a snag on her right shin. "Brought over a sponge cake, a batch of ginger snaps and some shortbread. I don't know how she coped in the war when there was rationing. She'd barely have been able to bake a cake a week."

"I suspect she blocks it out. A distant memory."

Her mum reached over. "Are you excited about tomorrow?"

Eunice nodded. "I am." It might not be Paris, but it was a job as a machinist in a respected garment factory in the West End. It meant she was going to be in the heart of London's rag trade. Far better than the small-fry factory she'd been at for the past two years in Hammersmith.

"Then I'm excited for you." Her mum patted her arm. "I know you want to do it your way. You wouldn't take my advice and get a nice office job, so it's good you took a step up to a bigger factory with better wages. You've worked hard, and who knows where this might lead? You'll meet new friends, and you might even meet the man you're going to marry."

Eunice rolled her eyes. Her mum thought an office job and snagging a good husband was the be-all-and-end-all. Eunice found the thought terrifying. "I'm not there to meet a husband. I'm there to learn new skills. Besides, I haven't met many men who can sew lately."

Her mum leaned forward. "They might be the supervisors. Maybe even the boss's son. What have I always said? Meet a man who can provide. It makes all the difference in life." She scanned the chipped kitchen cabinets, the grease-stained walls. "Tomorrow might be the day you meet someone who really matters. So keep a smile on your face and keep your hair nice. Just in case. You never know who might be round the corner."

Chapter Three

The swell and chatter of the crowd was all around them as Joan and Aunt Maggie walked slowly down the dusty stairs of the Dominion Theatre. It was a favourite haunt of Joan's, and she'd seen many films there. Tonight's starred Ian Carmichael and Janette Scott in *Happy Is The Bride*.

"What did you think?" Joan craned her head to see if it was still raining out the side door ahead. A barrage of black umbrellas told her it was. She stuck a hand in her bag to find hers, but couldn't feel it. Joan winced. She could still see where she'd left it on the hallway table. An umbrella was essential to London life, especially in March.

"Terrific, I loved it!" Maggie replied with typical enthusiasm. "I mean, if that had happened when I got married, it wouldn't have been funny at all. But it's a farce, that's the point."

"I suppose it is," Joan replied, jostled on either side as they got to the bottom of the stairs. "At least the women got more than a few lines, although it was still the men who came out the funniest."

Maggie already clutched her umbrella, her curly black hair out of control as usual. "The scripts are all written by men, that's the problem." She pressed the end of her closed umbrella into Joan's chest. "That's what you've got to change. Write some new scripts and make the women's stories the central plot."

They walked out into the side alley and around to the main street, Tottenham Court Road. It buzzed with life, the Dominion sign illuminated above. A red Routemaster spluttered as it pulled up in front of them, coughing diesel fumes into the air. The conductor jumped down from the open back step, shouting at the crowds to take it slowly as they pressed forward, desperate to get out of the rain. At the steps down to the tube station on their left, a crowd of umbrellas jostled for space, signalling something amiss.

"Tube's closed!" shouted a male voice. "Central line and Northern not working. Advice is to walk to Oxford Circus for other connecting lines!"

"Let's do that, then. We can get to Waterloo and walk, or get a bus." Maggie shook out her umbrella.

Joan gave her a pleading look.

"Where's yours?"

"On the hallway table." Joan threaded an arm through her aunt's so they could both fit underneath.

They stopped at the main crossing, waiting for the traffic lights to change from green to red. The rain drummed down on the umbrella, and Joan squeezed closer to her aunt in a bid to stop getting soaked. It was a ten-minute walk to Oxford Circus tube, so she didn't fancy her chances.

"Do you think that'll ever happen?" Joan waited until they were through the mass of people and a little way down Oxford Street before she restarted their conversation. It was a street she was well accustomed to, her workplace being just around the corner, off Wardour Street. They passed the cobbler who'd mended the heel of her shoe just last week.

"Do I think what will happen?" Maggie trod on a loose paving slab and water sloshed up both their legs as a consequence. "Bugger!"

Joan grimaced and shook her leg. "Plots with women as the central characters?"

Maggie glanced her way, stopping at the junction of Poland Street for a man on a bike who zigzagged down the road, a touch worse for wear. On the next corner, a woman in a very short skirt and a glittery top leaned on a street sign. Was she touting for work? They were near Soho, so there was every chance.

"I'd like to think so. Things are changing, aren't they? Women are not accepting that their place is solely in the home anymore, which is great. We've got stories to tell, too. It's your generation that needs to tell them."

Joan nodded. "Maybe I'll write a play about a factory of machinists and the crazy affairs that go on. All stories need drama, right?"

Maggie laughed as they approached Oxford Circus tube, its red-and-blue signage bold against the dark night. Nearby, a street vendor sold hot, sweet chestnuts in white paper bags.

Joan sniffed the caramel air, then clutched the wet metal banister as she made her way down the stairs into the tube station, concentrating hard on not slipping on the slick stone and metal steps.

"Mind out!" Maggie shook out her umbrella before folding it back up.

Joan gave up trying to stay dry tonight. It was a lost cause.

They both bought a ticket for London Bridge from the slanted ticket machines to their left, then strode through the gate and onto the giant escalator down to the trains. The familiar smell of cigarette smoke and oil filled Joan's airways as they descended. The tube always smelled like a car that'd just been serviced by a chain-smoker.

"These stories you're going to write about your factory. You're the one always telling me there are no men, so how are any affairs going to happen?"

Joan blushed. "Maybe the affairs could be between the machinists. Maybe they don't need men." Joan's brother, Jimmy, had a couple of homosexual friends who Maggie loved dearly, as did Joan.

Maggie glanced at her niece, her face soft. "I would expect nothing else from you," she said. "But if you want to get your play or film made, you might need to give the woman a man to love at first. When you're well known, you can do something more daring."

Joan beamed. She loved her aunt for so many reasons, but this was a key one. Nothing Joan said ever shocked her. She was sure her mum would have said exactly the same. But Joan would never know.

They reached the bottom of the escalator and walked through the grey tunnels, eventually being spat out onto a dark platform, waiting for their Bakerloo line train. Judging by the thickness of the crowd, they hadn't missed one recently, which boded well. Her friend Kitty had waited over half an hour for a tube last week, and then it had broken down in the tunnel.

Joan fished in her bag and pulled out a packet of Woodbines. She offered one to Maggie, who declined. Joan put an end into her mouth and asked a man nearby for a light. He obliged, before moving further down the platform. Joan and her aunt followed suit as more people crammed into the space. Up ahead, a tiny mouse raced across the platform and disappeared onto the tracks.

Joan took a drag on her cigarette, before turning to her aunt. "How's Uncle Derek's new job going, by the way?" They'd chatted briefly before the film, but about their own lives, not about Maggie's husband. He'd just started as a factory foreman at a brewery in Bermondsey.

"Going well, I think. I don't get a lot out of him. You know men." She raised both eyebrows. "And yes, I know you don't have a boyfriend yet, but you will. Plus, you live with Jimmy. Although, your brother is a rare breed. A man who likes to talk about his emotions."

Joan blew out smoke, a laugh catching in her throat. "Jimmy likes to chat more than any woman I've ever met."

"He's like your father. I don't know if it's working in the theatre that does it. Perhaps because you have to be quiet and whisper for the whole of the set, so when they can talk, they can't stop?" She paused. "How is my nephew? Still working at the Palladium? Still taking care of you?"

Joan nodded. "We take care of each other. I cook him a meal one day, and he does the same for me the next. I'm getting quite used to eating dinner cold on those days."

Maggie tutted. "You should heat it up in the oven."

Joan shook her head. "I can still hear Mum saying what a waste of money that is. Plus, it takes too long when I'm hungry. But we get along just fine. He cleans the bathroom, I do the kitchen, we negotiate the rest."

A breeze skimmed Joan's cheek, which signalled the train's approach. She sucked on the last of her cigarette, and then stubbed it out under her shoe. The train arrived, the rhythmic rattle of its wheels on the track soothingly familiar. It let out a pleading screech as it came to a drawn-out halt. Joan and Maggie got in, then sat side by side on the rough, dirty seats as the tube jerked before it pulled out of the station.

"Jimmy's going to make someone a lovely husband," her aunt added.

Joan nodded. He would. She dreaded the day that happened, though, because then she might be forced into getting married, too. At 18, Joan was happy to think about sharing her life with someone in the future. So far, though, the only man who fitted the bill was her brother. Every time her aunt brought up her future, Joan drew a blank.

"Work's going well, anyway? Contracts still coming in?"

Her aunt's words dragged Joan back into the present as the tube pulled up at Piccadilly Circus. She glanced out the window at the packed platform: they were about to be engulfed. Sure enough, within a minute there were people standing on her toes, hanging onto the hard plastic knobs suspended overhead. When the doors shut and the train lurched forwards, a woman opposite fell into a man's lap. She scrabbled to get up, apologising profusely. The man shook his head and offered his seat. She accepted eventually, her cheeks Routemaster-red.

Joan refocused. "So far, so good. There was that lull just after Christmas when we got a few afternoons off, but lately Mr Prestwick has been asking us to work Saturdays, too, which I'm happy to unless Jimmy's got me tickets to a show."

"Stanley's been on at me to take him to something else

ever since you took him to see Bill Haley and the Comets. I don't think I'll ever top that." Stanley was Joan's 14-year-old cousin, Maggie and Derek's son. They had four boys, so Joan was her aunt's honorary daughter. "Have you been to any dances lately? I know they're not really your scene, but you're only young once. You need to get out there, not just sit at home with your head in a book or writing your next opus." Maggie nudged Joan with her elbow. "Your mum would say the same thing if she were here."

That was true. "Kitty and Mari have asked, but they live in West London, and so the dances they go to are over that way. It's a bit far for a couple of hours dancing with a boy I don't have anything in common with." Joan had tried a few times and the result had never altered.

"It's not just to meet boys. It's to enjoy life, to have fun with people your own age. I worry about you, sitting in that flat on your own while Jimmy's at work. You're 18. You should be out there living it up. If you kiss a few boys along the way, all the better."

Joan shifted in her seat at her aunt's words. The thing was, she *preferred* sitting in her flat, reading or writing. Plus, she'd never met a boy who wanted to know anything about her. All they ever wanted to do was feel her breasts, press themselves against her and give her a sloppy kiss.

Kissing boys, even though all the love songs raved about it, wasn't top of her priorities.

"Maybe you could go out with Christopher to a dance nearby? I'm sure he'd be happy to escort you."

Christopher was Maggie's second-eldest son, and a real know-it-all to boot. The thought of spending an evening with him giving her a running commentary of all the girls who wanted to kiss him wasn't her idea of a good time either.

"We'll see," Joan said, as the tube pulled up at Waterloo station. She and Maggie fought their way through the maze of arms, legs and shoulders, breathing a sigh of relief as they made it to the platform.

"I mean it," Maggie said. She threaded her arm through Joan's. "It was one of the last things I promised your mum before she passed. That I'd look out for you, and make sure you were settled." She squeezed Joan's arm. "My little Joanie. I'm going to make good on my promise, okay?"

Chapter Four

Eunice slammed the black wooden door of number 24 Auckland House, then walked along the ocean-liner style corridor outside her front door. Today was the day her world cracked open that little bit more. No more working in W10: her new workplace was in W1. The centre of the action.

A door slammed behind her. "Eunice! Hold up!" David's footsteps echoed on the concrete as he drew up alongside her, then shrugged on his thick black jacket. His plumbing tools clanged in his canvas bag as it swung from his hand, a pack of Woodbines sticking out the top. As they took the stairs, a waft of stale urine almost made them choke, but neither said anything. They were used to it.

"Big day ahead."

"Why, what you doing?" Eunice gave him a grin.

"Ha ha."

They crossed the courtyard and out onto the road. It'd finally stopped raining, but the morning was foggy, the sun yet to burn through. Eunice was glad she'd worn her winter coat.

"You're late today."

David was usually at his site by 7am. It was already 7.30.

"We have to wait for the electrician to finish before we can carry on." He shrugged. "But enough about me. Today's the day you become far too big to be living here, right? The start of your destiny."

Eunice smiled. Of all the people in her life, it was David who listened to her the most. David who encouraged her dreams. She was always grateful to have him around.

A squat figure scuttled towards them out of the gloom, huffing under the weight of her shopping bags.

"Morning, Mrs Higgins. Can you manage?" David asked.

Mrs Higgins nodded, trying to catch her breath. "Thank you, dear, yes. I just went over to Florence's to get some ingredients. I'm making a birthday cake for her son. You know what she's like with baking. Only in this pea-souper of a morning, it was a job to find her place." She pointed a finger in Eunice's direction. "Your dress is still waiting to be finished, too. Pop by any night this week and I'll bake some scones so you can work on a full stomach."

Eunice nodded. "I will."

Mrs Higgins drew up alongside her and clutched her forearm. "Good luck today. Your mum was telling me all about your new job at the weekend. Bright lights, big city!"

"Thank you," Eunice said. "But I'm not going far. Just a bus ride away."

Mrs Higgins squeezed. "A bus ride for me. A whole new world for you. Now go. You don't want to be late on your first day, do you?"

* * *

Eunice jumped down from the bus and turned onto the pavement, the gasp of the bus's diesel engine leaving an acrid taste in her mouth as it carried on down Oxford Street. Her white cotton bag banged on her hip as she walked. Inside, she had a cheese sandwich, along with an umbrella and a hairbrush her mum had insisted on, "just in case you need to impress at short notice". Eunice had no idea what lofty events might happen in factories in town rather than in Hammersmith, but she'd taken the hairbrush anyway. Perhaps Queen Elizabeth herself, six years into her reign, would get bored and want to see what happened on the factory floor? In which case, Eunice might well give her hair a brush.

She turned down Wardour Street, its pavements narrower than the main road. The streets were packed, and every step she took, she walked into someone else and apologised. Opposite, the buttery pastry smells leaking from the door of Rayner's Pie Shop made her lick her lips. She hadn't eaten breakfast this morning, too nervous to keep anything down.

The first left was Heddon Street, the address on the piece of paper she clutched in her hot palm. Eunice stepped off the pavement, even narrower still, and glanced up at the red-brick building. It was as tall as the flats she lived in, perhaps even taller. Black chimneys billowed smoke from up high, and engraved concrete spelled out the name in large block letters. 'Prestwick Garments Factory'. Her new place of employment as a fully fledged machinist. The next step on her way to becoming a fashion designer. She was determined to make a success of it.

Eunice watched as a steady stream of women filed into the building. They looked like they belonged there. Did Eunice? She gathered her courage and went inside, climbed three flights of stairs, then stood back as the other workers clocked their timecards into the machine. She walked in and asked the receptionist for Mrs Armstrong.

An insanely glamorous woman appeared within minutes, her dark hair glossy, clipboard in hand, a folded overall on top. She wore a dark grey pencil skirt and a starched white blouse. It was the kind of skirt her mother tutted at, saying they left little to the imagination. Eunice, on the other hand, was desperate to buy one when she got her first new, improved pay packet. If she looked half as good as this lady, she'd consider it money well spent.

The woman smiled at Eunice and held out a hand. "I'm Mrs Armstrong." She handed Eunice the overall. "This is for you. Once you're past your probation period, you can call me Gladys. But only then." She glanced at the receptionist. "They get younger by the day, don't they, Roni?"

Roni glanced at Eunice and rolled her eyes, then gave a laugh.

Eunice followed Mrs Armstrong onto the factory floor, swallowed up in a haze of her Chanel No.5 perfume. The air was thick with chat and laughter, and most women she passed clutched white mugs filled with dark brown tea.

In front of her, six rows of six Singer sewing machines took up the main floorspace, with six overlockers down either side. At the far end of the room, six large cutting tables were pushed against the wall. Looking up, Eunice breathed in the tall-ceilinged space, and the taste of her future. Her skin tingled with excitement as Mrs Armstrong beckoned her to the machine at the end of the third row. This workplace was far bigger than what she was used to, but Eunice was ready.

"This is you. This whole floor is women's wear." Mrs Armstrong pulled back her shoulders, and pointed her manicured finger towards a large metal door on the far right of the room. "Through that door is men's clothing. Beyond that is millinery." She flicked her head towards the large leaded windows, the height of a few men. "Over the courtyard is undergarments. They're just setting about making the new range of women's underwear that sucks you in and gives you a flat stomach. There might be a stampede when the rejects are up for grabs, fair warning."

Eunice got on her tiptoes to try to see across the courtyard, but couldn't quite make it. The windows were too high.

"I'll come back to check how you're doing and give you your jobs for the week. As I'm sure you know, you get paid per piece you finish. Payment is on Friday lunchtime." Mrs Armstrong twisted around just as another woman arrived at the machine next to Eunice's. "Ah, perfect timing, Joan." She extended an arm towards Eunice's neighbour. "This is Joan, and she's been here for nearly two years, so she's going to take you through everything you need to know. Where the toilets are. When the breaks are. What songs to sing and when." The older woman smiled. "Joan is particularly good at the singing part, aren't you?"

Joan put her canvas bag on the back of her wooden chair and gave Mrs Armstrong a dazzling grin. "I don't want to blow my own trumpet, but if this factory ever forms a choir, I know who's going to get the lead."

"Modest as ever," Mrs Armstrong replied, but there was a warmth in her tone. She clearly had a lot of time for Joan. "Can I leave Eunice in your charge?"

Joan gave them both a firm nod. "I will teach her the ways of the factory."

Satisfied, Mrs Armstrong turned and walked back down

the rows of machines, greeting the women sitting at them as she went, her three-inch black heels clicking on the concrete.

Eunice turned to Joan and gave her a smile.

Joan returned it with interest. "Nice to meet you, Eunice." She held out a hand.

Eunice put her overall and bag on her chair, then shook Joan's hand. A tingle shot up her arm on contact. She blinked. "Just to be clear, I don't have to sing, do I?" That would be Eunice's worst nightmare. She couldn't hold a note.

Joan laughed, shaking her head. Joan wore her dark brown hair shorter than most women Eunice had met, but it suited her face perfectly. She stuffed her hands into the pockets of her trousers, then continued. "Only if you want to. We have Workers' Playtime on the wireless before lunch, and other shows throughout the week, too."

Eunice was used to Workers' Playtime, the lunchtime variety show. But her old factory never sang.

"Where are you from?"

Eunice gulped. Her throat always went dry when she met new people. It seemed particularly dry meeting Joan. "The White City. My parents are both from West London."

Joan nodded, taking that information in. "You sound posh. And you have an unusual name. Eunice."

Heat shot to Eunice's cheeks. It wasn't the first time she'd been told this. At school, she'd been teased for having a posh name. "My dad knew someone when he was growing up who was called it, and he always wanted to call his first daughter Eunice." She shrugged. "Although I heard that Nina Simone's real name is Eunice, too."

That got Joan's attention. "I love her new song, 'My Baby

Just Cares For Me'." She cocked her head. "She's called Eunice as well? Seems like you landed on your feet with your name. Better than Joan, I think we can both agree." She pushed in her chair, then motioned for Eunice to follow her. "The hooter for the start of work goes in five minutes, so we have to be quick." She walked past the front three rows of machines, getting hellos from all the other women.

"This is Eunice, everyone!" Joan hollered, indicating Eunice with her hand. "First day, so be nice!"

The women gave her warm smiles and waves. Eunice wanted the floor to swallow her up. She didn't seek out the limelight. But Joan, like Mrs Armstrong before her, was the opposite. Everybody on the floor was ready to greet her.

They walked past the cutting tables, and over to the corner with the tea trolley. Four women clustered around it, two just putting on their calf-length overalls, white with a light-red chequered pattern.

"The tea trolley is here in the morning and at lunchtime, and also comes around mid-morning and mid-afternoon," Joan said. "Free to all employees, so don't get thirsty. There are biscuits on the 10.30 round, so definitely don't miss out on that."

Eunice nodded, taking it all in. Free biscuits. Only two hours to wait.

"There's a canteen downstairs that serves decent food, although you have to pay up-front. But whenever they have toad-in-the-hole, put your name down. Best batter around." Joan pushed through the blue swing doors and took Eunice into a stairwell. The chill as they entered was noticeable, and Eunice shivered.

"The canteen's at the bottom of the stairs, and the loo's through that door." Joan pointed to her left. Her fingers were slim, her nails neatly trimmed. "Do you need the loo before we get started?"

Eunice didn't think so, but it seemed wise, so she nodded. She didn't want to be crossing her legs until the tea break.

Joan pushed open the door, then disappeared into the cubicle next to Eunice's. When they emerged, they stood next to each other at the bank of three sinks. She turned the soap in her hands, so pink, it hurt her eyes. She passed it to Joan. When their fingers touched, Eunice's hand trembled.

She frowned, catching her breath. When she looked up, Joan caught her gaze in the mirror.

"Where have you worked before?" Joan rinsed her hands, her gaze locked on Eunice.

Eunice's scalp tingled. "You wouldn't know it. Somewhere much smaller than this." She cleared her throat. As well as trousers, Joan wore a fitted white blouse and a red neckerchief. Eunice had never seen a woman wear one before, and she couldn't take her eyes from it. "My mum wanted me to leave the factory and get an office job, but that's not really me. I prefer making stuff, using my hands." She'd knitted her own scarves and jumpers since her grandma taught her when she was eight. Going into an office and becoming a secretary had never been in her plans.

"A factory is more down at heel," her mum had said.

Joan blinked, her eyelashes framing her deep grey eyes. "You'll like it here. They're a friendly bunch, and the owner of the factory, Mr Prestwick, is a good man. He pays on time and gives us all gifts at Christmas. You can't ask for much more."

They walked out of the loo and back onto the factory floor, just as the horn went for the start of the workday. Women scattered from the tea trolley back to their work stations. When she got to hers, Eunice put on her overall, doing up all the buttons from her chest to her calf. Her old work overall had been far too big, but this was a good fit. She hoped it boded well. Eunice pulled out her chair and settled in her seat. The Singer was newer, too. She took a deep breath. Now she just had to remember how to sew. She could do this.

"Get your machine threaded with that black cotton, and then I'll walk you through the patterns and where to pick up your pieces from the cutters."

At least she had Joan on her side. Eunice was very grateful. She glanced up to see Joan's enormous smile beaming down on her. She couldn't help but smile back.

"Ready?"

Eunice nodded. "Ready."

Chapter Five

Joan collected her wages from Roni's reception desk, then walked back to her desk, sliding open the square brown envelope. She fingered the notes and jiggled the coins. To her, money represented freedom. All around, chatter filled the air as women decided what to spend their wages on.

"That new pair of shoes in Brennan's shop window!"

"A good steak dinner with Tom. He needs a nudge to propose. That might make him do it."

"New nappies for the baby."

"It's going towards the television fund!"

As well as her half of the rent and food, Joan planned to spend hers on some new notepads for writing, cinema tickets and buying Aunt Maggie lunch tomorrow. It was her turn this year.

When everyone was settled back in their seats, Gladys put on the radio and turned it up. "And now on Workers' Playtime, it gives me great pleasure to introduce one of our newest and brightest singing talents, live from the Octagon Factory in Nuneaton, Julie Andrews!" said the host.

Joan leaned back in her chair. Julie Andrews on Workers' Playtime. It was quite the coup. "She was starring in *My Fair*

Lady on Broadway up until last month." Joan kept track via Jimmy's trade magazines.

"Good of her to come and do this, then." Eunice had been sat next to Joan for three weeks and was already part of the furniture.

"It is," Joan said. "I'd love to see her live. Perhaps she'll play somewhere in London soon. If my brother can't get me tickets, I might have to skip Friday pies to save money so I can see her."

"You haven't stopped going on about how much you're looking forward to your pie all morning, so you must *really* love her."

Joan did, in her own way. She liked that Julie wore her hair short, too. Plus, she was the perfect star, a combination of style, grace and raw talent.

Joan glanced over at Eunice. She had piercing green eyes, just like Joan's late mum. Eunice had style, grace and talent, too, along with a shoulder-length sheet of custard hair that had drawn Joan's attention ever since Eunice first sat down beside her. Joan didn't want to delve into the reasons why. It was too early.

Julie Andrews began to sing 'Wouldn't It Be Loverly' from the musical *My Fair Lady*. It was a popular song on the wireless, and the whole floor began to sway along. When it ended, the radio erupted with applause, as did their factory, everyone clapping their appreciation. Joan added a jubilant whistle, then turned to Eunice.

She had a strange smile on her face. Almost as if she were assessing Joan.

"Isn't she something?" Joan would love to write a script for

Julie Andrews one day. "Her voice is just so *big*. She deserves a larger audience. She should be in films next. I'd love to see her on the silver screen."

"I've only been to the cinema twice."

Joan frowned. How was that even possible? "Twice?" She couldn't fathom it. "I love the cinema. It's where I'm happiest." Joan went at least once a week. "Films take me away from the humdrum of everyday life, show me there's a bigger world out there."

"That's what fashion does for me," Eunice replied. "I read the papers, and any fashion magazines I can get my hands on."

Joan loved fashion, too. She loved anything creative. She sensed a kindred spirit in Eunice. She ignored the increased thud of her heart as she carried on. "You should come to the cinema with me. If for nothing other than the fashion. Film wardrobes are the stuff of dreams. Same with the theatre."

A smile spread across Eunice's face. "I'd love to." Her words were hushed, almost whispered.

"We'll set a date, then." Joan crossed one leg over the other, then smoothed down her tan trousers. She'd got grief for wearing them on the tube this morning. She'd given the fella a piece of her mind. No man was going to tell her what she could and couldn't wear. "Do you have big ambitions? Do you want to travel or do something grand?"

A smile ghosted over Eunice's face at the question, and her eyes lit up. Then she glanced down to the floor and shook her head. "Not really. Just the same as everyone else. To get married, have children, be happy." Her cheeks coloured at her words.

Joan's spirit dipped. "Nothing wrong with that," she replied.

"But I want something a little more. With the new feminism sweeping the country, we might be able to have it, too."

"Wouldn't that be something."

Just then, Kitty and Mari appeared between the pair. "Are you coming for a pie?" Kitty asked Eunice. She'd taken off her overall to reveal a bright yellow sundress, the same colour as Eunice's hair. "Friday tradition. You've said no two weeks running. We might get a complex if you say it again today."

Eunice winced, then tapped her bag. "I brought sandwiches."

Kitty narrowed her eyes. "I won't take no for an answer. Give your sandwiches to the birds on the way home." She glanced at Joan. "We need to discuss the Boat Race, too. Are you coming?"

Joan nodded. "Yes, to both."

Kitty patted the top of Eunice's machine. "You should come to the Boat Race, too."

"I love the Boat Race," Eunice said, suddenly interested. "I normally go with my neighbour, David, but he can't make it next weekend."

Joan's skin prickled. Of course there was a David.

"Ladies, can I have your attention please!" A booming voice at the front of the factory made everyone turn their heads. It was Mr Prestwick, the factory owner. He wore his usual pristine black suit and tie. The girls always joked he should really have been an undertaker. "I hope you all enjoyed Julie Andrews. What a talent she is! Just like all of you, my lovely talented women."

Joan smiled. Mr Prestwick was a kind-hearted man, and he knew how to get the best out of his workers. Flattery and double time. She knew what was coming.

"We've got a rush order today, and I wondered who might

like to come in and work tomorrow? I know it's Saturday, and that your time is precious. I won't ask you married ladies because I know you want to spend time with your husbands. But all you single girls, who would like to work? You'd be doing me a favour, and in appreciation, I'll pay you double time."

A murmur went round the floor.

"Can I have a show of hands?"

Kitty, Mari and Eunice all raised theirs, as did most other single girls and a couple of the married ones, too.

Kitty elbowed Joan in the ribs. "Why isn't your hand up?"

Joan grimaced. "I'm having lunch with my aunt. It's the anniversary of my dad's death, so I can't change it." They had lunch every year to commemorate the fateful day. Seventeen years. She'd hardly known him. It was her mum's death that still lingered around everything she did.

"Great stuff!" Mr Prestwick added. "Put your name down with Mrs Armstrong and see you here bright and early tomorrow. Thanks again, ladies!"

Eunice got up and took off her overall. "I'm sorry to hear about your dad."

Joan gave her a sad smile. "It was a long time ago. I was only a baby."

"Nice to keep the anniversary to remember him, though."

Joan nodded. It was. Plus, it meant a lot to Maggie, so it was a constant date in the diary.

"But I have to say, it'll be strange not having you next to me."

"Try not to miss me too much." Joan paused. "Are you coming for pie now?"

"Seems like it, doesn't it?"

Chapter Six

Eunice followed Joan down the cold factory stairs and out into the lunchtime air. It was the last week of March and up above, the sky was a strange blue mixed with the factory's grey smoke. In the distance, she could see the sun, but its yellow hue was dulled by the towering buildings covering its rays. None of that pressed down Eunice's enthusiasm for being in the thick of it. There had only been two cafes in walking distance at her last job, and none that served good pies. She couldn't wait to try the ones from Rayners.

A Lyons' Tea van rumbled past with its familiar branding, clipping the side of the pavement and almost ploughing into the lunchtime crowd.

"Careful!" Joan's fingertips dug into Eunice's upper arm.

Eunice lurched to the right, then grabbed Joan's arm to steady herself, before standing upright once more. She glared after the van, as did everyone around her, then caught her breath, one hand to her chest. She gave Joan a weak smile.

"Thanks," she told her. "Traffic is getting crazy on the roads, they don't need to jump onto the pavement."

Joan threaded an arm through Eunice's as they started to walk. "It's taken three weeks to get you to come for a Friday pie. It would have been a tragedy if you were run over before you'd even tasted one."

"Especially after I just got paid." Eunice ignored the fact her mum had suggested she might need to get a little more from her this week, because her dad had drunk too much of his wages. Her mum had taken to doing a bit of cleaning in the mornings for some of the more well-heeled households surrounding their flats, keeping her sister, Rose, off school to tend to her younger siblings.

Eunice was happy to help out, even if it did mean her Paris savings suffered. If her dreams were on hold, she could at least spend a little money on some immediate pleasures. Plus, if she didn't say yes this time, the girls might never ask again. She hadn't been a part of the in-crowd at her last workplace as she'd been too young. Now she was coming up 18, she didn't want to make the same mistake twice.

They walked in twos: Eunice and Joan in front, Mari and Kitty behind.

"Tell me: are you a liquor fan?" Joan asked. "Or do you simply go for pie and mash? There are those who swear by liquor; then there are those who'd rather eat their own eyeballs."

Eunice laughed. "I'm definitely in the first camp. My neighbour, David, is in the eyeball camp. His brothers take the mick out of him relentlessly, telling him I'm more of a man than he'll ever be." Why did she keep bringing up David? Joan was going to think he was her boyfriend. For some reason, Eunice didn't want Joan to think of her as anything but free.

Joan knitted her eyebrows together, then ran her gaze up and down the front of Eunice's body. "If your neighbours think you're a man, they might need to get their eyes tested. You look very much like a woman to me." She snapped her eyes onto Eunice's face.

Joan's words warmed her from the inside out.

Eunice slowed her pace.

Enough that Mari and Kitty walked right into them, lost in their conversation.

Joan blinked, then blushed. "Look where you're going!" she told her friends.

"It was you who stopped in the middle of the pavement!" Kitty replied, affronted.

Joan shook her head and they resumed their walk.

Eunice couldn't put a finger on why she was so skittish around Joan. But it was a comfortable skittish, if that were possible. Eunice got the feeling that whatever she said to Joan, her friend wouldn't belittle it or treat her as if she was odd. Even so, perhaps she needed to triage her thoughts before they rushed out of her mouth. It was a fault her mother always told her would get her in trouble one day.

She hated nothing more than proving her mother right.

They walked to the corner of Heddon Street, and queued outside Rayner's Pie Shop. Inside, four men were loading scratched white plates with pie, mash and liquor, served from large, round metal vats. Eunice's stomach rumbled. It had been a long morning. She sucked her index finger into her mouth. She'd caught it on a needle earlier, and she had a blood blister on the tip.

"Eunice is a liquor girl," Joan told Mari and Kitty.

Mari baulked, sticking her tongue out. "You know it's the water from the stewed eels, mixed with parsley?"

Conversely, Kitty clapped her hands. "We've got two for, two against."

Eunice raised an eyebrow in Joan's direction. "You're not a fan?"

Joan shook her head. "It's the way it looks. I'm all about eating food that's easy on the eye. Green is not my colour."

"She's the same when it comes to men. Doesn't like the green ones." Mari gave Joan a gleeful look. "Very picky when it comes to men, aren't you?"

"Picky is one word," Kitty told Eunice. "Impossible is another we might have used before." She put an arm around Joan. "Joan here is waiting for her knight in shining armour to come along on his white horse to fulfil her every need. We've tried to match her up with a couple of nice fellas, but every time, Joan shoots them down."

Joan gave a theatrical shrug. "I have high standards, what can I say?"

"Your standards might have to lower soon if you don't want to be left on the shelf. You know what they say: there's an optimal time when you can meet a man and get him interested, and that time is ticking away every day."

Joan shook her head and gave Eunice a look that told her this was a conversation they'd had many times before. "I'll know when the right one comes along." She leaned into Kitty, so their faces were almost touching. "And by the way, I think I'm still in the window. I'm not even 19, and it's 1958, *not* 1948. This is a time of opportunity. Not a time when women have to do whatever men tell them."

"Alright Emmeline Pankhurst, don't get your knickers in a twist."

The queue moved and the foursome shuffled forward, now just a few feet from the door. The smells coming from inside were divine, the shortcrust pastry and buttery mash making Eunice's mouth water.

Mari nudged Eunice, closest to the door. "Have a look inside and see if there's a booth, will you? I prefer to eat at a table than sit on the wall in the smog. Use your feminine wiles to try and make any men hogging the seats hurry up."

Eunice had no idea what feminine wiles were, but she did as she was told. When she walked in, two men were just getting up from a booth. She ducked her head straight back out. "There's one free," she told her workmates.

Mari flapped her hands towards the door. "Go get it!" She nudged Joan. "Go sit with her. We'll get the pies; you can get them next week."

Eunice walked straight into the men exiting, such was her desire to get the booth and win points with her colleagues. She slid into the black leather booth just as a waitress appeared, stacking the men's chipped white plates on her arm and wiping down the table with a grey cloth. She missed a small pile of mash, and Eunice poked it towards the edge of the table and then flicked it off with her index finger, in a move she'd perfected playing marbles with David on their flat drain covers when she was little.

When she looked up, Joan slid into the seat beside her. "Come to keep you company." She was taller than Eunice by a few inches. Eunice scooted left to accommodate Joan, and immediately slammed into the tiled white wall beside her.

Joan gave her an apologetic smile. "I've no idea who made these booths, but I think it might have been someone on hunger strike."

"It certainly wasn't someone who ate pie every day of their life," Eunice replied.

"Exactly! You'd think they'd widen the booths, considering what they're selling." Joan laughed heartily and Eunice smiled at the sound. It wasn't a laugh she was used to hearing in her family. Joan's laugh, in contrast to any Eunice had heard before, was loud and unselfconscious. Joan didn't care who heard her and what heads she turned. Eunice could well imagine her being picky when it came to men. She could also well imagine many men being rather intimidated by such a bold woman.

Eunice was grateful that Joan had been her neighbouring machinist and not one of the quieter girls. If she was going to make it in the fashion world, she had to learn to speak up and be heard. She could learn a lot from Joan Hart.

Her first three weeks had taught her Joan was a ray of sunshine in the factory, the one who led the tea trolley chats, the one people listened to. Eunice had gone home every night the last few weeks pleased she could now call Joan a friend. Someone who didn't live on her estate. She represented Eunice's first step outside the White City and into the wider world.

Joan turned and waved at Mari and Kitty, now in the shop and beaming at the table grab. She got up and got four knives and forks from a jug on the end of the counter. Within five minutes, the foursome were all seated, the green liquor nearly oozing off Kitty and Eunice's plates. When Eunice took a forkful, being sure to blow on it first, she closed her eyes and savoured the delicious mix of flavours: rich minced beef, buttery pastry, mash and vinegary liquor. The girls hadn't been hyping it up at all. These really were tip-top pies.

Mari and Kitty both added more vinegar and salt before they all tucked in.

"Did you ask Eunice about the Boat Race yet?" Mari asked Joan, blowing on her food.

"Not since earlier." Joan flicked her gaze to Eunice. "Would you like to come with us?"

Eunice nodded. "I'd love to." It would be the first year she and David wouldn't be watching it together. Times were changing.

Joan beamed. "That's brilliant."

"We normally watch it on Hammersmith Bridge. Not so far from you," Kitty said.

"Not at all. A hop, skip and a jump," Eunice replied.

"Grand," Kitty continued. "We're going to a dance in the evening if you fancy that, too. In Shepherd's Bush. There's a live band and normally a good pick of fellas." She glanced at Joan. "I'm not asking you because you never come to dances." She rolled her eyes in Eunice's direction. "Joan would rather have her nose stuck in a book than in a man's face."

"I have good taste, that's why." Joan waved her hand, then glanced at Eunice. "Are you going to the dance?"

Eunice swallowed. She was about to say yes, but she'd prefer it if Joan came, too. Mari and Kitty were lovely, but it was Joan she chatted to the most. Plus, the other two had both talked about men they had their eye on, so they might desert her. However, she had to be brave. Push herself to do more. So she nodded. "It's close to home, so that would be lovely."

Joan put down her cutlery, then glanced around the table. "In that case, I'll make a special exception and come, too."

"Sorry?" Kitty banged her ear. "I think I might need my

hearing checked. Did the great Joan Hart just say she was coming to a dance with us?"

Joan pursed her lips, though couldn't help but smile. "Okay, Miss Smartypants. I thought I'd make a day of it. Boat Race, dinner, dance. Plus, it's Eunice's first time, so she's going to need someone to talk to while you're both off smooching."

Mari raised an eyebrow. "You might meet the man of your dreams and be smooching, too."

Joan flicked her gaze in Eunice's direction. "Stranger things have happened."

Chapter Seven

Hammersmith Bridge was already busy for the annual Oxford vs Cambridge University Boat Race by 1pm. Aware of its popularity, the foursome got there early and were now squashed up against the ornate iron railings, the river so close, they could almost touch it. Joan was in the middle, with Mari and Kitty to her left, Eunice to her right. Kitty had brought homemade lemonade and Spam sandwiches wrapped in tinfoil, which had gone down a treat. Now they were onto Mari's offering: vanilla sponge her mum had made that morning. Mari unfurled the tea towel it was wrapped in and passed the slices to her friends.

Joan hadn't brought anything, but she was grateful for the snacks and drinks, which they ate as the crowd swelled all around them and along the riverbank. Hammersmith was one of the more charming bridges on the Thames, with tall parapets at either end and suspended steel sides that reminded Joan of her brother's old Meccano sets. This was the 104th Boat Race, a beloved annual event in West London. For a South London girl like Joan, this was one of the only reasons she ventured this far north and west: she loved the river and the feel of the day.

Up above, a patchwork of clouds had formed. Joan patted

her olive-green shoulder bag, then winced as she recalled she'd forgotten her umbrella *again*. She hadn't read the forecast in the paper this morning, but it was April, so showers were almost guaranteed. If it rained, she hoped she could duck under someone else's, or she'd look a state at the dance later.

"Who do you shout for, Eunice?" Mari asked. "We're all Cambridge here." She checked her watch. "They should be coming soon, it starts at 2.30."

Joan cast Eunice a look. "Say Cambridge, or there could be trouble." The light blues had been the winners more often throughout the contest and the decade.

"Of course, Cambridge," Eunice replied, before taking a bite of the sponge cake. She made a happy face. "This is delicious," she told Mari.

Mari smiled. "My mum is always baking. If you ever feel the need for cake, stop by our house. We're always overloaded and you only live on the next estate."

Joan watched Eunice, entranced at the utter delight on her face as she ate. Eunice wore her heart on her sleeve, unlike Joan. It was a trait Joan loved in other people. She was far more of a closed book. In Joan's experience, life had a way of pulling the rug from under your feet just when you were getting comfortable, so she preferred to stay alert. Prepared. Not to give too much away. But in the short time she'd spent with her, Eunice was the opposite. If Joan had to lay bets, she'd say Eunice had sailed through life to this point without too many problems. Nobody had died or left her. But Joan wasn't going to dwell on that today.

When Eunice turned to Joan, she had crumbs on the side of her mouth.

Before Joan stopped to think, she reached out a hand to wipe them away. As the pad of her thumb connected to Eunice's face, she whipped her eyes to Joan.

Joan's heartbeat thudded in her ears. She stilled, and the moment froze between them.

Eunice's gaze held her in place. What was she doing, wiping her face? Joan fizzed with embarrassment. There were only two people who did that. The first was a mother. The second was a lover.

Joan was neither. She hastily dropped her hand and cleared her throat. A stew of emotion swirled inside her.

"You had some crumbs," she stuttered, not able to look Eunice in the eye. She was sure her cheeks were the colour of a plum.

Eunice put her hand where Joan's had been, checking her fingertips for crumbs. Then she raised her eyes back to Joan. "Looks like you did a good job. All gone?"

Their gazes held, and Joan's stomach turned like it was on a spin cycle. She gave Eunice a curt nod.

A murmur ran through the crowd, and the moment popped between them.

Shouting and cheering further up the river caused the crowds around them to bellow, while everyone who was near to the railing began to bang their hands on it, making the bridge vibrate with noise. Electricity ran through the crowd as necks strained, looking for the first churn of the river. Joan leaned over and grinned at Mari and Kitty, as the bridge shook to the stamping of feet and hands. When she looked right, Eunice gave her a luminous grin.

Joan's stomach flipped again.

It had occurred to her she might be in trouble when it came to Eunice. Now, as her body trembled being so close to her, it came into sharper focus. However, it was the kind of trouble that made Joan feel alive. Standing shoulder to shoulder with Eunice, it felt like the life she wanted might be within her grasp.

The roar of the crowd doubled as the water up ahead began to move and the boats that travelled ahead of the rowers came into view.

"Come on Cambridge!" shouted a man behind Joan, and this was followed by a barrage of shouts for both crews. The crowd surged forward as everyone jostled to get a view of the boats. Joan's ribs crushed up against the railings of the bridge, and she leaned back in an attempt to free up some air. Next to her, Eunice let out a gasp and Joan reached out an arm, pushing back the man behind Eunice.

He held up a hand. "Sorry, but I'm getting pushed too."

"Stop pushing!" Joan shouted, then turned to Eunice. "You okay?"

Eunice nodded, catching her breath. "Thanks."

"Apparently, the Cambridge crew are far dishier, according to Mari. She saw two of them in the paper this morning," Kitty shouted along the rail.

Eunice grinned, then leaned over and shouted right back. "We're so close, we might be able to ruffle their hair as they row past."

"There should be a women's race in London, too. Equal-opportunity hair ruffling," Joan added.

Kitty rolled her eyes. "I don't want to snog them!"

Joan's body stiffened, but she kept her face as neutral as she could. If only her world was as easy as Kitty's.

Seconds later the crews appeared, Cambridge ahead by at least a full boat length. They pulled through the water, foam on either side of their thin vessel, and the shouting increased to exhilarating, deafening levels. Cambridge cruised along the frothy Thames, then disappeared under the bridge first, Oxford trailing still. Joan couldn't see them coming back.

As Oxford disappeared beneath them, the crowd fell back and Joan breathed out. The crush as the boats had approached the bridge had been very real and she dropped her head back to face the sky, then grinned at her friends.

"Cambridge all the way!" Mari punched the air, her cheeks pink with exertion. She shivered and stamped her feet. "Although every year, I think I might be crushed to death and die right here."

"It crossed my mind, too." Kitty grabbed Mari's wrist to check her watch. "Quarter to three. We should head home and get ready for the dance before these clouds turn to rain," she told Mari. The two of them lived on the same estate ten minutes from Eunice. "See you at the dance at 7.30?"

Joan and Eunice nodded, then walked towards the end of the bridge, swept along by the crowds. The air smelled of beer and good cheer. The Boat Race was one of those days that felt very much for Londoners, a day of togetherness for the city. Which was odd, when neither crew was from the capital. Still, it wasn't about the race at all. It was more about sharing an event on the river, and also, the start of brighter spring days.

Joan glanced up at the sky, pulling her blazer tighter around her as the wind whipped across the bridge. The crowds may well have crushed her, but they'd also kept her warm.

"What are your plans? Are you going home before the dance?"

Joan shook her head. "I wasn't going to as it's a bit of a trek. But don't worry, I can entertain myself."

Eunice hesitated. She stopped at the top of the steps that led down to the riverside, then glanced back to Joan. "That seems a bit mean. We could sit by the river while the crowds die down? Then get the bus back my way. There's not a lot of room at our flat, but you could freshen up before we go out."

"I don't want to be any bother." Joan meant it, too. "But some time by the river might be nice."

A smile crossed Eunice's face and she held out a hand, indicating the steps. "After you."

They battled their way down, going against the crowds, then found a nearby bench facing the river, grass and a pathway in front of them.

Eunice produced a flask of water and offered it to Joan. She took a long swig. "I was thirsty."

"That'll be from all that cake Mari's mum made."

"Must have been." Joan paused. She wanted to ask a question that had been on her mind since Eunice mentioned him the week before. "Your neighbour who couldn't make it today. Was it David?" She knew full well his name, but she was playing it cool.

Eunice nodded.

A chill worked its way up Joan's neck. "Is he your boyfriend?"

Eunice snorted. "No. He's lovely, but I've known him since we were little. He's like a brother to me. Just not as annoying as my own brothers."

Joan's shoulder muscles relaxed as a weight lifted. "No boyfriend in the wings, then?" She said it as lightly as possible.

"Nope, much to my mum's disappointment." Eunice raised her eyes to the sky. "Mothers are such a pain sometimes, aren't they?"

Joan pushed her tongue into the roof of her mouth. She hated when people said things like that. They didn't know how lucky they were. "Mine had her moments."

Eunice turned, then smoothed back her blond hair. "Had?" Colour drained from her cheeks.

Joan nodded. "She died three years ago. Cancer."

"Gosh, I'm sorry. What an idiot. Going on about my mum. You must think I'm terrible." She dropped Joan's gaze.

Joan shook her head. "Not at all. I'm sure if she was alive, she'd be annoying me, too. But she died when I was 15, so her saint status is preserved. Ask my brother. He was 20 when she died, so maybe she annoyed him, although he'd never admit it."

Eunice's face stayed stricken. "I really am sorry."

"Don't be." Joan swallowed down hard. "Mum always said you only get one life, and you have to play the hand you're dealt. It's what I try to remember on the bad days."

Silence settled on them, but it wasn't uncomfortable. Joan wasn't grasping for the next subject, which was unusual. Even awkwardness with Eunice came easy.

"You said your dad had passed, too?"

The wheels had clearly been going around in Eunice's mind.

"Yes," Joan said. "He died when I was a baby. I'd just had my first birthday. He worked in theatre and stage management. He was at the Café de Paris when it was bombed in 1941.

He was one of a number killed. My aunt and I go for lunch there on his anniversary now. We didn't used to when Mum was alive. She couldn't bear to go in. But I think my Aunt Maggie wanted to reclaim his memory. It's more her I go for. She knew him all her life. I didn't really. My brother Jimmy is more of a father figure to me."

"Wow."

That was a common reaction to Joan's story.

"So you're an orphan."

Something hit her in the stomach. Grief was a funny thing. She could still see her mum in her hospital bed, telling her not to call herself that. "It sounds like you're a terrible case who never had any love. That's not true, is it?" her mum had said. And it wasn't.

Joan clenched her fist and swallowed down hard. She didn't want to fall apart with Eunice, but something about her made Joan's normally solid walls wobble. "I am an orphan. But I've got plenty of family around, plus me and Jimmy live together and get along great."

"You sound like you won the brother jackpot. Mine are all under ten and annoying."

"They might come good in time." Joan turned her head skywards, where the clouds had got darker since they arrived. She hoped the heavens weren't about to open.

"I can't imagine a world without my parents. They've both got their faults, but it would be so strange if they weren't there. Especially as I'm the eldest." Eunice shivered. "I wouldn't want to be left in charge of five kids. I've seen what it does to my mum. She never has a moment to herself."

Joan glanced her way. "I thought you wanted kids?"

Eunice's kids would likely have the same heart-shaped face as her. The same striking cheekbones. The same button nose.

Eunice tilted her head. "I do. But I want to leave London and see what's beyond it before that happens." She glanced at Joan. "There has to be something more, don't you think?"

Joan smiled. "There was me believing when you said you just wanted to get married and have a family when we first met."

Eunice grinned. "I can be shy at first. I do want that with the right person. Doesn't everyone? But I want to carry on working, too. Go to Paris, see the fashion world. But I also want to design gorgeous clothes for everyday women. Well-cut lines, maybe something for a special occasion. I want to bring stylish clothes to the masses."

"Those are big London dreams." A drop of rain fell onto Joan's nose, quickly followed by another. The rain clouds had snuck up on them. Now, they had her attention. She raised her hand to her face, then stared upwards. "I'm sure you'll achieve all your dreams, Eunice Humphries. But now, I'd say that's our cue to get a wriggle on."

Together, they raced up the stone steps to the bridge, the rain coming thick and fast. Joan hadn't had the foresight to bring a brush or a change of clothes for later, and drowned rat wasn't the look she was going for at the dance.

Once they reached the pavement, Eunice turned to her, water running down her face. "I was going to suggest walking home, but maybe we should get the bus now? The stop's not far." She reached out a hand and took Joan's in her own. Then she broke into a swift run, leaving Joan with no choice but to follow. She was happy to.

They dodged a slew of people on the bridge as they ran, and managed to slalom the umbrellas. Joan breathed in the scent of the damp tarmac, the heady smell one of her favourites. Her mum had loved it, too, and it always brought her to the forefront of Joan's mind. Her mum had loved dancing in the rain. Singing, too. She'd have approved of their current predicament. Revelled in it, even. Joan's heart sang as well. Yes, she was getting soaked, but she was also holding hands with Eunice.

Eunice glanced her way, then grinned at her through the rain.

Joan's pulse skittered. She liked Eunice, didn't she? Liked her in the way she'd been trying to push down ever since they met. She blew out a long breath as they crossed a road and bounded onto the pavement of the main road. She had to revel in moments like this, holding hands with Eunice. Joan wasn't likely to hold anything else of hers. Especially not her heart.

Eunice pulled her into a doorway beside a bus stop. She put a hand to her chest, catching her breath, her golden hair stuck to her face. Eunice didn't look like a drowned rat. She just looked beautiful.

"I must look a right state." Joan ran a hand through her chestnut hair.

But when Eunice caught her gaze, she shook her head. "You don't at all." She put a hand up as if to smooth Joan's hair back, but stopped halfway, thought better of it, then cleared her throat. "You look alive. A bit wet, but alive."

Joan laughed, her heart beating loudly in her ears. Why had Eunice gone to touch her hair and stopped? It was similar to Joan wiping crumbs from her face today. Except Eunice had

53

instigated the action, not her. Joan licked her lips, her brain working overtime.

Could Eunice be feeling something for her, too? If so, was it friendship, or something more?

She couldn't ask. She couldn't imagine a time where that would be possible. Which was what made the situation all the more maddening.

Eunice hugged herself, then shivered. She was soaked through, her dress clinging to her breasts, her thin cardigan hanging from her shoulders.

Joan tried not to stare, but it wasn't easy.

"You're coming home with me, if only to get dry before we go out again."

"Are you sure?" Joan had meant it when she said she didn't want to be any trouble. Especially now she knew Eunice was from a family of eight.

But Eunice was having none of it. "Positive." She stared at Joan for a few moments, then glanced over her shoulder. "Here's the bus!" She grabbed hold of Joan's hand once more.

It was a move Joan could well get used to.

Chapter Eight

The bus ride back to hers was steamy: they weren't the only ones to be caught out by the Saturday rain. As she and Joan sat pressed together on the double seat, Eunice's mind whirred. Joan lived with her brother, just two in their flat. What would she think about her family and where she lived? She'd never worried about it with any of her other friends before, because they all either lived on the estate or in the surrounding ones. But Joan lived in South London, a different world. Did she live in a nicer flat in a better area?

Eunice wasn't sure why, but it mattered what Joan thought. Still, there was nothing she could do about it now. Joan would have to take her how she found her.

They got off the bus, crossed the main road and walked through to the courtyard. It was noticeably lighter, the clocks having gone back the weekend before. Nobody was playing football today, the grass still slick from the downpour. However, when they arrived at her floor, David sat on the steps with his older brother, Reggie.

When David saw them, he jumped up. "Hey! How was the Boat Race? Did Cambridge cream them again?"

Eunice realised she didn't know. She and Joan had been too busy chatting and getting soaked to find out the result.

"I think so. They were leading at Hammersmith at least." Joan stood next to her, hands at her side.

David eyed her curiously. "I'm David." He held out a hand and Joan shook it.

"Nice to meet you," she replied. "I'm Joan. I work with Eunice."

David gave her a warm smile.

Reggie got up and shook Joan's hand, too. "Did you forget your brolly?" he said to Eunice.

"No, we just decided to get this wet."

Reggie threw back his head and let out a throaty laugh. "She's prickly, our little Eunice. She didn't tell me she had such pretty workmates, either." He never missed an opportunity to flirt. It was why his girlfriends never lasted, much to his parents' annoyance.

"Hands off, Reg, you don't stand a chance." Eunice put a hand to his chest, a smile dancing on her lips.

Reggie pulled himself up to his full height, quirking an eyebrow as he did. "I'll have you know women find me irresistible."

"Not after I fill Joan in on the truth." Eunice pushed him backwards gently. "Anyway, we better go. We've got to eat and make ourselves pretty for the dance."

Reggie bowed, then waved an arm as if granting them access. "You're both pretty enough already."

"Save it for the mirror, Reggie." Eunice could hear his laughter as she opened her front door. "Hello! I'm home!" She turned to Joan, her lips pursed. "It can be a bit of a madhouse."

Joan shook her head. "Makes a change from mine, which can be too silent if it's just me."

Eunice thought that sounded just about perfect. She walked down the hall, trying to ignore the frayed carpet and smudged walls. She poked her head into the kitchen, where her mum was at the hob, the smell of onions and mince strong in the air. Saturday night was shepherd's pie, then treacle pudding and custard. Her sister, Rose, got up from peeling potatoes at the kitchen table and hugged Eunice, wrapping her arms around her and not letting go. Eunice kissed her hair.

"Hi, Mum." Eunice beckoned Joan inside. "This is my friend Joan from work. This is my mum and little sister, Rose."

Her mum turned, wiped her hands on her pink-and-white striped apron, then gave Joan a smile. "Goodness, you're soaked through! The kids have got the fire on in the other room if you want to warm up a bit. How was the Boat Race?"

"Good." Eunice had a sudden need to get away from her mum's gaze. "We'll just go and get dry, okay?"

They walked down the hallway, past the lounge where her brothers were arguing. Eunice grabbed a couple of towels. She indicated the white door on the right, then shut it behind them, her back pressed against it. Her heart squeezed in her chest. It felt like they'd survived round one.

"Your family seem lovely," Joan said. "Is this the girls' room?"

Eunice nodded, glancing at the bunk beds on the right, her single bed on the left. "I had my own room once, but I don't remember it. If I want my own again, I need to get married."

"And even then, it won't be your own." Joan licked her lips.

As Eunice followed the tip of Joan's tongue, her stomach swooped.

Joan cleared her throat and towelled her hair.

When she came up for air, Eunice handed her a brush.

"I can't imagine having this many people under one roof. In my life, it was only ever me, Jimmy and Mum. Now it's just me and Jimmy." Joan took off her black-and-white herringbone blazer and hung it on the end of the bunk beds. Then she combed her hair, brushing it back and to the sides.

Eunice was mesmerised. She loved that Joan's hair was shorter than most. She found it daring. She went her own way when it came to fashion, too. Whereas all the other girls at the factory were wearing flared skirts or sporting the latest minis, Joan favoured tapered trousers, fitted blouses, stylish belts and small scarves. She occasionally wore skirts in the summer, but declared them impractical during most of the year.

"I don't want a breeze flying up me every time the wind decides. Plus, it means less men are tempted to grab my behind. If they do, I grab them right back."

Eunice loved her strength. Tonight's neckerchief was green and white, which complemented her grey and black outfit perfectly.

Joan undid her black shirt, wafting the open sides to get some air. When she caught Eunice's gaze, she blushed and turned away.

Eunice almost stopped breathing as she caught a glimpse of Joan's breasts, encased in black. She had a crazy thought she'd love to reach out and touch them. She dismissed it, then cleared her throat. Eunice tried to come up with a topic of conversation, but her mind was blank. All she could see were Joan's breasts.

How they might look naked.

How they might look wet.

How they might feel under her tongue.

Eunice tensed at that last thought, as blood rushed to the tips of her ears. She was starting to have thoughts like she imagined Reggie would have. But Reggie was a boy. A man. Whereas she was a girl.

"Have you been to these dances before in Shepherd's Bush?" Joan did up her buttons, then turned back to Eunice. "Is everything okay? You're staring at me strangely."

The blood rushed to Eunice's cheeks and she shook her head. "I was just lost in thought," she said. "I'm going to change into my dress. Are your clothes okay? Not too wet?"

Joan shook her head. "I think my jacket took the brunt, so if I could hang that by the fire before we go?" She grabbed it and held it out.

"Of course." Eunice took it from Joan, and their fingers touched. A jolt of electricity shot up her arm, making her jump. The air around them sizzled as Eunice got trapped in Joan's stare.

What the hell was happening? She had no idea.

Her mouth went dry. She opened her wardrobe to get a hanger and tried to regulate her breathing. But suddenly, the room seemed too small, the air thick with anticipation. Maybe being in here with Joan was a mistake. But Eunice's charged body told her otherwise.

A sudden knock made Eunice jump. She clutched her damp chest, put Joan's jacket on a hanger, then opened the door. "Yes?" Her tone was shrill, and Rose shrank back.

"Mum says does your friend want to stay for dinner?"

Eunice's heart thumped in her chest as she turned to Joan.

Her vision swam as she stared at her. Eunice was having trouble deciphering words, shapes, the world. She didn't want to be here with her family and Joan anymore. Exposing Joan to dinner here seemed like the worst idea in the whole world. But she had to.

"Would you like some dinner?" It really was the very worst idea of her life.

"Mum says you don't want to be fainting on the dance floor," Rose added.

Joan smiled. "In that case, I'd love to."

* * *

They arrived at Shepherd's Bush Social Club just before 8pm. Dinner had gone on longer than Eunice had anticipated, and her mum warned them to be careful of Notting Hill. "Full of poofs and blacks, so steer clear." Shepherd's Bush wasn't that close, but the papers were whipping up a frenzy after the Windrush emigration from the Caribbean. From what Eunice understood, they were just normal people trying to make a new life. Her parents didn't see it that way.

"Your siblings made me laugh, especially your twin brothers, Graeme and Peter. They're so cute."

Eunice rolled her eyes. "They have their moments. But they spend most of the time hitting each other over the head with their cars. It drives us all mad. Then they fall asleep holding hands. They can't make up their minds whether they love or hate each other."

"I think you just described family in a sentence." Joan paused. "I like your shoes, by the way. Very sophisticated." Eunice wore a pair of black shiny heels, making her an inch taller.

"Thanks. I wear them when I want to impress."

Joan quirked an eyebrow. "Who are you trying to impress?"

"I'm not sure yet." But the fact Joan had already noticed them made tomorrow's blisters worth it.

It'd stopped raining, but the air still held a chill, especially now the sun had set. When Eunice and Joan walked up to the main door, the cluster of men smoking on either side eyed them like a buffet. Eunice sped up and pushed through the double doors with ease. Inside, the space was too bright, dotted with tables and chairs around the edge of the dance floor, a slightly raised stage at the front that housed the five-piece band. Three guitarists, a drummer and an accordion player provided the music, and a clutch of couples were already foxtrotting their way around the floor. At the back of the room, a tea urn sat on a table, along with trays of assorted biscuits.

Frantic hand gestures to the right of the room caught Eunice's eye: Kitty and Mari. They walked over to their table and got hugs as they arrived.

"We thought you'd had a change of heart!" Kitty was truly dolled up: her flowery dress shimmied as she moved, and her makeup glittered on her face.

"Just took a little longer than we expected," Joan replied. "Have you danced yet?"

Kitty shook her head. "We're waiting for the men to finish smoking and come and ask us. You know what it's like at these things. It always takes a while to warm up and for them to get their nerve."

"They're probably swigging whisky from a flask outside to work up the courage," Mari added. She smoothed down her equally flowery dress, a tight body leading out to a flowing skirt. Perfect for twirling. "I feel sorry for men, sometimes. They've got to do all the work, all the asking."

Eunice snorted. "Don't feel too sorry for them. The world is laid out on a plate for them. I'd do the asking if I could negotiate that deal."

Kitty's eyes widened. "A young feminist in our midst." She nodded at Joan. "Have you been on at her since we left?"

Joan glanced at Eunice. "Nope, this is all Eunice. I've said nothing at all."

Eunice shrugged off her coat, and Joan's gaze followed her every move.

"I still can't believe you designed and made that dress," Joan said. "It's incredible."

Eunice had done everything from coming up with the concept for the pattern to putting in the final dart, and her mum and Mrs Higgins had declared it 'head-turning'. A daring shade of turquoise, it made her eyes sparkle. Eunice couldn't quite pin down the look Joan gave her, but it was intoxicating. It made her feel like the most important person in the room. It made her skin tingle all over.

Half an hour later, Kitty and Mari were dancing with two of the smokers from outside. The floor was filling up, the men in suits and ties, the ladies decked out in an array of brighter fabrics. Eunice watched them spin around the floor, irritation tingling in her veins. Why did she have to wait for men to ask her to dance? Couldn't she just dance of her own accord?

"You know," Joan said, breaking Eunice's thoughts. "If you wanted to dance together, we could." She pointed at two couples on the far side of the room. "Those women are doing it." It was common practice at dances, because there were usually more women than men.

Eunice stood up and held out her hand. "Let's do it. But who's going to be the man?" Just saying those words made Eunice's blood flow faster. Did she want to lead, or did she want Joan to fill that role?

Joan took the decision out of her hands, wrapping her left arm around Eunice's waist, lifting her right hand into a ballroom frame and pulling their bodies tight. "I'm taller and I'm wearing trousers." She gave her a cheeky wink. "I'll lead." Joan pulled her shoulders back, and began to do just that.

In Joan's arms, Eunice held her breath as they hit the dancefloor. Twirled in the way Eunice had once thought might happen with a boy, but it never had. But now, in Joan's secure embrace, Eunice flew, her spirits lifting with every step. She couldn't wipe the smile from her face as Joan's fingers dug into her waist, as she breathed in Joan's heady perfume. She daren't look into her face for fear that Joan would see right through her. But dancing with her, their bodies crushed close, Eunice was pretty sure she was an open book anyway. If Joan could feel her heartbeat through her chest, she wouldn't be able to hide a thing.

She kept her head tilted to the left as she'd been taught, and her hand gripped Joan's, her frame solid.

However, what Eunice yearned to do was wrap her arms around Joan's neck, breathe her in and make everyone else vanish. And then do what? She wasn't sure. But she knew she had to hang on to this moment of closeness, when she got to dance with her preferred partner. So she pressed herself that bit closer as they spun, cocooned in their fragile world.

"You're a great dancer," Joan whispered, her breath hot against Eunice's ear.

Eunice twanged with pleasure at her words. "Thanks," she replied, her voice barely audible. They waltzed near the band, the drums loud in Eunice's ear.

The song ended and Eunice stepped back, applauding the band along with everyone else. She had a huge smile on her face.

"Thanks all, we're going to take a 15-minute break."

"Fancy a cigarette outside?"

Eunice didn't smoke, but she nodded anyway. If Joan left her now, she'd be bereft. Wherever Joan was, she wanted to be. It was an unsettling feeling.

But also, the most excited she'd felt in her entire life.

Joan grabbed her bag and Eunice's coat, then pushed open the doors. They stood to the right, next to a group of men with slicked back hair and suits. One of them nudged his friend as Eunice and Joan stood near them. Eunice ignored them.

Joan produced a packet of Woodbines and offered Eunice one. She took it. She had no idea what she was doing or who she was today. She didn't smoke. She'd never smoked, thought it was a grim habit. She didn't like the smell of smoke on her clothes. Yet, when Joan lit up her Woodbine and inhaled, Eunice would swear it was the most intoxicating thing she'd ever seen. The elegant way Joan held the cigarette. The way her eyes crinkled when she exhaled. The way she smiled at Eunice, just like she was doing now.

"What? You keep looking at me funny tonight."

Eunice shook her head like it was nothing. "I was just

thinking, I enjoyed dancing with you. Far more than any boy I've ever danced with."

Joan didn't drop her gaze. "I enjoyed dancing with you, too."

The moment pulsed between them, until Joan shook her head. "Sorry, I forgot to give you a light."

Eunice glanced at the cigarette in her fingers, then placed it between her lips.

Joan stared, a look on her face Eunice couldn't quite decipher, but one she knew she'd replay in her mind again and again later. Joan flicked the lighter and Eunice leaned into the flame, sucking down.

Big mistake.

As she inhaled, the smoke got caught in her throat and Eunice opened her mouth to suck in more air. It didn't help. She began to cough violently, her body convulsing as she gasped for air. Someone took the cigarette from her fingers and rubbed her back.

Eunice doubled over, hands on her thighs, trying desperately to steady her breathing. Eventually, the coughing stopped. When she straightened up, Joan's face was filled with concern.

"You okay?"

She wiped her streaming eyes. She must look a right state. She nodded her head in exaggerated fashion.

"I take it you don't normally smoke?"

Eunice shook her head. "I've always been curious, but I clearly need more practice."

Joan laughed. "The first go is always rough. Maybe you should give it a break tonight."

"Maybe." She smiled at Joan, happy to be laughing with

her. Her body was still alight with Joan's touch. So gentle, yet firm. Eunice had never been happier to be held.

"Excuse me." It was one of the boys in the group nearby. He had a quiff and a woollen jacket. "I wondered if you'd like a handkerchief?" He held out a crisp square of white cotton. "It's clean and you're welcome to it."

Eunice reached out. "That's very kind, thank you."

The boy cast his gaze to the floor. "You're welcome." He walked back to his friends.

Eunice blew her nose and wiped her face before turning to Joan. "I better check my face. I'll see you inside?"

* * *

Back by their table, Eunice and Joan chatted with Kitty and Mari as the band retook their places on stage.

"Okay folks. Boys, grab your girls, we're going in for a waltz to the sounds of Dean Martin. Please welcome to the stage our guest singer for the night, Johnny Haynes!"

Whistles and clapping from the crowd ensued, as men did as they were instructed and invited women to dance. Four approached their table; one was the man who'd given Eunice his handkerchief. He held out a hand to her, and his friend with the darker hair went to Joan.

"Would you care to dance?"

Eunice glanced at Joan, her muscles tightening. She didn't really want to, but she didn't have an excuse not to. So she nodded and painted on a smile. She saw Joan do the same, and as the band started up, the young man put his arm around Eunice's waist and pulled her close.

Eunice stiffened as their bodies pressed together. His

breath smelled of tobacco and whisky. She recoiled slightly.

In response, he tightened his grip on her. "Everything okay?"

Eunice gave him a faltering smile.

"Good," he replied, oblivious. "My name's Harry. You're Eunice, right?"

She tilted her head. "How do you know that?"

"Good guess."

Out of the corner of her eye, Eunice spotted Joan looking her way over her partner's shoulder. She widened her eyes and stuck her tongue out.

Eunice stifled a laugh, tripped over Harry's feet, then steadied herself.

Harry twirled her one way, then trod on her foot.

Eunice let out a shriek and dropped his hold.

"Sorry! I'm late to dancing, so I sometimes forget the steps." He invited her back into his hold and she accepted. "You're the first girl I've worked up the courage to ask. I promise not to tread on your toes again."

Eunice smiled at him. She couldn't be mad. He was trying his best. But it wasn't lost on her that Joan didn't even have to try. In Harry's arms, she felt heavy, like they might crash at any moment. But with Joan, the steps had felt light and they'd simply flown. Joan had transported her out of Shepherd's Bush Social Club and into another world. Whereas Harry had brought her back down to earth with a bump.

However, she didn't want to hurt his feelings, so she carried on dancing with him for the three-song set, before Johnny Haynes stepped down to great applause.

Across the dance floor, Joan's gaze sought her out. When

it found its target, Eunice's heart leapt like it never had before. So much so, she looked around to check if anyone else had felt the tremor. They hadn't.

"I have to go now." Harry's voice brought her back to the present. "Will you be here next week?"

Eunice stared at him, trying to make sense of his words. "I'm not sure."

Harry kissed the top of her hand. "I will be, and I'd love to dance with you again. I hope to see you then." He blinked, then grabbed his friend and they left.

Joan walked up beside her. "You looked cosy." There was an edge to her voice.

Eunice looked up, her feelings bunched in her throat. Joan's face spelt disappointment. She never wanted to be that to her. "Not really. I lost count of the number of times he trod on my foot. Anyway, he's gone now." She hoped that meant another dance with Joan was on the cards.

"I might go, too." Joan twisted her mouth left to right. "It's a long way home for me."

Eunice's stomach fell. "Right." There was so much more she wanted to say, but she had no idea how to say it. She wanted Joan to stay more than anything in the world. But to let Joan know that would be weird, right?

"I'll see you Monday." Joan's gaze lingered on Eunice, almost as if she was willing her to say more. To be brave.

But Eunice simply nodded. "You will."

Still Joan didn't move. It was as if she was glued to the spot.

Now Eunice had to say something. She took a deep breath. "Just to let you know, he was too bony." What was it with men? She'd preferred Joan's curves, her soft skin.

A light bulb switched on in Eunice's brain. What was she admitting to herself? That just one look from Joan stole her breath away, something she knew Harry could never do?

"He was?" Joan's voice lowered, along with her stare.

"I much preferred dancing with you." Where was this bravery coming from? She sucked in a long breath.

Joan's eyes widened.

Her smile pierced Eunice's heart.

"Eunice! Joan!" Someone grabbed hold of her arm and Eunice jerked back to reality. When she glanced at Joan, she was still there, still focused solely on her.

It was too much, and yet, it was all Eunice wanted. She hoped it wasn't written all over her face. Otherwise, she was in more trouble than she'd ever imagined.

But Kitty didn't seem to notice. "Are you coming? They're teaching us how to dance to that new doo-wop music from America!"

Eunice nodded, but never took her eyes from Joan.

"Have a good night." Joan gave her a sad smile, then walked away.

Chapter Nine

The next couple of weeks, Joan avoided any intimate moments with Eunice. She had to. Even though she was sure there was something in Eunice's stare that day, too. At the dance and at the Boat Race. The way Eunice had nearly reached out and swept Joan's hair from her face while they waited for the bus. Or had Joan just dreamt it? Very possibly.

It all had ominous echoes to Frances. The girl in her class who Joan had grown so fond of. Who Joan had kissed when they were 16. It had gone on for a couple of weeks, the two of them exploring each other's bodies tentatively, kissing constantly. Right up until the moment her mother caught them doing just that in Frances's bedroom, and threw Joan out, calling her "disgusting".

Joan had gone home that day and sobbed like she'd never sobbed before. She hadn't been able to hide it from her aunt or her brother. How she'd have loved to speak to her mum about it, but that could never happen. So she'd told Jimmy and Aunt Maggie. Jimmy had been kind, told her that her feelings were valid, and that she wasn't disgusting. That Frances's mum was the one who was disgusting. Aunt Maggie had said that teenage years were confusing, and maybe she'd overstepped the mark with Frances. That it could be just a phase. When Joan had asked what would happen if it wasn't, Maggie had told her she'd always love her, no matter what. That had made Joan sob even more.

Her brother and her aunt were trying to protect her. She knew what the world thought of women who loved other women. That they were deviant. Monsters. Not to be trusted. While Joan was pretty sure nothing was going to change for her, she couldn't take Eunice down, too. Eunice was an innocent in all this. She'd come along and captured something inside Joan. But it had to stay there. She had to keep a lid on her feelings. She knew how this ended. Maybe one day she might meet another woman who felt the same way. But for now, she had to be brave.

However, the past three weeks had been torture. Joan had been friendly with Eunice. All the easy chat between them had dried up, replaced with an invisible barrier. It'd been steadily building ever since Joan had pressed her body to Eunice's at the dance, and all manner of thoughts and feelings had shot through her. Spending time with Eunice had been magical. It had been one day. But that was enough.

This morning, Joan tried not to think about it. She didn't glance at Eunice's shimmering hair, and simply concentrated on her work. Machining pink flowery dresses. If she chatted less, she got paid more. Her mum would have agreed. Liz Hart had been a singer: an accomplished one, too. She'd always told Joan, "you only get paid when you sing". Similarly, Joan only got paid when she sewed.

Before the start of the second world war, Joan's mum had entertained at all London's hotspots: The Café de Paris, The London Jazz Club, or Feldman's as it was known back then. Her mum had worked all over, and particularly loved the clubs around Carnaby Street that showcased African and Caribbean music. Her parents had rubbed shoulders with all cultures and backgrounds. The world of entertainment was more forward-thinking than the world around it. Her mum would have been appalled at the papers and their racism right now. She'd always had a policy of inclusion for all.

The stage was where Joan's parents had met. It was why her brother worked in the theatre, and why she wanted to write plays or film scripts. It was a world she knew. A world she wanted to get back to. A world where, perhaps, her kind of people lived. She wasn't going to meet the love of her life in a factory, was she?

The wireless blared from the front of the room, and a murmur went around the workers. A few of the women turned to Joan. She'd inherited her mum's voice.

"You can do better than this, Joanie!" That was Crystal, shouting from row one.

Joan smiled. "Not this morning, sorry." She hadn't sung for a few weeks now. She hadn't been in the mood.

But the rest of the factory wasn't listening. "Come on, Joan!" said a couple of the girls nearby. Joan drew her lips into a thin line and shook her head.

Then somebody started a slow clap. The rest of the girls joined in. Joan kept her head down. She flexed her foot on the pedal, attaching an arm to the main body of the dress.

Then a velvety voice broke through the claps and the hum of the machines.

Eunice.

"I'd love to hear it. I haven't heard you sing since I started, only talk from the girls saying how good you are."

Joan turned her head and got caught in Eunice's deep emerald stare. Was she that easy to persuade? Apparently, when it came to Eunice, the answer was yes. Joan held her gaze, then gave her a nod.

The smile Joan received in return was all worth it.

She stood up and raised her hands, palms out, then lowered them slowly to hush the crowd. It worked.

"Okay you rabble," Joan began. Every time she sang, she thought of her mum. She had no longing to be onstage, but she'd learned how to control a crowd by watching her mum do it.

"You're the one with the microphone, so the one with the power. Always remember that. You're onstage, everyone's looking at you to lead."

She might not be onstage or have a microphone, but the premise was the same.

"Someone turn the wireless down and we'll have a quick sing-song." She turned to Gladys: she knew she was close by the waft of Chanel No.5 under her nose. "That okay with you?"

She held out a hand. "Be my guest."

Joan puffed out her chest, cleared her throat and then began to sing 'You Belong To Me'. She was rewarded with thrilled faces all round. When she went up a key on the second verse, singing of marketplaces in Old Algiers, she waved her arms for them to join in, and within moments, the whole floor was swaying to her rhythm.

Joan's gaze swept the floor, right to left. Over the machines, the huge metal pipes hanging from the ceiling, the enormous windows, the dappled sunlight on the brick walls. She took in Mari, Kitty and the rest of the girls, until she stopped at

Eunice. When she got to her, she couldn't tear her gaze away. It was impossible.

Her arms told the rest of the factory to join in as she reached the final verse, talking of jungles wet with rain. But Joan no longer sang to the factory. Now, her vocals were for Eunice alone. She couldn't help it. As she reached the penultimate words, and softly sang "you belong to me", her spirit and her hope soared. She'd never hoped for anything more in her life.

In response, Eunice mouthed the words right back to her, never breaking their stare.

Joan's breath got shorter as she approached the final flourish and she fought to get it back under control. She closed her eyes, thought of her mum, then powered through to the crescendo. When she raised an arm at the end in triumph, the whole factory whooped and applauded.

However, it was only Eunice's applause Joan craved. She bowed, soaking it up. When she turned to Eunice, the look on her face made Joan catch her breath. Eunice's smile was wondrous, it lit up the floor. Her eyes were shiny, like she could stare at Joan forever.

There was something there, wasn't there? Joan wasn't imagining it? How she wished she could ask. But this song, these last few minutes were the most honest Joan had been with Eunice in the past three weeks. Ever since the dance. When Joan sang, her emotions didn't lie. She couldn't sing and hold them in. Her mum had always told her that. She had to be true to herself. Maybe that's why there were so many more people in show business who didn't fit societal norms. People like her. They couldn't keep it in. They had to be authentic.

However, letting it all out came at a price. Now, she had to get on with her work, just like everyone else. But it wasn't that easy when she'd just opened herself up. Joan's chest heaved as she looked around. She caught Eunice's eye once more, and something threatened to bubble up. She had to regain control.

"Bravo!" a male voice shouted.

Joan looked up to see Mr Prestwick clapping as he walked to the middle of the floor. His first name was Bob, but Joan always thought he looked more like a Roger. He was dressed for the world's most glamorous funeral, as usual, his moustache waxed. "I don't often hear you sing, Joan, but it's always a pleasure!"

"Thank you so much," Joan replied.

"You know why I'm here, ladies. It's Friday, but we've got another rush order on. You know the drill: double time for anyone who can come in tomorrow. Married ladies, don't worry. But what about you single gals?" He rubbed his hands together, then looked left and right. "Hands up who can help me out? I'd be very grateful!"

Hands went up as they always did. Joan glanced at Eunice. Another day in the factory with her was heaven and hell all wrapped up in a neat bow. But when Eunice put her hand up, Joan's followed quickly. She couldn't help it.

"I knew I could count on you all. See you tomorrow at 8.30 sharp!" Mr Prestwick gave them a wide smile, then turned and walked off the floor.

Joan stood and smoothed down the front of her overall. "I'm just going to the loo."

Eunice nodded.

Joan walked through the factory, soaking up all the compliments thrown her way. She walked into the stairwell and welcomed its coolness. She could use a little of that where Eunice was concerned. She walked into the toilets, locked a cubicle door, sat down and put her head in her hands.

Pushing her feelings down only went so far, didn't it? Maybe she should get another job? But then, she'd never see Eunice again. That thought was the worst outcome of all. Because for all that Eunice caused Joan's heart to stop and start like a faulty watch, she still loved that it happened.

Life with Eunice was infinitely better than life without her.

She puffed out her cheeks and flushed the toilet, even though she hadn't used it. When she walked out to the sinks, the door opened and Eunice walked in.

Joan's resolve faltered. Then she pushed herself forward and turned on the taps, her eyes looking down at the water.

In moments, Eunice joined her at the basins.

"You've got an amazing voice. Your mum would be so proud."

Joan stared at the crack in the sink, before looking up and meeting Eunice's gaze in the mirror. "Thanks." *She wasn't going to cry.*

Eunice's mouth twitched. "Looks like we'll be working together tomorrow."

Joan nodded. She didn't trust herself to say too much else.

"I was wondering if you'd like to go for coffee after work. Or tea. Whichever you prefer." Eunice's cheeks coloured as she spoke.

Joan's insides stuttered. If she was imagining this spark between them, then it was the most peculiar thing she'd ever dreamt up in her life.

"Actually, I'm going to see a show at the Garrick tomorrow.

My brother is working on the set and he can get me in for free."
She paused. "We could go for coffee and then go to the show
together. I'm sure Jimmy could put your name on the list, too."
The words were out before Joan's brain had time to protest.
When Joan risked a glance at Eunice, a smile graced her lips.

"I'd love to."

Joan blew out a long breath. "Great." And it was. Eunice
was coming to the theatre with her. It was a date. Only, not
a date.

Joan rinsed her hands, then grabbed a paper towel from the
stack, drying in between her fingers with concentrated effort.
"I wasn't sure if you'd be free." She glanced up. "Whether or
not you met that boy again and were seeing him." She didn't
want to know. But at the same time she *had* to know.

However, Eunice shook her head, then awarded Joan
another smile.

Eunice's smiles gave Joan life.

"I did meet him the following week. I dragged David and
Reggie along, too. They agreed he was too bony. Plus, he was
a bad kisser." This time, Eunice's smile didn't reach her eyes.

Joan flinched. That was a gut punch. She was pleased he'd
been bad, but she didn't want him to kiss Eunice at all.

She straightened up and turned to Eunice, looking her
right in the eye. "If nothing else, you have to find someone
who's a good kisser. It's important." Joan so wanted to reach
out and show Eunice just what she meant. Heat surged
through her.

Eunice gazed at her. "I agree," she replied, not missing a
beat. "Kissing is very important."

Joan's throat went dry. Her mind blank.

Still they stared.

The door opened and Sheila, the chief cutter, walked in.

"Hey girls!" she said, before disappearing into a cubicle.

Both Joan and Eunice took a step back, then cleared their throats. The air was filled with so much left unsaid — and this time, Joan was convinced it was a two-way street.

"We should get back."

Eunice nodded. She opened the toilet door and waited for Joan to walk through.

When Joan's body brushed Eunice's, she shivered.

"I'm looking forward to tomorrow night already," Eunice added.

Joan gave her a smile. "Me, too."

Chapter Ten

Eunice let herself in the front door. She hoped she could sneak in unseen. It was Friday, so no doubt her dad was down the pub. All three of her brothers were playing football out front. That left Mum, Rose, and Mabel to navigate. She held her breath, then slipped past the kitchen, the wireless blaring. She got past the lounge and to the threshold of her room when the door opened, revealing her mum.

Eunice jumped back, and clutched her heart through her chest. "You gave me a fright!"

Her mum steadied herself on Eunice's shoulders. "Vice versa! I was just putting your clothes away and I gave your room a quick dust." She kissed Eunice's cheek, then stepped back. "You're freezing. Is it cold out there?"

Eunice nodded. "Windy. I'm surprised the boys are still playing football. I would have thought the wind would have blown the ball all the way to Loftus Road by now." Loftus Road, the home of her dad's beloved Queen's Park Rangers, was just a five-minute walk away.

Her mum stepped into the hallway. "Come and have a cup of tea with me in the kitchen before I put the fish on. I feel like we haven't had a proper chat since you started your new job. You've worked half the weekends and been out with your new friends." She put a hand on Eunice's arm. "I want to know how you're doing."

She couldn't say no to her mum. "Let me just splash some water on my face and I'll be with you."

Eunice shut her bedroom door, then flopped onto her bed. For now, she'd have to put today on the back burner. Joan singing to her. The moment they'd shared in the toilet. She wasn't sure what was going on, but it was powerful. This *thing* between them frightened her to death *and* lit her up. But she couldn't tell her mum that. She couldn't even tell David, who had always been her confidante. If she didn't understand, nobody else would either. She had to paint on a smile. Even though, everywhere she looked, she saw Joan.

Five minutes later, when Eunice had gathered her thoughts, she walked into the kitchen and washed out the teapot, swilling the tealeaves down the sink. The tap leaked at the bottom as it always did. Her dad was meant to fix it last week, and the week before that. He was a handyman at the local hospital, and hired out his services around the estate, too. His own home was the least well-tended of them all.

Eunice warmed the pot — her mum would have a fit otherwise — then put the kettle back on the stove to boil. The drying rack overhead was full of the family's smalls. Eunice pulled it down and felt one of her brother's socks. It was dry. She began folding the laundry. If she left it up, it would smell of fish. Her parents weren't devout Catholics, but they wouldn't dream of eating anything else on a Friday.

"You are good. I'm going to miss you when you leave."

Eunice folded Graeme and Peter's once-white vests, her face creased. "Where am I going?"

"You know what I mean. In a year or two you might be married. Then it'll be down to me, Rose and Mabel."

"You could ask the boys to help."

Her mum waved a hand. "They're boys, what do they know?"

The kettle whistled, and Eunice made the tea. Her mum got teacups and saucers, and brought over a Lyons' cake tin, too.

"I thought we were waiting on Mrs Higgins' weekly delivery?"

"We are. But Hilda baked some shortbread and brought it round. It pays to have good neighbours." Hilda was David's mum.

"Apparently it does." Eunice poured the tea and added milk, then took a shortbread. She sucked on it, remembering how Joan had sucked on her pie at lunchtime. How enticing her lips had looked. Eunice cast her gaze to the floor. Thank goodness her mum couldn't read her mind.

"How's this week been? Are you working again tomorrow?"

Eunice nodded. "We are. Double time again. I can put it towards my Paris savings."

Her mum patted her hand. "You and your dreams. But it's good to dream."

"I'm going to Paris. It's not a dream. It's a plan." She knew her mum meant well, but she didn't want to be patronised. "Also, I'm out tomorrow night, so don't worry about dinner for me." Out with Joan. Just the thought made her smile.

Her mum raised an eyebrow. "Out with who? On a date with that boy again?"

Eunice wrinkled her face. "I told you that was going nowhere. No, I'm going out with Joan. Her brother works in the theatre and he can get us into a show for free."

Her mum sat back, assessing Eunice. "Joan again? You two seem to get on well."

Eunice shifted in her seat. "We do. She's nice. I like her a lot."

"Does she have a boyfriend?"

Eunice's throat went dry. "No."

Her mum took that in for a couple of seconds. "Is she fussy like you, too?"

Eunice didn't respond. She'd heard this all before.

"Don't roll your eyes at me," her mum said.

Eunice thought she'd managed not to.

"What was wrong with the last one? What was his name?"

"Harry. He was nice. Needed a bit more meat on his bones. But he was just a bit dull. I told you before, I want to meet someone who I connect with." Just like she did with Joan. If only Joan was a man, her mum would be off her back.

"You've been listening to too many love songs, that's your trouble. You're 18 next year, nearly a woman. You've got to stop rejecting all these men and being so fussy. I know you think you're special, and you *are* special. Special to me, your dad, your siblings. But you have to at least date one of these fellas. You've never had a boyfriend, and you should have one. Just to get a feel for it. He might not be Mr Right, but he could be Mr Right Now." Her mum sat back, pleased with herself. "Haven't all your other friends had boyfriends? Don't you want one?"

Eunice shrugged. She'd always found the thought a little repulsive, but assumed she'd grow out of that. She was still waiting.

"It'll happen when it happens. I'm not worried about finding a man. There's plenty of time, I'm hardly past it."

"Of course you're not."

"Well, then." Eunice folded her arms across her chest. Maybe there was a reason she didn't have these chats with her mum too often. Self-preservation. She sighed. "I'm not going to go out with someone just to please you. I don't want to lead someone up the garden path."

Her mum bit into her shortbread. "You might find once you've walked up it, you like it more than you think. You should have a relationship, pretty girl like you. Otherwise, people will talk."

Eunice threw up her hands. "Let people talk. I'm not going out with someone for everyone else's benefit. This is my life, nobody else's." She didn't want to end up in a marriage like her parents'. She'd often wondered how they got together, because they seemed to have nothing in common apart from their children. "How did you know when you met Dad?"

Her mum's smile didn't quite cover her face. "We met through his brother. I thought he was a bit of a smart alec, which at the time I found attractive. So I walked up the garden path with him, and by the end, I liked him more."

Eunice wasn't convinced. "I hope I feel more than like for my future husband."

"I grew to love him. You can do that, too. Loving someone isn't a given all the time. That goes for everyone: your husband *and* your children."

A knock on the front door interrupted them, followed by footsteps in the hallway. Moments later, Mrs Higgins padded into the kitchen, carrying a bag of treats. "Hello you two!"

If she could feel the tension in the room, she didn't show it. Eunice was grateful for the interruption.

"I brought cakes, rolls and scones." Mrs Higgins put her bag on a chair. She took out two tins of treats.

Mum hopped up and traded her full tins for two empty ones. "I cleaned them out, ready for next time." She paused. "Would you like a tea? It should still be hot."

Mrs Higgins' face lit up like this was the best offer she'd had in days. Perhaps it was. "That would be lovely." She wheezed as she sat. The smog troubling London wasn't agreeing with Mrs Higgins' asthma. Lately, her wheezing preceded her.

"Have you seen a doctor about your asthma?" Mum asked.

Mrs Higgins waved a hand. "I've got my medication. They'd only tell me to stop eating so many cakes. Plus, every time I go to the doctor I pick up something new. I'd rather stay here where I can control things." She sipped her tea, then tapped the table. "I had some exciting news today, though. I got a letter from my nephew saying he's coming to visit over the summer. He's just back from national service. He's 20 and wants to see London."

"Is he your brother's son?" Mum asked.

"Yes, Kenneth. A lovely young lad."

Eunice could see the cogs whirring in her mum's head already.

Sure enough, moments later: "A young man coming to London. I'm sure Eunice would be happy to show him around, wouldn't you?"

Eunice squashed down a sigh. "Of course." She couldn't say no to Mrs Higgins. "When is he coming?"

Mrs Higgins frowned. "He wasn't specific, but I think he was suggesting August? But I'll have to check."

August was three months away. If promising to meet Kenneth got her mum off her back, Mrs Higgins could have come up with the perfect plan. This way, she could spend more time with Joan and not have to dance with more dull, bony boys.

"Let me know. I'd be happy to take him on a tour of the city. Who better than a born-and-bred Londoner?"

"That would be wonderful!" Mrs Higgins replied. "Who knows, you might even get on."

Eunice smiled, Joan's lips reappearing in her mind. "I'm sure we might."

Chapter Eleven

Joan twirled in the road outside Prestwick's, showing off her new coat. It was pea green, and she loved it. "What do you think? I can roll in the grass now and not worry about stains. Just dog poo."

Eunice snorted. "I love it. But then, with your height, you can carry most things off." She grinned. "When I become a famous designer, will you be my model?"

Joan raised an eyebrow, then bowed. "It would be my honour, m'lady."

Saturdays in the factory always felt different, despite them doing the same job in the same spot. It was the weekend. They shouldn't be at work, but they were. Plus, the radio had blared all day, which made everyone giddy.

Now, Joan had a fat pay packet burning a hole in her pocket, and she had Eunice. Just like today, tonight felt different, too. With just the two of them, it almost felt like a date. Although, this was better than any date Joan had dragged herself to before. For starters, it was a date she wanted to be on. All day long, Joan had stared at Eunice's golden hair, an ornate clip drawing her eyes to its tightly drawn up bun. When the horn signalled it was time to go, Eunice pulled the clip free, and her hair had fallen into an artfully tousled mass around her shoulders. She looked like a film star. She had Joan won already.

"Shall we go to Carlo's? It's a new place that's just opened on one of the side streets off Covent Garden. Jimmy told me about it and said it's great. Italian."

Eunice nodded. "I've never been to an Italian restaurant," she said. "Scrap that, I've never been to a proper restaurant before. Unless you count pie and mash shops, which I don't."

Joan stopped walking, giving Eunice a look. "You've never been to a restaurant?"

She shook her head. "Nope."

Joan held out a crooked arm. "In that case, let me escort you to your first Italian experience. Before you know it, you'll be jetting off to Milan and drinking tiny coffees out of tiny cups. They have fashion there, too, right?"

"Chance would be a fine thing." Eunice grinned, then threaded her arm through Joan's and they set off down Wardour Street, the crowds of people on the pavements meaning they were constantly stepping into the road, avoiding cars and vans in the process.

They passed the film studio Pathé, not the only one on Wardour Street, which was a bit of a film mecca. Jimmy told Joan she should hang around there in her lunch hour and sneak a script into one of the offices, but Joan was still working up to that. The shutters were down on Hancock's Camera Shop, its bright orange front still shimmering in the evening sun. Conversely, the many cafes and restaurants were getting into their stride at just gone 5.15pm. Their awnings were out and ready for business, and as they passed Fred's Bistro, the smell of tomatoes filled the air.

They hit Shaftesbury Avenue with its wealth of theatres. Joan breathed in the bright lights of the West End, her spiritual home. She took Eunice's hand to cross the main road, and didn't let it drop as they elbowed their way through the Leicester Square crowds. Once onto Charing Cross Road, Eunice's pace slowed as they passed Daphne's, a posh hotel with a hugely impressive floral display, along with a doorman in a peaked cap.

"I've never been in a posh hotel, either. I always wanted to go to one, like The Savoy."

Joan raised an eyebrow as she pulled Eunice past the door. "Maybe we can make your dreams come true one day. But let's tick the restaurant off first. One step at a time."

However, when they arrived at Carlo's, Joan's face slumped. Inside, the lights were off, and the chairs stacked on top of tables. A sign in the doorway read: 'Closed today. Re-opening tomorrow.' Joan cast her eyes to the still-blue sky. She'd imagined a red-and-white chequered tablecloth, candlelight, romance. She'd been living in one of her scripts, clearly. "The best laid plans. Your Italian experience will have to wait." She tried not to drop to the floor and cry.

Eunice twirled on the pavement and pointed at a cafe over the road called Dale's Den. "What about that?" The sign in the window said it did the best fish and chips in London. "We could swerve Italy and go full-on England? Plus, it looks a bit posher than most fish and chip places."

Joan peered across the street. Eunice was right. It had candles on the tables and it was busy. She shrugged. "Good as any."

The cafe had ten tables all close together, its windows thick with steam. The inside warmth was welcome. They peeled off their jackets and hung them on the backs of their white wooden chairs.

Eunice wore navy earrings that dangled from her lobes and a navy pencil skirt. She'd topped it off with a fitted peach blouse that framed her ample breasts perfectly. "I love that colour on you, by the way. You've got an eye. I think you're going to make a fantastic designer."

Eunice cast her eyes to the table, then back up to Joan. "Thank you. That means a lot."

When their gazes met, Joan almost forgot how to sit on her chair. She gripped it for reassurance. Desire thudded in her chest in place of a heartbeat.

A man with tattoos broke the moment, a small notepad in his hand. He grabbed a blue biro from behind his right ear and gave them a welcoming smile. "What can I get you ladies? The fish and chips are delicious and comes with a pickled gherkin and a pickled egg on the side. Our homemade lemonade is also recommended."

The entire cafe appeared to have taken his advice, fish and chips and lemonade on most tables. Joan looked at Eunice. "I'm fine with that if you are?"

Eunice nodded. "Sounds perfect."

Joan's stomach grumbled as the man left with their order, the smell of salt, vinegar and fried food dazzling her senses. She hadn't eaten much all day. She'd been too nervous about tonight, and too focused on her work. But now she was here, the nerves were calmed and her hunger was back.

"It's nice to spend some time together. We haven't been able to chat much at work since the Boat Race and dance." Eunice didn't quite meet her eye as she spoke.

Joan shook her head. "It's been flat out, hasn't it?"

The man reappeared with a fresh candle stuck into the top of an empty wine bottle. He put it on their table and lit it. "A bit of romance for you, ladies."

Eunice's cheeks coloured red as the man disappeared.

"Why should romance just be for men and women? Friends can have it too, can't they?" Joan matched her words with a bold stare.

Eunice met her gaze then. "I don't see why not." When she raised her hand to her face, her fingers trembled.

Their food arrived, and Joan had to agree: it was a contender for the best fish and chips she'd ever eaten. Although equally, it could also be the company she was keeping. Everything she did with Eunice took on a magical, otherworldly glow when it was just them. When they added other people, family, friends or dancehall boys, things got complicated. But just the two of them? Something brilliant happened. Food tasted better. Colours got brighter. The world simply became more radiant. Just like Eunice's smile.

"What's this play about tonight?"

Joan rested her cutlery on the sides of her plate. "It's called *Kismet*, and it's a musical version of a play from 1911."

"That's old. I can't imagine being old, can you?"

"I just hope I get there. My parents didn't."

Eunice cringed. "Me and my big mouth."

Joan shook her head. Nerves swished her inside. "It's fine, honestly. But if I'm lucky enough to survive, I want to have achieved all my dreams. Written plays. Seen them performed. Become *someone*."

Eunice's face lit up. "You want to write plays? That's

next-level clever, but if anyone can do it, you can. I want to have achieved my dreams, too. And I'll definitely have been to Paris by then."

"And maybe Rome."

"Maybe."

"We'll get to Carlo's another day." Joan wagged a finger to back up her point. "Anyway, tonight's play is about a poet, but it's also about the poet's daughter who falls in love. Kismet means fate or destiny." Joan gulped as she said the final line.

Eunice stared right at her. "Do you believe in destiny? Like, two people meeting and knowing they should be together? Even if everything about them says they shouldn't be?"

What was Eunice saying? Joan's cheeks flushed at the implication. "I do," she replied, her throat dry. "Sometimes, love just happens. I've heard about it in songs, and I've watched it in films. But I'm sure it happens every day to normal people too."

Why was she saying this out loud and not in her head? This was not Joan at all.

The candle flickered to her left, and opposite, the glow around Eunice increased.

"People like us?" Eunice asked, her whole face expectant.

Joan nodded. "Exactly like us."

* * *

They walked through Soho, a frisson of excitement running through Joan because her aunt and brother constantly told her not to. Soho was rife with crime and prostitution, but Joan loved it anyway. It was a bit late to tell her not to walk through Soho when she'd been doing it with her mum since she was small. Joan loved the crackle of energy under her feet. Tonight was no exception as they walked down Dean Street. She spied two men walking on the pavement opposite, one with a leather jacket and blond quiff. She frowned, then gripped Eunice.

"Look over there," she hissed under her breath. "It's Tommy Steele!"

Eunice turned her head right, clocked him, then eyed Joan. "Oh my god, it is! Wait until I tell my sister Rose, she loves his new song!"

They followed his retreating figure down the street, brushed off their excitement, and carried on walking.

"I'll never tire of that, you know. The thrill of living in London."

Eunice nodded. "I feel sorry for people who live elsewhere. Like Norwich. Or Bolton."

"Why live anywhere else? It's the capital city. This is where the action is." Joan lit a cigarette as she walked, and offered one to Eunice.

She declined.

"You saved yourself a lot of money not smoking."

"More money for Paris. Also a capital city, also where the action is," Eunice replied, with a grin.

Joan crossed a side road, dodged a Lyons' Tea van, then stopped in front of a bustling cafe with two tables on the pavement outside. She pointed up to the sign and Eunice followed her finger.

"Bar Italia," Eunice read.

"If we can't go to Carlo's, I thought a coffee and dessert here seemed appropriate. It's still not Paris, but we'll work on a French bistro next time." Joan took a drag on her cigarette.

"You know London so well. I feel like a tourist with you."

Joan shrugged. "It comes from growing up around here, spending my childhood in clubs and theatres. You learn where to eat and drink." She ushered Eunice inside. "This one comes recommended. It was a favourite of my mum."

Eunice squeezed Joan's arm. "Then I'm sure I'll love it, too."

Joan took a steadying breath as she walked in. Every time she did, she could see her mum at the counter with her espresso. If she concentrated hard, she could still smell her here. Smoke, silk and coffee. Now she was here with Eunice.

Joan ordered two espressos and one cannoli from the manager, Paolo, who greeted her with a hug. He'd known her mum, and always remembered her. She guided Eunice to the chrome and leather bar stools that lined the inside wall. Joan finished her cigarette and collected their order from the marble-topped counter.

Eunice fidgeted in her bag and pulled out her purse. "Let me give you some money."

Joan shook her head. "My treat."

"But you paid for dinner."

She shrugged. "You can pay next time. I'm showing you my Soho, my London. Allow me."

Eunice took a moment, then put her purse away. "Okay." She sipped her coffee and made a face. "It could do with some milk."

Joan laughed. "It's how they drink it in Italy, apparently."

"Was your mum a fan?"

Joan nodded. "She was." She glanced around the room. "She loved everything European. Said they did things a little more extravagantly, with a touch more panache. I guess that's why I want to see the world, to fulfil my mum's dreams. She'd been to Rome and Paris, but she always wanted to go to Berlin. She never made it."

"What was her name?"

Joan blinked. "My mum? Elizabeth. Liz to her friends. Only my aunt called her Elizabeth. And my dad, apparently."

A smile lit Eunice's face. "That's my middle name. Eunice Elizabeth Humphries. Maybe I'll change it to Eunice Liz Humphries."

"I think Eunice Elizabeth Humphries is just perfect." More perfect than Joan could possibly hope. "I love that you share a name with my mum."

Eunice licked her bottom lip. "I do, too."

Joan held Eunice's gaze, steadied her breathing and pointed at the cannoli. "Have some of that. My mum swore by them."

Eunice picked it up with a frown. "What is it?"

"Fried pastry with cream cheese. It's called a cannoli. Trust me, it's amazing."

Eunice took a bite and closed her eyes. "Now I *really* want to go to Milan, too." She smiled at Joan, then shook her head. "You are not like anyone else I've ever met in my life, you know that?"

Joan stared at Eunice. "You're pretty unique yourself."

"I feel so... easy with you. I was just telling my mum the other day," Eunice began, then stopped. She winced, then shook her head.

"What did you tell your mum?"

Another shake of her head. "Nothing. It's not important." She sipped her coffee and took another bite of the pastry. "What time is it? We don't want to be late to the show."

Eunice tapped her foot on the chrome bar of her stool.

Something had got Eunice agitated. Joan had no idea what. "We've got plenty of time," she replied. "But if it makes you feel better, we can finish up and go."

Eunice sucked on her top lip, then nodded. "Let's go."

* * *

In all honesty, the show could have been terrible. Joan paid more attention to the glorious fact she could sit next to Eunice in the dark for a couple of uninterrupted hours. Yes, there was a big audience all around them. And yes, there was music, sound, actors. But the person Joan paid most attention to was Eunice. She was all-encompassing.

At the interval, Joan offered to get ice cream, but Eunice shook her head.

"I'm still full from dinner and cannoli." She sat forward, hands on the chrome railing, looking down at the stage. Free tickets meant they were in the gods, on level three. "One day, when I'm a famous fashion designer, we'll sit down in the stalls. In the posh seats. We'll be so close, we'll be able to see the actors' faces."

Joan smiled. "I look forward to it."

Eunice sat back and glanced at Joan. "Thanks for bringing me, though. This is the first time I've seen a musical."

"First cannoli. First musical." Joan put a hand to her chest. "Tell me you've had fish and chips before."

Eunice laughed. "Never by candlelight." Something passed over her features. A look. An emotion that Joan couldn't quite pin down. She'd love to know what Eunice was thinking.

"That was pretty special, wasn't it?"

"It really was."

The second half began, and the love story see-sawed. At one stage, when it seemed all was lost, Eunice's breath caught, then she wiped away a tear.

Joan pulled a handkerchief from her bag and offered it to Eunice. She accepted.

Moments later as the story turned even more precarious for the lovers, Joan reached out and took Eunice's hand in hers, settling it on her lap.

Eunice's breath stilled.

Joan glanced sideways, gave Eunice a smile, then squeezed her hand. It was hot to the touch.

Eunice squeezed right back.

She and Eunice held hands for the rest of the performance. It went to the top of the chart marked 'Happiest Half Hour of Joan's Life'. When the cast took their final bow and the pair got up to leave, sadness washed through her. She wanted to sit next to Eunice and hold her hand all night.

Outside, Charing Cross blared too bright, people bustled too fast, the rain drizzled too wet. The magic of the show was quickly washed away. Joan's fingers itched to wrap themselves around Eunice's once more. However, that bubble had burst.

"How are you getting home?"

Eunice pulled an umbrella out of her bag, then nodded up the street. "Tube from Tottenham Court Road. And I better get going or my mum will send out a search party."

"Of course." Joan ran a hand through her hair. She'd forgotten her umbrella again. When she stepped out into the rain, she was going to be soaked. "I'm going over the bridge, so I'll say goodbye. I really enjoyed tonight." She gazed at Eunice. "Thanks for coming."

"I had a fabulous time." Eunice stared right back.

Joan wasn't sure how they should leave each other. Eunice's full red lips were inches from hers. She knew how she *wanted* it to go. But that could never happen. Could it?

Before Joan understood what she was doing, she leaned forward and placed her lips on Eunice's cheek. It was velvety soft.

Eunice shivered at her touch.

When Joan eased back, they both stared again. Her heartbeat roared in her ears. She wanted to reach out, pull Eunice close and kiss her properly. But she didn't. Her fingers clenched at the futility of it all.

"Bye, then." Eunice blinked, then almost ran from Joan.

Joan watched her disappear into the crowds, then turned for home.

* * *

It was late by the time Joan got in. She walked all the way home, wanting to be with her thoughts. Through Covent Garden, past the restaurant they'd eaten in. Over Waterloo Bridge, the Houses of Parliament and Big Ben to her right. Not that she could see them. It was too foggy, especially by the river. She was grateful to get to the other side, then navigate her route home. So familiar, she did it on autopilot.

After Mum's shows, which Joan had watched from the wings, she'd always bought Joan a sweet treat, latterly from Bar Italia. Then they'd walked home, her mum enthusing about London. She'd loved the city so much, and her enthusiasm rubbed off on her daughter. Joan couldn't imagine living anywhere else. She missed her mum so much, especially on a night like this. Her mum would have known what to say. Joan's heart ached as she walked past London Bridge station, past the concrete blocks of Guy's Hospital, then rounded the corner to her block of flats.

Jimmy was home when she got in. He popped his head around the doorframe and gave her a grin.

"I'm just making toast. Want some?"

She nodded. "Yes please." Joan shucked her jacket and bag, then walked through to the kitchen and slumped forward as she sat down, her head rested on top of her crossed arms. When she looked up, Jimmy stared at her, in between concentrating on buttering the toast. The smell made her smile, even though she wasn't hungry. On the stove, the kettle heated, too.

Jimmy made the tea and brought the buttered toast over to her. He gave her a knowing smile. "Right then. What's all the sighing about? I'm no detective, but if I had to guess, I'd say it's about this friend of yours you took to the show tonight?"

Joan blinked, then sat up. Was she that transparent?

"No need to look so shocked. I remember you crumbling about Frances a couple of years ago. Plus, I've got eyes. You're not chasing boys like most girls your age." He took a bite of his toast and chewed. "So, this girl. Eunice, did you say?"

Joan nodded. She didn't trust herself to speak. If Jimmy knew, did the factory know, too? Panic slid down her.

But then she remembered that Jimmy knew her. *Really* knew her. He'd been there all her life.

"I'm not going to tell you off. You know me better than that." He smiled at her. "I'm a sensitive fella, you know."

"And you can cook. You want to be careful. People will start to talk." She smiled at the irony of her words.

Jimmy laughed. "Let them. I know whoever I marry will think I'm a wonder. Or I'll be like every other schmuck in town, trying to work out what she wants." He reached out and patted Joan's arm. "You look like you're at an impasse. A woman-driven impasse."

Joan blew out a long breath. There was no point trying to hide it. Plus, maybe Jimmy was a good stand-in for her mum. He'd proved himself to be so over and over again. "You could say that. I was just thinking I miss Mum so much." She pouted. "She started our late-night toast sessions, didn't she?" The three of them had put the world to rights many times.

"She did." Jimmy met her gaze and their sad smiles mirrored each other. "I miss her every day."

Nobody understood what it was like to lose Liz Hart like they did.

"But I'm here. And you want my advice?"

Joan nodded. "I'd love it."

"I know you had your young heart broken by that other girl a couple of years ago. But you're older now. There's even more at stake. So tread carefully. When it comes to women, nobody knows what they're doing. You're not immune just because you're a woman too."

Joan let out a strangled laugh. It was good advice. Only, it was a little too late. Joan was already in way over her head.

"That's exactly what Mum would say." She paused. "But is it worth it? I'm older, yes, but nothing's changed. People either die — like our parents — or they leave. Frances was just another person I lost. Will Eunice be any different?"

Jimmy tilted his head. "That's the million-dollar question. But you won't know until you try."

Chapter Twelve

Eunice had been right. Once she agreed to take Mrs Higgins's nephew out for the day when he came in August, her mum took a step back from her 'you need a boyfriend' campaign. It couldn't have worked out better. Kenneth — what sort of name was that? — lived in Birmingham. Eunice had heard of it, but it might as well have been on the other side of the world if it wasn't in London. She'd never been there and doubted she ever would.

All of which meant that taking him out came with no strings attached. It was one day. Hopefully he wouldn't be too much of a bore, and then Eunice could get back to her life, and he could get on the train back to Birmingham and *his* life. It was perfect. Eunice was almost grateful to Kenneth for giving her three months of peace.

She'd made the most of them, too. In the past 12 weeks, she'd got to know Joan that bit more. She'd learned about her mum and dad. She'd even met Joan's brother when she went to their flat one Saturday afternoon. He was taller than Joan, but he had her smile and her laugh. Eunice could have sat and listened to them both all day. If she were that bit older, maybe she'd have been drawn to Jimmy. But she wasn't. It was his sister who made her smile.

Eunice's job was going well, too. She and Joan laughed all day, as did the whole factory. Their sing-songs were weekly now, with Joan holding court and Eunice spellbound. Weekend work was plentiful, which meant her Paris fund was swelling. And in Joan, she'd found a friendship so perfect, it made Eunice purr.

David had always been the friend she loved the most. The one she confided in. Her mum had always thought it strange she didn't have a close female friend. It had simply never happened at school. It had always been her and David. While he still was her best friend, she hadn't seen so much of him this summer. He'd got a girlfriend named Susie, and Eunice had got a Joan.

Her friendship with Joan was on a different level to anything she'd ever had before. It had an electricity that thrilled her. An intensity that scared her. But after a few charged evenings out in April and May, they'd settled into a rhythm. Eunice still looked at Joan and wondered what it would be like to kiss her. She had no idea where those thoughts came from, but they didn't scare her as much anymore. They were as natural as breathing now. She and Joan shared a connection. They had what Eunice had longed for with a man. If it had to be with a woman, she'd accept it as it was. Joan was enough.

The pair had spent lazy summer Saturdays walking the river, shopping, having coffee and laughing over the past three months. They'd gone to the cinema, Joan giving Eunice the low-down on the films she liked and the films she didn't. Joan had many opinions on films. Her knowledge of them and their actors always amazed Eunice, and it was one of the many things she admired about her. Eunice also loved reading while

Joan wrote. She'd promised to write her into a script soon. Eunice had never been more thrilled.

Joan was so much more cosmopolitan than her. She'd grown up in a different world. She still lived in a different world outside the factory, having so much more freedom than Eunice. And yes, it came at a price, but to Eunice, what Joan had was tantalising. She didn't have to do chores for her family. She didn't have to wash up dinner for eight every night. She had space and time to herself. Eunice could only dream of that.

Meeting Joan had shown Eunice that the world she lived in could be different to the one she'd grown up in, and for that she'd be forever grateful.

They hadn't shared a meal or an evening out at the theatre since they saw *Kismet*. Eunice had hoped Joan would invite her again, but it hadn't happened. She got the feeling Joan was holding back. That perhaps they'd stepped over a line that night, and going any further would have been impossible to row back from. Joan had applied the brakes to her tactile nature. She paused when she went to touch Eunice now. Her eyes darted away when they met in the toilets at work.

But sometimes, when it was just the two of them, Joan let her guard down. When she did, Eunice did, too. In July, they'd lain on the warm summer grass in Kensington Gardens, Eunice with her chin propped in the heel of her palm, and talked about their plans for the future. To their right, beyond the tall hedges, the bronzed statue of Peter Pan stood proud. The boy who never grew up. Right then, Eunice wasn't fussed about doing so, either. She wanted to freeze time and stay right there, beside Joan. The Canadian geese squawked on the Long Water nearby, while Joan ran her hand up Eunice's forearm. Just her touch was enough to ignite a fire inside Eunice. When she'd stared at Joan, then at Joan's hand on her skin, the moment had pulsed between them. Then Joan had taken her hand away.

Eunice wanted to know what the next step was. She had no idea. It scared her to even think about it. But it scared her even more that it might never happen.

Eunice put down the basket of wet laundry and opened the door to the drying room. Every floor on their block had one, a massive space with washing lines to dry your larger items. Two of the eight lines were free, so she set about pegging out the clothes. She stared into the dusky late summer night, the open windows creating a breeze for the washing to dry. One day, this wouldn't be her life.

When she got back to the flat, Mrs Higgins was in the kitchen chatting to her mum.

"There she is! Just the girl I want to see." Mrs Higgins paused. "Or should I say, woman?" She grinned. "Just to let you know, Kenneth arrives tomorrow. Are you free to show him around on Saturday?"

"This weekend? I thought it was the next one." Eunice tried to keep the disappointment out of her voice, but she wasn't sure she managed it. Tomorrow was Friday, and she'd hoped to spend Saturday with Joan, who'd promised to cook for her. They'd planned to crack open some schnapps her brother had brought back from Holland, too.

But Eunice couldn't say no to Mrs Higgins. Not after she and Kenneth had given her a glorious summer.

"No, it's this weekend. It's not a problem, is it?"

Eunice glanced at her mum, whose face was like thunder.

She shook her head. "Not at all. I've been looking forward to meeting him." She owed him, after all.

"Fantastic! I'm cooking him dinner tomorrow, but I'll bring him over on Saturday morning? I know he'll be dying to meet someone his own age." She walked towards Eunice and pinched her cheek. "It's going to be so nice to have company for a change!"

Mrs Higgins left, blowing kisses to them both.

When the front door slammed, her mum put both her hands on the kitchen table and stared at Eunice. "You hadn't forgotten, had you?"

Eunice blushed. "Of course not."

"More plans with Joan?"

She cast her gaze to the floor, before looking back at her mum. "Make up your mind. When I was in school, you wanted me to have a friend who was a girl. Now I've got one, you want me to find a man."

"You can have both, but you have been spending an awful lot of time with Joan. It's all about balance." Her mum paused. "Plus, finding a man and settling down is what will make you happy."

Eunice nodded. She wasn't in the mood for a fight. They'd have to agree to differ.

* * *

Kenneth had a winning smile and Tommy Steele blond hair. He was also tall, with broad shoulders, and dressed in a natty suit with a wide kipper tie. Just the type of man her mum would favour. Eunice didn't have to look up to know she was grinning from ear to ear.

"Your aunt tells us you just completed your national service?"

Kenneth nodded. "Somehow, I got conscripted, even though some of my friends avoided it. But it wasn't too bad. A year in Wiltshire, a year in Dusseldorf. It sounds impressive, but it was a lot of sitting around not doing much."

"He's running himself down. He learned a great deal. All of which he can put into practice when he becomes a manager at his uncle's clothing factory."

Eunice's ears pricked up.

Her mum jumped in before she could speak. "Eunice works in a clothing factory. You've already got so much in common!"

Great, they could talk about bobbins and overlockers all day. Eunice squeezed out a strained smile.

"You youngsters go and have a lovely day." Mrs Higgins squeezed his arm. "But mind out for those hooligans. Did you hear the commotion again last night? The Teddy Boys are kicking off against the blacks." She shook her head. "Terrible it is. They're all lovely people." Race riots had been rumbling for a few days now.

"Don't stray into Notting Hill, okay? That's where the trouble's been," her mum added.

Eunice shook her head. "We won't. I'm taking Kenneth on a tour of central London."

It took a few minutes to get out the door, but they managed it. Kenneth gave her more of his charming grin as they walked down the stairs and out into the courtyard. Her brothers were playing football with four of their friends.

"Have a nice day with your boyfriend, Eunice!" Peter shouted.

Eunice gave him two fingers, which made Kenneth snort.

"Do you have annoying younger siblings, too?"

He shook his head. "Two older sisters. That's why I laughed. That was me a few years ago. I am the annoying younger sibling."

They turned onto the path and walked to the bus stop. Up above, the sky was the same colour as Joan's eyes, a silky grey. The forecast promised it would brighten up later. Eunice wasn't sure she would, though.

"I just wanted to say thank you, too. It's very kind of you to take me out for the day, take pity on me. I love my aunt, but it's nice to spend time in the city without her. I dare say you might know a few different places, too."

"I work in town, so you're with the right woman." Ugh. Had that sounded weird?

"That's what I'm hoping," Kenneth replied.

They took the 94 bus, Eunice going upstairs as she always did. They sat next to each other, their bodies pressed together on the small seats. She'd done this with Joan many times and never questioned it. With Kenneth, it was a little too intimate for their first hour together. However, the bus was packed with Saturday shoppers going to town, so she had no choice.

They jumped off at Marble Arch, and Eunice ushered him into Selfridges to marvel at the food hall. She pointed out the cannolis on the Italian counter, and her heart panged. Just like her before the summer, Kenneth had never heard of them. Now, she and Joan were regulars in Bar Italia, and Paolo greeted them both when he saw them. Kenneth insisted on buying them both a pistachio cannoli, declaring them 'delicious!' Guilt overwhelmed Eunice as she ate hers. She had to stop thinking about Joan. She had to show Kenneth a good time, or she'd never hear the end of it.

They dipped down to Oxford Street for the shops, and he cooed over her factory building. He was definitely trying. She took him to Carnaby Street with its independent shops and cool vibe. To the South Bank to see the Royal Festival Hall, built in 1951 for the Festival of Britain. They bought cheese and ham sandwiches with coffee, then sat on a bench on the South Bank, shielding their eyes from the sun.

Kenneth took off his jacket and laid it carefully beside him.

"This is your first job back after the army, then?"

"It is." He sipped his coffee. "Although I might have to go to Scotland for a while first, but I'm trying to push back on that. My uncle has a friend who wants to teach me some things. But yes, I'll be working in a clothing factory, so maybe you can teach me the tricks of the trade so I can win over my staff?"

Eunice had always assumed that management knew what they were doing. She'd never thought they might be questioning their moves. "You've never worked in a factory and you're going in as a manager. How does that work? Don't you need experience?"

He blushed at her words. "It's not what you know, it's who you know sometimes. My uncle owns the factory. He needs new blood, and he doesn't have any sons. So he asked me if I was interested. Both his daughters and my sisters are all happily married, and their husbands have jobs. Plus, my uncle and I have always been close." He shrugged. "I got lucky. Unless I hate it."

"Just remember to say thank you to your workers and be grateful. You can't run your factory without them. Give them praise and give them bonuses. And overtime." She prodded Kenneth's knee with her finger. "All staff like the opportunity to earn more money at double time. I'm saving up for my Paris trip by working weekends."

He glanced at her. "You're going to Paris?"

Why had she told him that? That was a little too personal. She'd already decided that today was going to be surface level, nothing more. Only, she hadn't accounted for Kenneth being so easy to be with. He seemed nice. He wasn't trying to be something he wasn't. He'd already told her that he'd hated the army. He was far more honest and straightforward than any boy she'd met before. A little like David.

"That's my plan." Still, Eunice felt like she'd said too much. Like Kenneth would tell Mrs Higgins and then everyone would know her plans and think her a little too big for her boots. She'd only told her mum, David, Joan. That was it.

"Just to be a tourist? See the Eiffel Tower?"

Eunice shook her head. "I want to work in the heart of fashion. To do that, you have to go to either Paris or Milan. I just feel like there will be inspiration there."

Kenneth finished his sandwich before he spoke. "Inspiration for what?"

She was in too far to pull back now. *Damn it, Eunice.* "I want to be a fashion designer. I sew dresses and skirts every day, and that's great. I enjoy my job, and I love my colleagues." Especially one in particular. "But I'd love to get in on the process a little earlier. To come up with designs for ordinary women. I'm not talking about couture, which is what I'd see in Paris. I'd love to make a boutique range of course, but have it affordable for a special occasion. But mainly, I'd like to design more stylish, everyday clothes for women."

Kenneth listened to every word. Again, not a trait she'd discovered in most men she'd met. "I love your passion. I never really knew what I wanted to do, and now I've been given an opportunity, I want to take full advantage of it." He paused. "Maybe you could come and work with me in Birmingham and be our next designer." He laughed. "I've no idea if we even have them in-house or how things work, but I'll let you know."

A fizz of excitement flew down Eunice. It was true what Kenneth said. It wasn't what you knew, but who. "If you're looking, I'd be interested," she said. "Although I'd have to work from London. I could be your eyes and ears on the ground in the capital."

Kenneth grinned. "We might make a great team." His eyes searched her face. "You'll be known throughout the land. We can tell the story of how it all started on the South Bank, right here on this bench."

Eunice blushed and looked away. She wasn't doing anything wrong. She was simply entertaining Mrs Higgins' nephew. Being a good neighbour. But somehow, doing that felt disloyal to Joan. Which was crazy. She shook her head. She didn't have time to stop and analyse her feelings. They had sights to see.

She finished her sandwich and brushed down her dress. She was eager to move, and not sit here anymore, chatting to Kenneth. She didn't want to give him the wrong idea.

He wasn't Joan. Eunice had told her she had a family thing. She hadn't told Joan she was seeing Kenneth. She'd tried, but she'd been unable to get the words out of her mouth. She wasn't totally lying, though. Mrs Higgins was *almost* family.

"Your dress is lovely, by the way." Kenneth stood up and put his jacket back on.

Eunice glanced down at her fitted baby blue outfit with white jacket. Her mum had insisted she pull out all the stops. "You like it? It's from a boutique in Soho." Buying it had eaten into her Paris fund. Working in central London wasn't good for that.

"It looks very chic."

Eunice blushed, then muttered her thanks. "Shall we go?" She paused. "And can you not say anything about Paris to your aunt? It's sort of my secret thing."

Kenneth gave her a salute as he balled up his sandwich bag and put it in his paper coffee cup. "You can trust me, I've been in the army. Where to next, tour guide?"

Eunice pointed with her finger across the river. "Houses of Parliament and Big Ben, then up to Trafalgar Square and Covent Garden."

"Are we going to meet the prime minister for coffee?"

"I asked, but Mr Macmillan is getting a haircut this afternoon." She gave him a grin.

Kenneth tipped back his head and roared with laughter. "You are not what I expected when my aunt told me about you. Not by a long shot."

* * *

They went to dinner at the same place she and Joan had dined at, mainly because it was somewhere Eunice knew would be good. Kenneth declared them the best fish and chips he'd ever had, and Eunice had smiled and chatted, but her heart hadn't been in it.

Kenneth was lovely, but being there with him only highlighted what was missing. The spark she had with Joan. The breeze that was their relationship. She and Kenneth were getting on fine, but they'd only just met. They didn't have a relationship of any sort. No shared glances. No thwarted smiles. No in-jokes. As the day wore on, Eunice found herself resenting their time together, which was harsh. It wasn't anything to do with him.

It was to do with Eunice and where her heart lay.

With Joan.

Maybe what she and Joan had *wasn't* enough, despite what Eunice tried to convince herself. As the day wore on, she was coming more and more to that conclusion.

They ended by going to the cinema to see Elvis Presley in *King Creole*. Eunice welcomed the respite from talking. She closed her eyes in the darkness. Coming to see a musical only made her think of Joan more, if that was possible. What was Joan doing right now? Sitting on her window seat writing? Listening to the wireless?

They caught the 94 bus home, walked up the stone steps of her block, then bid each other goodnight. Kenneth gave her a shy smile as he walked away.

Eunice was just about to open her door when he called her name. She looked up.

He walked back towards her. "I was just going to say. I'm planning on coming back in a few weeks, mid-September hopefully. I wondered if you'd care to have another day together? I really enjoyed this one."

She stared at his handsome face. His dark stubble. She should find it more attractive. Maybe she would in time?

Kenneth was head and shoulders above the other men she'd met. Perhaps she just needed to walk up the garden path with him. Just like her mum had suggested.

She nodded. "I'd like that." A sharp pain hit her in the stomach, but she ignored it.

"Great. I'll let my aunt know when I'm coming. It was lovely to meet you, Eunice."

"You, too, Kenneth."

Chapter Thirteen

After the warmth of the summer, September brought a rush of russet-coloured leaves, with darkening days as the last embers of the season fought for attention. Today the sun shone, and Joan felt invincible in her pea-green coat as they headed out on their lunchtime stroll. She threw a carefree arm around Eunice, easy to do seeing as she was a fair bit taller. Joan liked the height difference. It seemed right.

Two women walking by on the other side gave Joan and Eunice a look. Joan clocked it. Did they think they were a couple? Sometimes Joan imagined they were. However, Joan could work with what they had. She had to. She didn't want to risk it all by asking for more. She'd loved this summer, and she was hoping she and Eunice slipped into autumn just as smoothly, with no changes.

They reached the corner of Old Compton Street and carried on down to Shaftesbury Avenue. A man selling *The Star* waved a headline that told of a calming of the race riots in West London. Eunice had told her the same this morning when Joan asked. She didn't like to think of her being in the thick of any trouble.

"What are you doing tomorrow?"

Eunice slowed her stride. "I might be busy."

Joan squeezed her shoulder. "Doing what? I thought Saturdays were ours." For the past three Saturdays they'd been inseparable. Lunch by the river. Time spent in Joan's flat. Going to the cinema. They'd even fallen asleep one afternoon on Joan's bed. She'd woken up with Eunice draped around her. It had been bliss.

Eunice wriggled out of her grasp as they crossed the main road and walked towards Chinatown, its red lanterns swaying in the breeze. "I've just got a thing. With a boy." Her voice dipped at the last moment.

Joan's stomach dropped, her breath caught. "A boy?" She almost choked on the words. "I didn't know there was a boy in the picture." When had Eunice had time to see a boy? Her weekends had been spent with Joan or her family. Or so Eunice had said. Had there been a boy all along?

Eunice shook her head. "There's not really. It's just a favour for a neighbour. Mrs Higgins, who lets me sew at hers? She bakes for the family, too. Her nephew came to town last month and I took him out. He's back tomorrow and I said I'd take him out again." She shrugged, avoiding Joan's gaze. "It's not a big thing at all." Eunice sped up, putting a slight distance between them.

It seemed like a bigger thing than Eunice was letting on.

However, Joan didn't want to freak Eunice out, so she let it slide. She caught up with her as they hit the spot between Piccadilly Circus and Leicester Square. As usual, the pavements thronged with people. On the corner, two men sold glass animals from wonky trestle tables. Joan had no idea who bought them, but they were always here, so somebody did.

They dodged a couple of passing cars, crossed to Haymarket and walked down.

"Are you spending all day with him? It's just, there's a CND rally on."

Eunice turned. "CND?"

"Campaign for Nuclear Disarmament. It's a new group, trying to stop any more world wars. Because the next one will kill us all. Anyway, Jimmy's going and a couple of his friends. I'm going to tag along if you fancy it."

Eunice paused, then shook her head. "Last time we were together all day."

Joan's spine tensed. She ignored it and bit the inside of her cheek. "You never said."

"It didn't seem important." Eunice gripped the back of her neck with her right hand, and gave Joan a pained look.

It was important.

They both knew.

Joan begged to differ. "Is this a boyfriend-girlfriend thing?" Fear bubbled up in her throat. She'd thought she and Eunice were a *thing*. That they had all the time in the world. But it wasn't true.

Keep it cool, Joan. Keep it cool.

Eunice shook her head. "No, just a neighbour thing. He lives in Birmingham, so we're not likely to start going out, are we?"

"Stranger things have happened. My cousin met a man who lives in Bristol when he was in London for the weekend. She lives in the middle of nowhere now, somewhere called Frome." Joan's mind still boggled. "I can never imagine living out of London."

"Me neither, hence it's going nowhere, whatever he might want."

"So he does want something?"

Eunice sighed. "I don't know. We never discussed his intentions. But he's a man, and don't they normally?"

Joan bit her lip. Yes, they normally did.

It was *exactly* the thing she wanted, too. To hold Eunice in arms. To kiss her, love her, never let her go. But that wasn't in the script, was it? Even though she wrote them. The irony wasn't lost on her. Perhaps it was time to write her own script, especially for the two of them?

They walked on in silence for a few more moments. Joan balled her fist by her side and squeezed. She hated that she couldn't say a word.

"Are you bringing him to town?" she asked finally. She didn't want to know. But then again, she did.

Eunice stalled. "Probably. We did last time."

"Then bring him to the rally. I'm bringing my aunt, I'd love you to meet her. Plus, your neighbour's nephew — what's his name?"

"Kenneth."

Sounded prissy. "Kenneth can meet Jimmy and his friends. They can talk boy things."

"He just finished his national service. He might not be against war."

"That might be the reason he *is* against it."

Eunice stared, then nodded. "Okay. I'll bring him."

* * *

Joan knew it was a mistake as soon as she saw Eunice.

The thought of Kenneth hadn't been real while he'd just been a figment of her imagination. But now he was in front of her, bright as day. Plus, he already looked at Eunice like he wanted her. Joan didn't blame him.

She saw now as she'd never seen before that if she wanted anything to happen with Eunice, she had to tell her. They'd come so close a couple of times, then both backed away. All she knew was the campaign for nuclear disarmament wasn't the closest cause to her heart today. That honour went to Eunice Humphries, with her sunlit hair, her hesitant smile, her heartbreaking eyes.

Eunice waved as they approached, picking their way across Trafalgar Square, stepping over pigeons like they were prized possessions.

The crowd was larger than Joan had imagined it would be, with a couple of hundred milling around the large fountains. She stood at the base of Nelson's Column where she'd arranged to meet Eunice and Kenneth at midday. Eunice was bang on time.

Joan ground her teeth together as she kissed Eunice's cheek. She breathed her in. How she loved her smell. Flowers and her future.

Kenneth was all smiles, boxy shoulders and hair wax. He was handsome, if you liked that sort of thing. He looked like a corporate Tommy Steele. His suit was a little too much for a Saturday. Definitely too much for a CND rally. She glanced at Jimmy with his scuffed leather boots, turned-up jeans and braces over his black jumper. She wasn't sure he and Kenneth would have much to talk about.

"Lovely to meet you, Joan." Kenneth offered his hand.

"Eunice has told me so much about the factory. Apparently without you, she'd have been lost."

Eunice blushed under Joan's gaze.

"I'm sure she'd cope just fine. She's a very capable woman." Joan shook Kenneth's hand.

Joan introduced Aunt Maggie, Jimmy and his friend, Frank. Frank had hair past his shoulders and clutched a banner with a CND sign on it.

"Down with war!" he told them, brandishing his banner.

Joan kept an eye on Kenneth as he nodded his agreement.

"It's lovely to finally meet you, Eunice." Aunt Maggie's curly hair whipped in the lunchtime breeze. "Joan has told me so much about you. You've been such a good friend to her."

"I hope to continue to be." Eunice gave Joan a scorched look that made her tremble. One there were far too many people here to witness. Particularly her brother and her aunt.

A truck selling ice cream pulled up nearby. It was mid-September, but it was just about still warm enough.

"Can I get everyone an ice cream? I'll buy a mix of flavours?" Murmured agreement, and Kenneth ran over to the van.

Joan could feel her brother's gaze on the side of her head as she watched him go. Her muscles unclenched slightly. "He seems nice," she told Eunice.

Eunice nodded. "He is. Grateful to have me as his tour guide."

"He doesn't look like he should be at a CND rally, though," Frank added. "Bit overdressed."

"He's here, though, isn't he?" Maggie's tone held a warning. "Be kind, Frank."

Frank rolled his eyes, but shut up.

"When's the rally due to get going?" Eunice smoothed down her coat and clutched her handbag. She looked anything but comfortable.

"There's not really a set time. It's more when the megaphone turns up." Joan wanted to sweep Eunice far away. To their normal Saturdays, when it was just the two of them. They always worked. Other people sullied the water.

Kenneth arrived back juggling six ice creams, the remnants running down his fingers. He laughed as he handed them out, then licked the melted ice cream.

Eunice pulled some tissues out of her bag and offered him one.

Kenneth took it, smiling as if this was something Eunice did all the time. Like they were a couple.

Joan stiffened. Acid crept up her windpipe. She swallowed it down. Was this really only the second time they'd met? She licked her ice cream, but all she tasted was coppery fear.

"What are your plans later?" She didn't want to know. But then, she did.

"We thought we might go to the cinema or a play. Eunice took me to a lovely little fish and chip place last time, so we might head back there, too. What was it called? Dale's Den?" Kenneth rested his hand on Eunice's arm as he asked.

Joan's jaw clenched. She'd taken him to *their* cafe? *Their* spot? Had they held hands by candlelight? Kissed as they left? Exactly what Joan had wanted to do?

How dare he.

She was the one who made Eunice feel like the princess she was.

She was the one who'd lain on the riverbank listening to Eunice's dreams.

This was *her* future he was stealing.

Eunice wouldn't look at her. She simply nodded. "Something like that."

Kenneth licked his ice cream, then checked his watch. "It was lovely to meet you all. We better run if we want to catch that photography exhibit your friend David told us about. It sounded super."

Eunice finally glanced up at Joan. "Sorry," she mouthed. Then she let Kenneth take her hand and pull her away.

Joan couldn't find the words.

Her brother put an arm around her. He pulled her close and kissed her hair. "It's going to be okay, Joanie. You wait and see."

But Joan wasn't sure it was. Not while she was too scared to tell the truth.

Maybe now was the time to be brave.

Chapter Fourteen

Eunice climbed the stone steps to her flats, Kenneth behind her, his breath heavy in the air. Today had been strange. Meeting Joan at the rally had thrown her off course. She hadn't wanted to go with Kenneth. She'd wanted to stay with Joan, her aunt, her brother. But Eunice had made a promise, and she had to keep it. The first couple of hours had been thorny. But Kenneth was so upbeat, so kind, that Eunice couldn't make him suffer all day. It wasn't his fault.

The day had taken on an otherworldly feel. As if it was happening to someone else altogether. Especially when Kenneth started being gallant. Pulling out her chair in a cafe. Opening doors for her. And then, on the 94 bus home, he'd taken her hand in his.

Eunice hadn't pulled away. She couldn't. She'd simply stared at their joined hands, at the looks of strangers on the bus. How they smiled at them, as if they were any other couple coming home from a date on a Saturday. Somewhere along the timeline of today, Eunice knew that's what today had become. A date. Kenneth had subtly turned it into one, and she had no choice but to comply. It was how Eunice had been brought up.

Boys asked you out. They bought you dinner. They held your hand.

Then they kissed you.

Eunice pulled up outside her front door and turned to Kenneth. She knew what might come next. The one thing on the list that hadn't been ticked off — with Kenneth or Joan. They'd both asked her out, both bought her dinner, both held her hand. But now Kenneth stared at her with a strange look on his face. A question on his lips. He shifted from foot to foot, and didn't meet Eunice's eye right away. When he did, he took a deep breath, then smoothed down his greased hair. He was about the same height as Joan. But Joan had better lips.

"I had such a fabulous time today. I've looked forward to it since last time. I'd love to do it again soon. My new job's going to take up a lot of weekends, but maybe I could come back soon and see more of the city with you?" He paused. There was sweat on his top lip. He waited for an answer.

Eunice's heart thumped in her chest. Kenneth was the acceptable choice. The sensible choice. He had so much going for him. He had a job, he had charm, but most of all, he was a man. Eunice knew what society wanted. What her family wanted. Kenneth was the easier option in so many ways. She couldn't shoot him down right away. She wasn't that girl.

So she nodded. "Of course. That would be great."

Relief dripped from Kenneth. "For a minute there I thought you were going to tell me to sling my hook."

Eunice laughed, then dropped his gaze. "That would have been awkward." He didn't need to know the truth.

Emboldened, Kenneth took her hand. "You're the most interesting girl, Eunice. Pretty, too." Then he leaned forward, pulled her close and pressed his lips to hers.

Eunice stood in his embrace. She closed her eyes, and let

Kenneth kiss her. His firm body pressed into hers. He was far from bony. Yet Eunice still wasn't relaxed. Kenneth's kiss lasted less than ten seconds, but the whole time, Eunice searched for a connection. A spark. Something that made her want to come back for more.

It wasn't there. When was it going to happen? Kenneth was the fourth boy she'd kissed. He was far and away the best boy she'd kissed. And yet. He still wasn't what Eunice had always imagined. She wanted romance. She wanted fireworks. Kenneth lacked matches.

He pulled back, then gave her a shy smile. "I'll write to you, I promise." He took her hand and kissed her fingers.

Still nothing. Perhaps Eunice was at fault. Perhaps her wiring was off. All her other friends had boyfriends and they talked of passion. Even David had a girlfriend. Eunice was determined to keep trying. Perhaps she was a slow learner.

"Does this mean you're my girlfriend? Because I'd love it if you were."

Eunice met his gaze. This sweet, handsome man was asking her to be his girlfriend? He had no idea what he was letting himself in for. She was missing some vital ingredients when it came to romance. But maybe Kenneth could help her find them? In the meantime, he still lived in Birmingham. Which meant she didn't have to kiss him that much at all. Perhaps Kenneth was the perfect boyfriend.

"I can be." Somewhere in her mind, a door slammed shut.

Kenneth blew out a long sigh. "Fantastic!" He kissed her lips again.

A cold breeze swept through her. She tried not to dwell on what she wanted. "That's settled, then."

* * *

"How was last night? You slipped in like a ghost. Your dad and I were up but we never even heard you." Her mum hung the last of the family's underwear on the kitchen drying rack, then winched it up overhead. The bigger items lay in a white plastic basket at her feet. From another room in the house, a thud reverberated, followed by shouting.

Eunice buttered her toast at the kitchen table, adding extra to the corner as she did every time. She wished she could have breakfast in peace. "It was fine."

The words Eunice hadn't said loitered in the room.

"Just fine?" Her mum stuck her head out of the kitchen. "Stop hitting your brother!" she shouted. Then she shut the door, pulled out the chair opposite and sat. "You look tired."

Eunice made sure she kept her face as straight as she could. She'd slept fitfully, her mind churning with what was wrong with her. That she couldn't feel anything towards Kenneth.

She chewed on a mouthful of toast, then reached out for the marmalade. "We had a nice time. We had dinner, went to the cinema." Eunice scowled, then looked up. Her mum needed something or she wouldn't let it lie. "He's asked me out again."

There it was. The smile her mum had been trying to suppress now ruled her face. "So are you together?"

Eunice's body tightened, as if someone was twisting her from the inside out. She nodded. "Kind of. Yes." She had no idea words could hurt so much.

"That's wonderful," her mum beamed. "He seems lovely. Mrs Higgins will be thrilled, too."

Eunice stared at her mother. She was sure Mrs Higgins *would* be thrilled. Her mother certainly seemed to be. Both of them appeared capable of more emotion than Eunice. What was wrong with her?

She put her toast down and got up. She walked around to the washing basket. "Shall I hang that out for you?"

Her mum blinked. "That would be lovely, thank you."

Eunice picked it up, balanced it on her hip and walked out. Her mum might well have more questions than answers, but Eunice wasn't prepared to talk right now.

She pulled the door shut behind her, then glanced at Mrs Higgins' green door. Kenneth was going early, but she didn't want to risk running into him. Too many people had an opinion on Kenneth. She turned to go to the drying room, but when she looked up, her heart lurched.

Joan stood at the top of the steps, then walked towards her.

A herd of elephants trampled through Eunice. Her grip loosened on the basket, but she managed to clutch it at the final moment, the plastic digging into her hip. She wished she'd put makeup on, but there was nothing she could do now. When Joan stopped in front of her, it took everything Eunice had not to throw the basket over the wall and kiss her. Instead, she clenched her toes and tried to avoid looking into Joan's soft grey eyes. That would be her downfall.

"Hi." Eunice's words were a whisper. Was it just her, or were Joan's trousers making her legs look longer today?

Joan gave her a faltering smile. "Hi." She pointed to the washing. "Were you on your way somewhere?"

"To the drying room." Eunice could only deal in facts when it came to Joan. Her emotions, while dormant with Kenneth, were far too much when it came to her. She nodded past Joan and they walked. "What are you doing here? You live miles away."

Joan let out a strangled laugh. "I could say I was just passing, but I'd be lying."

They arrived at the drying room door. Eunice glanced at Joan, her face taut. She doubted she'd slept well, either.

"I needed to talk to you," Joan said. "After yesterday."

Eunice ground her teeth together and tried not to let the wobble that was happening inside her show.

When she walked into the drying room, David's mum, Hilda, was inside, putting the last of her laundry in her basket.

"Hello, Eunice!" She walked over to her. "I hear you had a second date with your young man yesterday." She put her free hand on Eunice's forearm. "If it doesn't work out, you know I've got David waiting in the wings. I can get rid of his girlfriend. You just say the word." She gave a chuckle as she left.

Eunice didn't dare look at Joan. She walked over to the furthest line and put her basket down. She shook out her dad's work overalls and pegged them, just as the door shut and she heard Joan's footsteps. She smelled her, too. If she hadn't been made of bones, Eunice was sure she'd have melted to the ground right there. Every hair on her body tingled as Joan pulled up next to her.

Eunice took a deep breath and pulled out two of her brother's school shirts. She hung them from the hem down, just as her mum had taught her. "Good skills to have for when you get married and have your own kids," she'd told her.

Right now, it was a good skill to focus on doing properly. Anything to avoid Joan.

"How was your second date with Kenneth?" Joan's words fizzed in the air.

Eunice attached the final peg and looked up. "It was fine."

Joan's stare was steady.

Eunice's heartbeat was anything but.

"He seemed nice."

She could hardly breathe. Eunice nodded. "He is."

Joan gulped. "Which is why I'm here."

Eunice didn't understand. She bent to get another item of clothing, but Joan put a hand on her arm.

Eunice trembled under her touch. An alarm blared in her head.

"Stop." Joan paused. "Please."

Eunice's breath caught in her throat. Joan's second word came out with a slightly scorched tone.

Eunice did as she was asked. When she dared to look at Joan, her chest heaved. She glanced over Joan's shoulder. The door was shut. They were completely alone. Eunice had no idea what was going to happen next. It was at once terrifying, but also thrilling. She knew now they'd been on this threshold for so long.

Something had shifted, and Kenneth was responsible. Now, Eunice could hardly breathe.

"I hated seeing you with him yesterday."

Oh my god. She was actually saying it.

"I wanted him to be awful. Ugly. Charmless. But he was neither. He seemed... nice. And I could see he was very taken with you." Joan reached out a hand and took Eunice's in hers.

They both shook.

"Eunice Elizabeth Humphries, look at me."

Eunice closed her eyes and raised her gaze. She counted to three, then opened her eyelids. What she saw nearly broke her. Joan's eyes were shiny, her breath quick. Joan had cracked open the door, but Eunice could see the terror on her face. She wanted to reach out and tell Joan it was all going to be okay, but she couldn't. Because she had no idea if that was the truth. She couldn't promise Joan a thing. But oh my, she wanted to. She wanted to promise her the world. Even though she had no idea what that meant.

Eunice glanced to her right, but couldn't see the door. They were hidden behind the washing.

"I can't bear the thought of you being with him. I spent last night tossing and turning in my bed. Because Kenneth can do what he wants, can't he? He can swan in from Birmingham, take you out, buy you things, and then eventually he'll ask you to marry him. Because that's what happens." Joan shook her head, her cheeks flushed red. "But he's got no right to be so taken with you. He can't fall in love with you." Her breath caught. "Not when you're already taken."

Eunice squeezed Joan's fingers tight, her stomach flip-flopping. "I'm already taken?" The words slid out as a whisper.

Joan stepped forward. "You are." Her thumb stroked the back of Eunice's hand, and Eunice shivered. The way Joan's lips parted when she spoke had her mesmerised.

"By who?"

Joan dropped Eunice's hand, then cupped her cheek.

It was all Eunice could do not to purr.

"By me."

Heat poured down her in waves. Everything Eunice owned swayed: her vision, her breath, her heartbeat. She already knew this moment was one she'd remember for the rest of her life.

It happened as if in slow motion, but then so quickly, it caught her off-guard. Eunice blinked. As her eyelids sprang open, Joan's perfect pink lips pressed onto hers.

The world faded away as Eunice sank into Joan's bold, delicious kiss. Sparks of pleasure rippled across her skin. A low hum zinged in her ears. Joan's arm circled her waist, strong and firm. That much was like Kenneth. But the rest? It was night and day.

Joan's lips on hers were everything. Eunice was vaguely aware she was standing in the drying room. Hardly the spot she'd imagined for her first dynamite kiss. As Joan spoke to her in a language she fully understood, a firework burst in Eunice's soul. Followed by another. In moments, a full-blown display began.

Eunice *finally* had her dream. The one that had taken up residence in her heart ever since she started at the factory six months ago.

Joan had truly swept her off her feet.

Something roared inside her, and she realised it was her heartbeat.

Joan's lips slid over hers, and Eunice wilted in her arms.

They broke apart, both gasping for air.

Their gazes locked.

"Oh my god," Eunice said.

Joan said nothing, just stared.

Then Eunice reached up both hands and pulled Joan's mouth back to where she needed it most. Now the door was open, Eunice wanted to break it down. Tear it off its hinges.

She didn't care what anybody thought. She only knew what she felt. What she wanted.

What she wanted was Joan.

The second kiss was even better than the first. It was beyond anything Eunice had ever experienced before. This time, Joan slid her tongue into Eunice's mouth, too. Was it possible for too much emotion to flood your system? Could she short-circuit herself? It certainly felt that way.

Eunice's hands worked their way around Joan's body, and one landed on her bum. She squeezed. Joan groaned into her mouth.

Eunice's brain unpicked everything she'd ever been taught and threw it on the floor. Stamped on it. What was happening? How was it possible to be this turned on? Feel this much passion?

They broke apart for a second time when Joan went to move forward, walked into the laundry basket and almost fell on top of Eunice.

Eunice burst out laughing, then steadied herself, before they both stopped and stared. The tension in the air was so thick, it was almost suffocating. Eunice tried to piece together her thoughts, to make sense of what had just happened. She couldn't. None of it made any sense. The only thing that made sense to her was Joan. Nothing had ever had more clarity. But take them both out of here, that's when the clouds came.

She wasn't going to think about that right now.

Instead, she stared at Joan. "I don't fully know what just happened…"

The door of the drying room flew open.

Eunice jumped backwards as if she'd just touched an

electric fence. So much blood rushed to her cheeks, she was surprised there was enough in the rest of her body to keep her upright. She glanced at Joan, then looked over the top of her laundry. Thank goodness they were camouflaged a little. She stood on her tiptoes to see who it was.

"There's always one sock that jumps ship and wants a life of its own, isn't there?" Hilda held up the rogue sock and rolled her eyes at Eunice. "Are you going for the world record for taking the longest time to hang out your washing?" She tapped her watch. "Chop, chop, while there's still warmth in the air."

Eunice murmured something, then waited for Hilda to disappear before she turned to Joan. Whatever magic spell they'd both been under had well and truly popped, but Eunice was desperate to get it back. She licked her lips. "That was incredible—"

"Eunice!"

Eunice jumped out of her skin. It was her mum. She pulled the washing down and poked her head over it. "Yes?" *Please don't come any nearer.* It was important her mum didn't see Joan. Not right now.

"What are you doing? Can you come? Peter's clonked Tony over the head and there's blood everywhere. I need a hand."

"Of course!"

Her mum nodded, then turned on her heel.

Joan's back was against the wall, her face white. She blew out a breath. "I better go," she said, not meeting Eunice's gaze. "This is too risky and you don't want to be seen with me. I don't know what I was thinking coming here. It was a mistake."

Eunice frowned. "What are you talking about? It didn't feel like one to me."

"Nor to me!" Joan screwed up her face. "It's just... what happens now? Kenneth still exists, and it's not like we can be together, is it?" She paused, then shook her head. "I have to go."

Eunice wanted to pin her to the wall, kiss her again. Instead, she watched her leave, open-mouthed.

Joan had swept her off her feet, then left her hanging.

Chapter Fifteen

Monday morning.

The day after yesterday. September 22nd.

The day after that kiss.

Joan slammed the cutlery drawer with more force than necessary. As the drawer crunched on her bones, she let out a yelp. "Fuck!" She yanked it open with her other hand, then squeezed her fingers round her injured hand. She wasn't concentrating this morning. How the hell was she ever going to concentrate on anything again after she'd kissed Eunice, told her how she felt, then run away? She'd spent all day yesterday wondering why she'd run. She'd concluded that she had to. Eunice would eventually, so it was better to get in there first.

She rubbed her hand again, then winced. Her mum wouldn't be impressed, would she? Instead of playing the hand she'd been dealt, Joan had simply folded. At least the pain in her hand distracted from the pain in her heart.

"Where's the fire? What's happening?" Jimmy stood in the doorway in his long johns and white T-shirt. "Why are you destroying the kitchen or yourself this morning? I've been lying in bed, and all I can hear is slamming, stomping and yelling."

Joan sighed. "Sorry. It's just one of those days." She pointed to the side. "There's tea in the pot if you want one."

Jimmy poured a cup, then sat opposite her, his gaze never wavering. "Aren't you going to be late for work?" He glanced up at the kitchen clock.

Joan shook her head. "I'm not going in today."

Jimmy stared at her. "You never have a day off. Even when you're sick."

"Then I'm due one, aren't I?" Joan took a sip of her tea.

"This is to do with Eunice, I take it?"

She glanced up. He knew?

Jimmy gave her a sad smile. "It's hardly a surprise after Saturday. The look on your face when she introduced Kenneth." He paused. "I told you, women aren't easy. You have to fight for them, especially the good ones. But sometimes, the good ones get snapped up. You have to lick your wounds and move on." He put a finger to his chest. "I'm speaking from experience. I'm sorry she's got a boyfriend, but you can't avoid her forever. You work with her."

Joan's heartbeat was loud in her ears. "I know." He didn't know the half of it, but she wasn't going to correct him. He didn't need to know she'd kissed Eunice. That Eunice had kissed her back. That she'd felt Eunice's breasts through her top and thought she might die on the spot. She couldn't face her today. Tomorrow, she'd see how she felt. "I just need a day, that's all."

"Fair enough." Jimmy folded his arms across his chest. "By the way, I have news. My contract at the Garrick runs out next week, and I've been offered a job in Guildford. But it does mean I'm going to be staying in digs for an extended period, so you'll be home alone. Obviously, you've got Maggie and her crew just across the way. But I just wanted to check that's okay before I say yes?"

Joan nodded. "Of course. You've done it before."

"I know. And you're older now, too. But I just need to check you're not going to go stir crazy on your own nursing a broken heart."

Joan rolled her eyes. He was nearer to the truth than he thought, but she wasn't going to let on. Her heart wasn't broken. Yet. "I can cope. I'm a big girl. I'll miss you, though."

"I'll get the train back when I have a day off. But go over and see Maggie when I'm gone. I know you like peace and quiet, but it's good for you to get some family time, too."

Right now, peace and quiet sounded ideal. "It's fine. It'll give me space to write, won't it? No excuses. When do you leave?"

"Next weekend."

* * *

Joan didn't make it into work until Wednesday. By then, she was bored of her own company. Plus, she needed to start earning money again. Her heart raced as she walked onto the floor, her colleagues greeting her and asking after her health. She told everyone she was feeling much better. And she was. Until she drew up at her machine. Just the sight of Eunice's hair flowing down her back made Joan's pulse race. When Eunice turned, Joan's stomach swooped as if she was on a swing.

She'd taken a chance and written her own script. But had it bombed, or had it got the green light?

Joan gave Eunice a tentative smile. "Hi."

Eunice blushed pillar-box red. "Hi," she replied. "I

wondered if you were ever coming back." The last bit was said as a whisper.

Joan sat down, busying herself with her machine. She didn't know what to say in return. She'd wondered the same thing, too.

A silence hung between them. "Are you feeling better?"

Joan glanced across, holding Eunice's gaze. "Time will tell." She paused. "How are you?"

"Better now you're here."

What was Eunice saying? That she wanted Joan here? Had Joan done the wrong thing running off the other day? She'd love to know, but now wasn't the time to ask those questions. She had to focus on what was in front of her. Sunshine-yellow dresses. She was grateful for it.

* * *

At morning tea break, Joan made her way over to the tea trolley. She poured a mug of tea the colour of bricks, then helped herself to a Rich Tea biscuit.

"You feeling better?" Mari flipped the lever on the tea urn and held her white mug under it as the black liquid spurted into her cup.

"I am, thanks." Joan glanced up.

Eunice walked towards her.

Joan's heart thumped in her chest. She clutched her mug and focused on Mari.

"Were you being sick? There's a bug going round our estate where you can't stop vomiting."

Joan nodded. "I was," she lied. Eunice walked right by her and on to the toilets. Joan breathed in her scent. Sunlight streamed through the windows and followed her, lighting her up like the goddess she was.

"Joan?" Mari frowned. "Are you okay? You seem a little spaced out. Are you still feeling bad?"

Joan blinked. "I'm fine. Just... still recovering." She put her tea down on the table. "Actually, I might just nip to the loo and splash my face." She walked away and through the main swing doors, out onto the cold, draughty stairwell. As Joan eyed the toilet door, she paused. Eunice was on the other side. Did she want to speak to her? Should she follow her in or should she wait?

She'd wait. Joan pressed her back to the cold wall of the stairwell, her blood racing in her ears.

Moments later, Eunice appeared. When she saw Joan, her eyebrows rose up her forehead.

Eunice was so perfect. Nothing would ever change that. Even if she flashed forward 60 years, she would lay money on Eunice still being beautiful. Her soft hair, her emerald-green eyes, her warm smile.

"Hi," Eunice said. "Were you waiting for me?"

Joan ground her teeth together. "I guess so. I wasn't sure you'd want me to, but here I am."

Eunice walked over and stood beside her.

Having her this close made Joan immediately want to reach out and pull her closer. To press her lips to Eunice's once more. But she couldn't. Not right now. Would she ever do it again, or was the weekend a mirage? When Joan looked at Eunice, her face was strangled with emotion, too. Was she thinking the same thoughts? Did she want to kiss Joan, too?

"I was worried about you this week."

Joan leaned more heavily on the wall. "You were?"

"Uh-huh. You left quite abruptly."

Joan sucked in a breath. "I know. It was just... a lot."

Eunice licked her lips, then snagged Joan's stare again. "But I didn't understand what went on. Did you run because you regretted it?"

The swing doors whooshed open.

Joan glanced up and pushed herself off the wall.

Kitty grinned at them both. "What are you two doing out here?" She paused. "Whatever it is, you both look guilty. You need to work on your poker faces, ladies!" She gave Joan a wink, then went into the loo.

Eunice pursed her lips and sighed. "This isn't the best place to discuss this."

Joan shook her head. "It's not." She paused. "Do you want to go for a coffee after work later?"

Eunice shook her head. "I can't. I'm helping Mrs Higgins with some painting. I promised her on Monday, and she's keeping me busy until the weekend."

Frustration fizzed through Joan. This week was going to be torture now. Knowing that Eunice wasn't scared. That something else might happen.

"What about the weekend? My brother's working, you could come over and I'll cook you dinner. Make up for when you ditched me for Kenneth. They've started selling fish fingers at our local shop finally."

Eunice stared at Joan. "It'd be just the two of us?" Her gaze dropped to Joan's lips.

Dammit, Joan wanted to kiss her. Her breath sped up. She nodded. "Yes, it would."

Eunice's pause was two long breaths. "That could work."

"It's a date, then." Joan shook at her own words. "I mean, not a date, but, you know."

Eunice pushed herself off the wall. "Yeah," she replied. "I know."

Chapter Sixteen

Eunice shut Mrs Higgins' front door and walked the few steps to her own. When she got there, she heard shouting behind it. Her brothers were arguing again. She decided to let them simmer down and walked to the stairwell, then climbed to the top floor. When she got there, David was already leaning over the balcony, cigarette in hand.

Eunice smiled as she walked up beside him. "Great minds think alike."

He offered her a cigarette. She shook her head.

"What brings you here?" David bumped her hip. "I thought you'd be in your room writing love letters to Kenneth, spritzing them with your perfume."

"You know I don't waste perfume like that."

David laughed. "What are you doing up here?"

She shrugged. "Usual. My family are too loud, so I'm just grabbing some quiet time. Same as you."

David turned his head. "How *are* things with you and Kenneth, anyway? Is this a thing that might turn into something more?"

Joan flashed into Eunice's mind. She pushed her aside. "I don't think so. He lives in Birmingham."

David shrugged. "People move."

"Not us. We're London people." She paused. "He did kiss me, though." But it was nothing compared to how Joan had kissed her. Nothing at all.

David glanced at her, one eyebrow quirked. "And I'm guessing from the tone of your voice and your body language, it wasn't great?"

Eunice stilled. "It was…" Just like every other kiss she'd had from a man. Flat and uninspired. Whereas Joan had given her a kiss she couldn't stop thinking about. Which was all wrong and yet somehow, right. "It was fine. Just not amazing." She paused. "How about you with Susie? Do her kisses make your toes melt?"

David smiled as he turned to her. "I love kissing her."

Had Kenneth enjoyed kissing Eunice? She'd love to know. "What about Susie? Have you asked her?"

"Asked her if she likes kissing me?"

Eunice nodded.

"Of course not. Are you crazy?"

Eunice laughed. "I dunno. It's just, I've kissed a few boys now, and none of them have felt right."

"That's because you haven't kissed me." David puffed out his chest.

Eunice punched his arm lightly. "Of course that's the reason. You're the greatest kisser of all time."

"I've got a trophy I'm that good."

Eunice sighed. "But seriously. I've seen the films."

"No you haven't."

She laughed. "I did see some this summer. With Joan." A spark of heat landed in her stomach and worked its way south. Joan had made her feel the way no boy ever had. "Plus,

I've read books. I expected to have met at least one boy who could kiss by now. Someone I loved kissing. Who swept me off my feet." She stared out into the autumn evening. It had happened. But not with who she'd expected.

"Kenneth might just be crap at kissing."

Eunice sighed. "Maybe."

David grinned. "Do you want me to kiss you? For the sake of comparison, obviously."

She let the option roll across her brain, but quickly dismissed it. "I'm not kissing you. You're... David."

He mimed a dagger to his heart. "Hit me where it hurts, why don't you." He gave her an exaggerated pout.

"You know what I mean." She was already kissing enough people without adding David to the mix.

"Maybe it will just take time. Absence makes the heart grow fonder. Isn't that how the saying goes?" He paused. "Are you courting now?"

Eunice stilled. He'd asked, and she'd said yes. Then, she'd promptly kissed someone else. She was really bad at courting. "We are, I think."

"You think? Poor Kenneth. He hasn't made a great impression on you, has he?"

"Apparently I've made one on him. Mrs Higgins was telling me earlier that he's told his parents about us, and he can't wait until he can come back and see me."

"Sounds like he's smitten. Are you going to give him another try or let him down gently from afar?"

Eunice had no idea. She couldn't even think about Kenneth right now. Her brain was too taken up with Joan and this weekend. Kenneth hadn't truly been on her mind until now.

"I'll carry on." It seemed the easiest thing to do, particularly when he wasn't here. He was easy to court when he lived three hours away.

Whereas Joan lived a tube ride away. Eunice was taking that tube to London Bridge tomorrow, and going to see Joan. Just the thought made blood rush to her cheeks. She stared out, remembering Joan's lips on hers. They weren't easy to forget. Kenneth was already relegated to a distant second.

"Where did you just go? Your face came over all dreamy, and you looked like you were miles away. I'd guess you weren't thinking about Kenneth?"

Eunice blushed some more, then shook her head. "Nothing. Just thinking about work." Or about a certain someone from work.

And the fact it was less than 24 hours before she could kiss her again.

Chapter Seventeen

Joan set the kitchen table with the good cutlery, then straightened the place mats one more time. She'd spied them in a window display this week and thought of Eunice. They were of street scenes of Paris.

Joan checked the kitchen clock, made sure it was still working. It was. She went to the drawer and got spoons for the dessert. She'd bought tinned peaches and evaporated milk. She glanced up at the clock again. She'd told Eunice to come any time after 5pm. It was five to. She glanced down at her clothes. She'd paid special attention to them today. Her trousers, her shirt, her underwear. Because today might be the first time someone else was going to take them off.

At three minutes past five, a knock on the front door made Joan jump. Her breath caught in her throat. She smoothed down her top, straightened her chiffon scarf, and walked to the door. She'd never been so nervous about a visitor in her life. She didn't want to think about why it was so important. That it could be the start of the rest of her life.

Eunice stood on the other side of the door and she was a knockout. She had her autumn camel coat on, and her good shoes. The ones she'd worn to the dance. The ones she wore when she wanted to impress. Joan ushered her in, peering round the door to check nobody was watching. Especially Aunt Maggie or her family. She wanted tonight to be about her and Eunice, and nobody else.

She took Eunice's coat and hung it on the hallway rack. She liked the way it looked there. Then her eyes took in Eunice. She was poured into a hot-pink dress with a fitted body and flared skirt, and she smelt divine. Joan gulped, then showed her through to the kitchen. The late evening sunlight bounced off the kitchen counters.

Eunice stood, staring at her.

Joan shivered under her gaze. "Sit, please." She pulled out a chair.

Eunice tucked her dress under and sat. She picked up her place mat. "Are these of Paris?" She glanced up. "I love them."

Joan flushed with pride. "I bought them yesterday. There's no French food tonight, but we can still immerse ourselves in Paris."

"I love that, thank you." Eunice gazed at her.

The air sparkled with magic. Joan took a deep breath, got the matches and lit the grill. "We've got fish fingers, peas and tinned potatoes. Plus dessert. I hope you're hungry."

"Starving." She got up and stood next to Joan. "Can I help?"

Joan glanced sideways and their eyes met. The urge to kiss her right now was overwhelming. But they should eat first. Joan had no idea where tonight was going. She didn't want to jump the gun. However, when she sliced the already cooked potatoes, her hand trembled.

Eunice glanced down, clocked it, and covered Joan's hand with her own. "I'm nervous too, if it helps."

Joan gulped. "That might make it worse."

They ferried salt, vinegar and ketchup to the table, then Joan served the meal.

Eunice declared it a triumph. "I haven't had fish fingers before. Mum says they're too expensive for all of us. So you gave me Paris and new tastes."

Joan smiled. "I think we've both developed new tastes over the past few weeks."

They stared at each other. Moments ticked by. Joan forgot to breathe. She got up, cleared the plates, checked the grill was off, then sat down again. Only, now it was worse. Because there was nothing to do. Dinner was eaten. Now, it was just the two of them. It wasn't even 6pm.

Joan tried a smile but she was pretty sure it came out wonky. Her whole body was a mass of jitters.

"Thank you for dinner. Nobody's ever cooked for me before."

"I'm glad I was the first."

"I'm glad, too."

"Was your mum okay about you coming tonight?"

Eunice nodded. "She asked if there were boys coming, too. When I told her no, she was fine." She stared a little more. "I told her your aunty lived close by, too. But I'm glad your brother's out. This week at work has been awful."

"Agreed."

Eunice was silent for a few seconds. "Did you regret last Sunday? Is that why you ran?"

Joan shook her head. Regret misted her thoughts. She'd played a bad hand, but how to explain it? "I thought you'd regret it. When your mum came in, you looked like you wanted the ground to swallow you up. Plus, there's Kenneth."

Eunice ran a finger down the side of her place mat depicting the Eiffel Tower. "There is," she replied. "He kissed me last week. When he did, I felt nothing." She raised her head. "When you kissed me, I felt everything."

Her words poured down Joan like honey. Outside, someone shouted, but Joan couldn't work out what they said. All she could hear was the beat of her own heart, and the words that had just slipped from Eunice's lips reverberating in her soul.

Eunice liked when Joan kissed her.

Holy hellfire.

"You didn't want me to run?"

Eunice shook her head. "No." Another pause. "The opposite, in fact."

Joan had dreamed of Eunice saying something like that. Now it was here, she wasn't sure what to do with it. Her body jumped with nerves. She couldn't sit still. She got up and grabbed the tinned peaches, then bowls from the cupboard.

When she turned, Eunice was next to her.

Eunice took the bowls from Joan's hands and put them on the side. Then she took Joan's right hand and pressed it on top of her breast.

Joan sucked in a breath. What was Eunice doing?

She looked into Joan's eyes. "This is what I wanted you to do next."

How she'd wanted to do that, too.

Joan was done skirting the issue. She gathered Eunice in her arms and seconds later, stared into her velvety green eyes. She pressed her lips to Eunice's again, and the spark that had ignited the moment Eunice arrived at her door burst into life, a surge of heat rampaging through Joan's body. She'd been waiting for this moment all her life. For a woman she wanted to want her back. She'd tried to deny it. Tried to push it aside.

Now the fire had been lit she wasn't going to let the embers die.

If their first kiss had been delicious yet tentative, this one was anything but. Eunice's hands clamped on Joan's bum, her body pressed into Joan's like they came that way. As a pair.

Joan wasn't complaining.

But it was Eunice's kisses that skittled Joan's remaining resolve. As if the first time was a trial run. This time, Eunice didn't hold back. Had Eunice been waiting for this moment all her life, too? Joan daren't even think that was true.

Joan slid her lips from Eunice's mouth, then placed hot, wet kisses down Eunice's jawline, her neck and her collarbone. Joan couldn't go any further, because the rest of Eunice was fully clothed. Was she going to stay that way? Joan wasn't pushing for anything. Eunice's kisses were more than enough for now.

Within seconds, Eunice's lips were back on Joan's, this time her tongue pushed into Joan's mouth, demanding more.

Joan was happy to give.

Eunice pushed her up against the kitchen counter, where her hands reached for Joan's breasts. Joan's buttons popped as Eunice's fingers laid claim to her.

Joan pulled back, her breathing ragged, her eyes wide. Eunice was pushing her further than she'd ever gone before.

They gazed at each other for a few long seconds.

"Bedroom?" Joan could scarcely believe she was uttering that word.

Eunice gulped, then nodded.

Joan pulled her towards the kitchen door before she lost her nerve. At her bedroom door, she stopped and gazed at Eunice. "Are you sure?"

"No. But I'm even more sure I don't want you to stop kissing me." Eunice's hand trembled as she crushed Joan's with it.

Eunice looked around Joan's room. They sat on the bed, and she stroked Joan's coarse green blankets. "I wanted to kiss you last time I was on this. I thought you had to be married to have a double bed."

An image of them both in white wedding dresses flashed through Joan's mind. She'd marry Eunice on the spot, but that was never going to happen. They were two women. That was not their lot in life. "I got lucky," Joan replied. Then she didn't want to talk anymore.

Her lips found Eunice's again, transporting her away to a place of bliss. Who knew this was what kissing could be? Joan hadn't been searching for a prince, having worked out a few years ago she'd prefer a princess. She'd finally found her. Eunice was the person she was meant to kiss all along.

They fell onto their backs and rolled on the bed, all the while their lips fastened together. Joan's hands caressed Eunice's body, then her fingers got tangled in her golden hair. She clamped a hand on Eunice's breast.

Eunice groaned into her mouth.

Joan couldn't breathe. Not only because Eunice's tongue brushed hers and stole her breath, but also because the question of 'what happens next' was lodged in her throat.

When they eventually broke apart, they stared, their

breath heavy. Joan's body hummed with delight. She'd never felt this much for anyone in her life.

Eunice sat up, turned and flicked up her hair. "Unzip me?"

Joan gulped, then did as she was asked. Somebody had sewn this zip into this dress in a factory just like theirs. She'd put zips in a thousand times, maybe more. But she'd never thought about the person who undid it. Never thought it would be her. She knew she was going to think about this moment every time she sewed a zip from now on.

The dress fell from Eunice's shoulders with ease, and she stepped out of it, along with her slip. She was left in her pants and bra, both white. Her pale skin was almost the same colour. She sat back down.

Desire licked Joan like a flame. She leaned forward and dropped hot kisses onto Eunice's shoulders, then lower to her collarbone. She pulled her closer, cupped Eunice's breasts and buried her head between them. She'd found her gold at the end of the rainbow. It had been Eunice all along.

Eunice gasped, then held Joan's head there. "This feels…" she began.

Joan raised her head and their gazes locked. "I know," she replied. In seconds, she reached around and unclipped Eunice's bra. Joan could hardly believe this was happening. She sucked one of Eunice's nipples into her mouth.

Why had nobody told her life could be this good?

Suddenly, time sped up. Joan's kisses covered every inch of Eunice's skin as she pushed her onto her back, pressing into her.

Eunice squirmed beneath her. "You need your clothes off, too," she said through patchy breath.

Joan stilled, then nodded.

Eunice sat up with her, and Joan was transfixed by her breasts. She took them in her hands and licked them.

In response, Eunice pulled her head up roughly and kissed her again.

Shedding Joan's clothes was stop-start, but they managed it. Joan had thought getting naked with Eunice would leave her feeling exposed. In fact, it was the opposite. The way Eunice stared at her, she'd be happy to stay like this forever.

They rolled back together again, this time both of them exploring the other's bare skin. Then Joan's fingers skated down Eunice's body and between her legs, under the edges of her underwear.

Eunice sucked in a breath so large, she almost swallowed Joan whole.

Joan stared at her.

They both froze. They were on the precipice. Everything they'd done so far had felt incredible. But this was the next stage. Joan knew what she liked. She'd touched herself enough times. But she had no idea what it might feel like for someone else to touch her. Just the thought made her body heat to nuclear temperatures.

"You feel so amazing." Joan's fingers were on top of Eunice's knickers. She moved under them and they connected with Eunice's coarse hair.

Eunice shook, her eyes wide. "Have you done this before?"

Joan moved her fingers further down. She shook her head. "Never."

Eunice moved her head and kissed Joan. "I'm so scared."

Joan trembled. "Me, too," she whispered. "If you want me to stop…"

Eunice shook her head. "God, no," she rasped. "I'm just glad you're doing it with me."

"I couldn't think of anyone more perfect."

Joan moved Eunice's underwear down and she kicked them off. Then she slid her fingers until they connected with Eunice's wetness. She closed her eyes and stroked Eunice slowly.

Eunice let out a moan that was exactly what Joan wanted to hear. As Joan moved the tips of her fingers, she watched Eunice's face contort.

This was the most spectacular thing she'd ever done. She was in bed with another woman. They were having sex. Was this sex? She had no idea. Whatever it was, it almost took Joan's breath away. She trembled. It started in her stomach and seeped into her bones.

"Is this okay?"

Eunice moved her hips and groaned as Joan slid her fingers down. Then, almost of their own accord, they were sucked inside Eunice.

When that happened, Eunice's mouth opened wide. "Ooooh, Joan," she groaned. Eunice screwed her eyes shut and lifted her bum off the bed.

Joan slid slowly in and out. She knew if she touched herself, she'd be wet. She had no idea if she was doing this right, but the way Eunice was reacting, she was going to carry on.

With every circle, touch and thrust, Joan got to know Eunice that little bit more. When Eunice opened her eyes, she showered her with kisses. As Eunice's chest turned pink, then her face, Joan concentrated on getting this right. She wanted to give Eunice her all. Joan was in this moment with everything she had.

Moments later, Eunice's body twisted, and her face scrunched.

Was Joan hurting her?

Eunice's eyelids fluttered open, and she gave Joan the briefest of encouraging nods.

That was all she needed. Joan slid back inside just as Eunice's walls began to pulse, and Eunice groaned into the air with renewed force. As she came, she pressed her head back into the pillow. Joan had never seen a more beautiful sight than Eunice in full flight. Elation flowed through her as Eunice soared. She was the most gorgeous woman on the planet, and she was hers.

Moments later, Joan lay beside Eunice, her fingers stroking her hip, then her breasts. How were her breasts so perfect? How was everything about Eunice so perfect? How was Joan meant to transition back to real life now, back to Eunice just being her friend when they'd shared this moment? She had no idea.

She opened her eyes and gave Joan a grin. "I don't know what to say." She flung an arm around Joan, then slung a leg over her hip, too.

Her wetness was slick on Joan's thigh. So this was what happiness felt like. Was this how normal girls felt when they were with boys? Joan couldn't imagine they ever felt what she was feeling right now. On top of the world.

"Was it okay?"

Eunice's gaze melted onto her. "Okay? It was spectacular." She ran a finger down Joan's cheek.

Joan reached her mouth around and kissed it.

"It was everything. You were everything. I can't believe I was your first." She paused. "You haven't done anything with a boy, either?"

Joan frowned. "It never really interested me."

"Me, either." Eunice sucked on her top lip. "You think there's something wrong with us?"

Joan shook her head. "No, I think we're perfect. You and me against the world." She got lost in Eunice's lips once more. It was easily done. When she pulled back, breathless, Eunice gave her a grin.

"You and me against the world sounds perfect." She moved her leg and rolled onto her back with a sigh. "There's just one thing, though."

Joan propped her elbow on the bed, then her chin in her palm.

Eunice's gaze went to Joan's breasts and she kissed them. Like that was the most natural thing in the world.

For Joan and for her, it suddenly was.

"What's that?" Joan asked.

Eunice knocked her elbow so Joan flopped backwards, and then climbed on top of her. She pinned Joan's arms either side of her head, then kissed her hard.

"I haven't touched you yet." Eunice stared down. "I'm scared to."

Joan licked her lips. Just the thought of it made her pulse race. "Don't be."

Eunice sat up and ran her hands through her hair.

Joan's breath caught in her throat. Eunice, naked and straddling her, was an image she was going to replay for quite some time. She sat up and kissed her. She never wanted to stop. Eventually, Joan moved Eunice off her, then took her hand.

Joan spread her legs. "Just touch me. We can do this together." Her heart thumped as Eunice's fingers slid down Joan's skin, through her hair and then to her very core.

When they hit Joan's wetness, she arched her back. "Oh, hell," she said. She closed her eyes.

Eunice stared. "Am I doing it right?" Then she moved through Joan and into her.

Joan hoped she lived to tell the tale.

If she didn't, she couldn't think of a better way to go.

Chapter Eighteen

Eunice woke up the next morning and stared. Where the hell was she? Then it all came back to her. Dinner with Joan. The Paris place mats. The uneaten dessert. The night of hot passion. So filled with desire, she could still taste it. Her body still tingled with the sugar rush of sex, but what happened now? She tried to still her mind, to not think about that, but it was hard. A few months ago, she didn't even know it was possible to kiss a woman, never mind have sex with her. Now, she'd spent the night doing just that and loving it. Revelling in it. Wanting to do it again and again.

She sat up, her heart racing. Where was Joan? This was her place, her bed. A double bed. Joan had told her last night it had been her parents' bed, then her mother's before she died. Eunice had been glad she didn't know that beforehand.

She swung her legs out of bed, glancing down at her body. She was no longer a virgin. Or was she? Did sleeping with a woman count? She had no idea. She hoped it didn't show up on her body. Were people going to stare at her all the way home, a knowing look in their eyes? She pushed those thoughts out of her head. Right now, she had to find Joan.

She threw her knickers back on, then grabbed her bra from the floor. Joan had hung up her dress on the outside of her wardrobe. That was kind of her. Eunice slipped it back on, then stroked the wooden hanger. A part of Joan's life she hadn't seen before last night. She knew so much more about it now.

Joan stood on her balcony just off the kitchen, leaning over the railing, soaking up the late September sun. She wore beige shorts, and a black short-sleeved shirt with white buttons. When Eunice walked up behind her and put a hand on her bum, she jumped.

When Joan saw who it was, she smiled.

Joan's smile could light a dark night.

She transferred her cigarette to her other hand, stroked Eunice's back through her dress, then stopped. Joan glanced up and across the courtyard to the balcony opposite. An older man with a bald head peered over his paper and sat up straighter when he saw Eunice. They both knew they couldn't touch each other on this balcony where there were prying eyes.

For the first time in her life, Eunice had to watch her actions. When she saw Joan's bare arm, her natural reaction was to touch it. Now, she couldn't. They were no longer just friends, easy in each other's company. Had they ever been, truly?

Unease settled in Eunice's stomach.

"That's Mr Harridge. Mum was friends with him, used to chat across the balconies. He's always on his, rain or shine." Joan paused, then turned her head. "How are you?"

Eunice nodded. She'd woken up so happy. But within minutes, a swirl of emotions had blotted her day. "Good."

"You looked so perfect sleeping this morning, I thought I'd leave you." Joan sucked on her Woodbine.

"How long ago did you wake up?"

"About an hour ago."

"Can I have a cigarette?" Eunice folded her arms across her chest.

Joan frowned. "You don't smoke."

Eunice raised an eyebrow. "If there's ever a morning to take it up, it's today, wouldn't you say?"

Joan grabbed her pack from the kitchen, brought it out and held up her lighter.

Eunice balanced the cigarette between her lips. When she glanced up, Joan stared at them. Eunice knew exactly what she was thinking. Because she was thinking it, too. She ignored the liquid desire in Joan's eyes. Tried to shuffle her emotions back into order, but she'd have made a lousy croupier. Instead, she sucked on her cigarette. Then she choked, tears streaming down her cheeks.

Joan patted her back. "Smoking doesn't seem to agree with you."

Eunice straightened up. She needed something to do with her hands so they didn't go straight to Joan. This was as good as any. If she only smoked this morning, so be it. Was this why all the characters smoked in books and films when they were having affairs? Eunice had gone to bed a girl, and woken up a woman. The world looked brighter, bigger, sharper. As if everything she'd ever known before had dissolved, and now all she had was the present.

"What have you been thinking about in the hour you've been up?" Eunice leaned on the black metal railing, echoing Joan's stance.

Joan twisted her head and gave her a sad smile. "What's going to happen now. If you're going to freak out. If this is just a one-off." She sighed, then stretched her back, both hands gripping the railing. "What's happened to me overnight? It's like you've given me a truth pill. I'm not someone who talks about things. But last night seems to have short-circuited my brain." She took a long drag on her cigarette, stood up, then nodded through the doorway. "You want to go inside and I'll put the kettle on?"

Eunice leaned on the kitchen counter as Joan lit the hob. Once the water was heating, she turned. When their gazes met, they both closed the few steps between them before they even knew what they were doing. Then Joan's lips were on hers, the taste of cigarettes strong on her breath. Eunice broke away to stub out her own, then they kissed like there was no tomorrow. Which there might not be. Because their future wasn't clear. Was last night a one-off? Did Joan want it to be? Eunice hoped not, but she was in no position to make demands. She had a boyfriend. Sort of.

They stayed clasped, and kissed until the kettle started to sing. Then Eunice reluctantly let Joan go. She sat at the table, head to the ceiling, until Joan sat beside her, plonking mugs of tea in front of them. Eunice stared at the tea. She didn't even know what it was anymore. It was meaningless. The only thing that meant anything to her was Joan.

"You want the peaches we never ate last night?"

"Not really." Eunice couldn't think about eating after that kiss. She never wanted to eat again. She'd just live on Joan's kisses. She was aglow, exhilarated. She'd read about love, but she had no idea what it felt like. Was she falling in love with Joan? If love felt like every part of her was spinning, then yes.

Eunice closed her eyes briefly. Falling in love with Joan

would be the sweetest thing ever. Coming back here, going to bed with Joan would be a dream. However, dark clouds covered her heart even as she thought that. None of this would be easy. She'd known that from the start. Last night and that kiss had just made it ten times better, but also ten times harder.

Eunice stared at Joan. She was so perfect, with her short hair, her perfect cheekbones. She was pretty and handsome all at the same time. She was *everything*. "I just want you." She kissed Joan's fingers. They trembled under her touch.

Joan flexed her hand, then took a sip of her tea. "Last night was... just so much." She paused. "But what about Kenneth?"

Eunice ground her teeth together. What about Kenneth? "He's not important." She really wanted that to be true.

"He's still in your life."

"I know." She stared at her tea. "My mum loves that, as does Mrs Higgins."

"And you?"

She shrugged. "He takes the heat off. Plus, he's convenient because he's not nearby." Eunice eyed Joan. "Maybe that's what we need to remember. While I'm still seeing Kenneth, my mum's not going to badger me into getting a boyfriend. She likes him. This gives us good cover to spend time together, right?"

Joan pursed her lips, then nodded. "I suppose you're right. Just don't go falling in love with him, okay?"

Eunice reached out and grabbed Joan's hand. "I guarantee that's not going to happen. My heart's already taken."

* * *

They spent the rest of the morning in bed, exploring each other's bodies some more. Eunice couldn't believe she had any more to give, but every time Joan touched her, it was like she filled right back up with yearning all over again. She understood desire now. Eunice wanted to live there, in Joan's bed, and never leave.

She blew out a long breath, then raised Joan's hand in the air, their fingers tangled together. Eunice never dreamed one person could give her so much pleasure. Particularly not a woman. But after hours in bed together, she already knew forever wouldn't be enough.

"I'm not going to be able to take my eyes off you at work tomorrow."

Joan turned her head. "I'm glad to hear it. If this is one-sided, I'll be very upset."

Eunice laughed, then brought Joan's fingers to her mouth and kissed them. "I'm going to be watching your fingers too, now they're so precious to me. Making sure no needles attack them. They're going to be needed for so much more."

Joan growled, then rolled on top of her. "Don't get me started. You have to go home at some point today. I'm going to be sad enough as it is." She kissed Eunice's lips.

"I've got a family dinner to sit through. Sunday roast with my dad a bit tipsy from the pub. My brothers arguing." Eunice sighed. Real life was too much to contemplate. "At least you get peace and quiet."

Joan shook her head, then rolled onto her back. "At least you have something to take your mind off things. All I have is my own thoughts."

"Didn't you say you had your next screenplay to write? The one starring me? I've given you some fresh material, haven't I?"

"You certainly have. I feel like I have something to say today. Something hopeful." She kissed Eunice's cheek. "We're not virgins anymore."

Eunice turned to her. "Does it count with a woman?"

Joan narrowed her eyes, her stare dark. "It does for me."

Eunice stared right back. "It does for me, too," she whispered. "Have you kissed a woman before?"

Joan stalled. "One. Briefly. But never like I kissed you." She paused. "How about you?"

A shake of the head. "You're the first." Eunice paused. "You think we could get out of marrying a man altogether? Build a life just me and you?" Just saying the words made her heart soar.

Joan grinned, then propped herself up on her elbow again. "Of course we could! Times are changing. Women's rights are coming more to the fore. We're not just men's property and we're not just baby-making machines." She raised a hand in the air. "We'll move to Paris together, and you can become a famous fashion designer. I can learn French and become a playwright. We can become a famous celebrity couple and everyone will want to be us. It'll be like Calamity Jane, if she'd got together with Katie like she should have all along."

Eunice frowned. "Who's Calamity Jane?"

Joan made a face. "You have so many films to catch up on." She kissed her lips. She tasted of cigarettes and lust. Eunice wanted to lick her lips dry. "All you need to know is that I'm Calamity, you're Katie, and Wild Bill Hickok and Danny Gilmartin can make do with each other."

Eunice smiled. "Okay, Calamity. Let's move to Paris and be together."

Joan touched Eunice's cheek. "It's not impossible. If we want it, we can have it. It's what my mum always used to say. You've got to play the hand you're dealt." She stared into Eunice's eyes and held her in place. "Last night we were dealt a hand of cards. This morning we were dealt another. There will come a time when we have to decide to stick or twist."

But now was not that time. Now was a time for Eunice to press her lips to Joan's, and lose herself totally.

However, all the while, there was a kernel of excitement growing inside her. Maybe they *could* work out, just the two of them. It was exactly what she needed to hear after the last 24 hours. Maybe they could work in Paris. Maybe dreams could come true.

Eunice never wanted this to end.

She'd never felt happier in her entire life.

* * *

Eunice bolted up the stone steps to her flat, her eyes bright, her spirit up. She hadn't even known it was possible to feel like this. Like she truly belonged in the world. The whole of the walk over London Bridge, which she forever knew would hold this memory, as well as the entirety of the tube ride home, she'd wondered if people could see the change in her. How her muscles ached in all the right ways. How she was now finally a woman. But nobody seemed to notice.

It didn't matter.

Eunice knew. The new her was visible in every step she took.

However, as she pushed open the front door, and the smell of Sunday roast hit her nose, her bravado faltered. *This* was her normal world. Did she fit in here anymore? What if her mum could see right through her? What if she knew what had gone on? Her mum had an uncanny knack of doing so. She always wheedled out what Eunice was thinking.

But this was one time Eunice had to hold tight. She couldn't tell her mum. Not only would she be shocked, but she wouldn't understand. *Nobody* would understand. But that was fine with Eunice. Because it wasn't for anybody else to understand. It was for Joan and her alone. They could have a future. But Eunice had to take it one step at a time.

Her mum was at the stove stirring a metal pot, probably filled with cabbage. Her two sisters were setting the table. They smiled up at her as she walked in.

"Hello love," her mum said. She walked over and kissed Eunice's cheek.

Being touched by someone other than Joan felt alien. Eunice stiffened in her embrace. Could she smell the change in her?

Mum let her go. "Everything okay?"

Eunice nodded, even though it was a lie. Outside, everything had felt like an opportunity. Like the world was suddenly hers for the taking. Whereas in this flat, where Eunice was known as the eldest daughter, the next to be married, it felt like the death of her dreams. Within these four walls, there was no room for manoeuvre. Her life was already mapped out.

"Fine." Eunice pressed down her nerves. "I'm just tired."

Her mum nudged her. "Were you up all night? I know what it's like when you girls get together."

Blood rushed to Eunice's cheeks as she nodded. "We were." She wasn't lying.

"Get washed up. Dinner's in half an hour." Her mum grabbed her arm. "Also, there's a letter for you on your bed. From Kenneth. He seems keen." Her mum's smile was so big, it nearly fell off her face. "Keep hold of that one. He's from a rich family. He could be your ticket out of here and to a better life."

Eunice gave her mum a stiff grin, then went to her room. She already had a better life waiting for her with Joan. Right now, she chose that.

Chapter Nineteen

Joan had been accused of strutting before. Her mum had encouraged it. She'd said if men could strut, why couldn't women? They'd practised it walking home from her mum's shows. As Joan walked across the Thames today in the murky October morning, not even the fog and the chill in the air could dent her mood. Joan was 100 per cent strut. She glanced up at the grey sky and thought of her mum. Joan's heart still ached, but at least it was familiar now.

She had no idea what her mum would say about the past few weekends with Eunice. Of how Joan's life was panning out. She'd thought about blurting it all out to her dentist this morning, but he'd had his hands in her mouth, so she didn't get the chance.

A shiver ran through her as she dodged through the crowds at the end of Waterloo Bridge, then across the Strand and up the cobbled streets of Covent Garden. On her left, the six Roman columns outside the Lyceum Ballroom were festooned with balloons, and banners were up and ready for the staging of tomorrow's Miss World competition. Joan rolled her eyes. Women in swimsuits parading around for the benefit of men didn't exactly correlate with her feminist ideals for the modern world. She hoped Miss World would run its course soon enough, and women could be appreciated for their brains as well as their beauty. She appreciated women for both.

Okay, one woman in particular.

At 8am, the city was just coming to life. Across the street, a man pulled out a striped restaurant awning. She walked the slight incline, then turned left into Covent Garden. In among the cobbles and the striking stone architecture, flowers stalls covered the square, with sellers shouting to grab your attention.

"Get your freesias, your roses, your lilies here!" The man's hands were covered in dirt, but it was all in a day's work for him — just like getting covered in lint was for Joan. She walked past the cafes and restaurants, taking delivery of bottles of Sunfresh orange juice and Robinsons squash. Across the road from Covent Garden tube station, The White Lion pub rolled barrels of Bass Mild and Whitbread Bitter to their cellar door. Up ahead, the Lyons' Tea Shop was in full swing, serving tea, coffee and breakfast to hungry tourists and commuters.

Joan zipped through Soho, breathing in the smell of bacon frying from a handful of greasy spoons. She trod the familiar pavements of Old Compton Street with its piss-stained alleys, past a lone prostitute still working, and then up Wardour Street.

Today was Friday. Which meant tomorrow was going to be the fourth Saturday in a row Eunice had stayed at hers. They'd get to spend another 24 glorious hours in bed. She now knew the contours of Eunice's skin. How she wriggled when Joan nibbled the side of her neck. How she loved her breasts to be touched and caressed. Joan wanted to spend months getting to know the ebb and flow of Eunice's body.

She'd had three weekends in a row, yet it felt like she'd only just scratched the surface. She already knew she'd never get bored of Eunice.

She was on the corner of Heddon Street when she heard her name. When Joan turned, Kitty pulled up alongside her, holding out her arms, a wide grin on her face.

"What do you think? Do you like my hair? Clive's sister's a trainee hairdresser and she practised on me last night. I got this done for free!"

Joan nodded. Kitty would marry Clive for less. "Looks fabulous."

They pushed through the main factory door and climbed the stone steps to the third floor, crashing through the door to be greeted by the normal Friday morning chatter. Joan's heart fizzed as she walked up the rows of machines, stopping at hers. Eunice was already there. She looked up as Joan approached. Something passed over her face that Joan couldn't quite place. She ignored it, even though her heart lurched.

"Morning." Joan wanted to reach over and run a hand down Eunice's shiny hair, but she refrained. Words formed on her tongue, but she couldn't say any of them. It wasn't just the two of them anymore. They were in public. They had to behave as if they were just good friends.

"Morning." Eunice put her eyes down.

"Morning, Eunice, ready to crack the dress record today?" Kitty was the current holder for the most dresses sewn in one day, but Eunice had levelled it last week. There was no formal championship, but it was a highly prized fake trophy in the factory. Kitty gave Eunice her best glower.

Eunice flexed her fingers. "Ready and waiting."

"Loser buys the pies at lunchtime. What do you say?"

"Prepare to buy me lunch."

"Fighting talk. Let's go!"

* * *

"You look pretty today."

The crimson that stained Eunice's cheeks was the finest Joan had ever seen. She reached under the table and took Eunice's fingers in hers. Just the stroke of them around her own made her heart swell. Keeping her feelings at bay throughout work was easy when she had something to do with her hands, when her focus was elsewhere. But here in the pie shop, thighs pressed together, it was so much harder.

She glanced up to the counter where Kitty was flirting with one of the men behind the counter. It was effortless, and nobody batted an eyelid, because it was normal. Expected.

Joan hadn't expected Eunice. "Before they get back, is everything okay for the weekend? You're still coming tomorrow?"

Eunice furrowed her brow and shook her head. "My mum's not keen on me staying away again. She's suspicious there's a boy involved. She keeps going on about Kenneth, saying how he's a good bet. Plus, she wants me around for Sunday morning and to help with the kids as we've got company coming for lunch." She dropped her head. "I might be able to get out in the evening, though. We could go to the dance. I know it's not private, but at least we'd see each other."

Joan's bravado dropped. "Did he send another letter?" Kenneth had talked about coming to see Eunice soon. Every time Joan pictured it, it made her stomach curdle.

Eunice nodded. "The third in a couple of weeks." She ran a fingertip across Joan's knuckles.

Something deep inside her stirred. Just the slightest touch from Eunice was enough.

"Don't worry, I'll put him off. But tomorrow, I can't come over."

When Joan looked into Eunice's eyes, she saw disappointment reflected back at her. She gulped and went to say something, but the words stuck in her throat.

The clatter of plates made both Joan and Eunice jump. Out of sight, they untangled their fingers. Joan painted on a smile as she greeted her friends.

"What are you two looking so secretive about?" Kitty sat in the booth opposite, one eyebrow raised.

Joan curled her toes in her shoes. "Nothing." Her nerves jangled so much, she was sure she rattled.

Kitty looked from one to the other. "You sure? Is it about a boy? I came into the loo the other day and you had your heads together then, too. Is it the fellas from the dance?"

Eunice wriggled next to her. "It's not about fellas. We were just saying about the dance. There's another one on tomorrow at the club. Are you going?"

Both Kitty and Mari nodded, forking beef and onion pie into their mouths. "Course. Clive and Douglas are picking us up from mine." Mari paused. "Are you coming again?"

Eunice glanced Joan's way. "I was thinking I might. If Joan's up for it. My mum would be happy with me doing that."

Joan didn't need asking twice. If that was the way she could see Eunice, she was all for it. She nodded. "Count me in."

Mari's mouth hung open. "That settles it. It must be about a boy. Joan never agrees to come to a dance so easily."

Joan sighed. "People change, Mari."

"When there's a boy on the horizon, they do."

* * *

Joan had to clear her throat three times before Eunice looked up. She shifted her gaze to the door out to the back stairwell, then got up and headed that way. It was a path they'd trodden a few times over the past week, and it still made her palms clammy with anticipation. She pushed open the door, walked casually into the furthest cubicle and pulled the door closed. Seconds later, the main toilet door opened, followed by footsteps, then a light tap on her cubicle.

Joan moved aside and Eunice appeared.

She slid the lock closed.

Eunice's hands slid up Joan's cheeks almost before Joan could process what was happening. Then her mouth bruised Joan's in a hurry, pulling Joan's head downwards, claiming her as her own.

Joan pulled Eunice close, her arms encircling her waist, the buttons of their overalls clicking as they bumped together.

Eunice's tongue ran across the front of Joan's teeth, then her hand travelled to Joan's right breast and squeezed.

Joan groaned into her mouth, then pressed herself against Eunice. When they pulled away, they both gasped for breath. Joan dug her fingers into Eunice's slim waist and moved her head back, so it rested on the cubicle wall.

"I've been wanting to do that since you told Kitty you were going for the record today."

Eunice smiled. "I always want to kiss you. It's a shame we have to work, but at least I get to look at you all day."

"You can't be looking at me, otherwise you wouldn't be breaking dressmaking records."

"I want to impress you with my skills in between times."

Joan raised an eyebrow. "I don't think it's possible for you to impress me any more than you already do." She undid the two top buttons of Eunice's overall, pushed the material aside, then did the same with the top underneath. Joan lowered her head and placed hot kisses down Eunice's neck, across her collarbone and pressed her nose into the soft skin at the top of Eunice's left breast.

Eunice moaned, then covered her mouth with her hand.

The door to the toilet opened, and two pairs of footsteps clacked on the stone floor, then two locks shut.

Joan clung to Eunice and held her breath as the two new toilet-dwellers went about their business. Her heart thumped in her chest as they grinned at each other. She knew they were taking a chance. If they were caught, they'd both be fired. But right now, with the imprint of Eunice's lips on hers, Joan would happily accept her fate. She and Eunice were far more important. After the past few intoxicating weeks, she'd risk it all.

She reached across and pushed the toilet flush, kissed Eunice's lips silently once more, then walked out. Eunice locked the door behind her as agreed. Joan washed her hands, greeting a couple of co-workers from the floor. She waited until they left, cleared her throat twice, then Eunice emerged. She grinned as they stood together at the basin, adrenaline pumping through her veins.

Eunice turned the tap off and dried her hands. Then she lunged at Joan and pressed her lips to hers once more. "I never knew I could want someone as much as I want you."

The door swung open and Mari walked in.

Joan's heart almost vaulted out of her chest.

Eunice went a peculiar shade of white.

Mari gave them a broad smile, then wagged a finger in their direction. "Don't think I'm not on to you. You're acting very strangely. I'm going to find out what's going on. Mark my words."

Chapter Twenty

Eunice hated the dance like she never had before. Being so close to Joan but not being able to kiss her was worse than she could possibly have imagined. Conversely, Kitty and Mari had twirled around the room with Clive and Douglas, having the time of their life. For them, dancing was where they came alive. Whereas Eunice and Joan had to bottle up everything they felt and act like they were having a good time. They danced with a couple of fellas, then made their excuses and left early.

They didn't talk much as they got off the bus, the sharp wind of the October night cutting Eunice's skin. She wanted to take Joan's hand, but she couldn't. Her body ached to touch her. Her mum always told her that life as a woman was tough. However, once she'd met the right person, Eunice had assumed it would get easier. She had no idea how wrong she'd been.

Was she in love with Joan? All she knew was she thought about her night and day. She couldn't wait to be in her arms. She looked forward to work and breathing the same air as her daily. She didn't want to think of a world without her. Eunice couldn't imagine feeling this way about a boy. Feeling his hard body against hers. The thought made her queasy. Joan's body was firm and soft all at the same time. It fitted Eunice's perfectly. And when they were together, naked, the rest of the world dissolved into nothing. Everything became fluid and soft. Eunice never wanted to escape.

In public, as tonight had proved, it was a totally different story.

They turned into the courtyard of Eunice's flats and climbed the stairs. They still hadn't spoken. The disappointment of the dance was still upon them, so many things left unspoken. Eunice's body was wound tight with tension. She imagined Joan was the same. They were both liable to explode at any minute.

Joan stopped at Eunice's floor and glanced her way.

Eunice shook her head, took Joan's hand and dragged her up to the fourth floor. To the top balcony, the place where she and David had put right much of the world's ills. When they got there, Joan produced her cigarettes and offered Eunice one. She shook her head and waited for the end of Joan's cigarette to light orange against the dark of the night. She could watch Joan inhale all night long. The way she smoked was so much better than the way anyone else did.

That went for most things when it came to Joan.

She was exquisite.

"I shouldn't have come."

Eunice shook her head. "Don't be silly." She took Joan's fingers in hers.

Joan stared at their hands, then pulled hers away. "I hate having to hide away with you."

"We don't have any other choice."

"I know." Joan sighed. "I just want the world to wake up. I want to shake things up."

"Like Calamity Jane?"

Joan gave a wry smile. "Just like her. But with less horses."
She sighed. "I hate seeing all those boys able to ask a girl to
dance and it's just accepted. It makes me…" She paused, then
held her clenched fist up to the sky. "It makes me want to punch
someone. Or something." She tipped her head and exhaled a
line of smoke. "Why can't we dance together like them?"

"It's just the way it is." Eunice wished with all her heart it
wasn't, but it was. "We can be together again soon, properly."
But she knew her words were hollow.

Joan turned to her. "Come back to mine now."

Eunice's spirit sagged. "You know I can't." She desperately
wanted to. "My mum needs me here because my aunt, uncle
and cousins are coming for lunch and she needs the help."

Joan took a silent drag on her cigarette. "And then Kenneth
arrives and who knows when I'll get to see you again?"

"You see me every day at work."

"That's not the same."

Eunice stepped closer to Joan and snaked a hand around
her waist. "You're what I want." Joan's body stiffened beneath
her fingers.

"Am I?" Joan eyed Eunice, her face creased with doubt.
"Or is this just an interlude in your life, until you sail off into
the sunset with some bloke?"

Eunice pulled her closer. "That's simply not true. It's you I
want to be with." She hated the look of hopelessness in Joan's
eyes. This weekend was meant to be for them, to spend some
time together. Even if it wasn't at Joan's, just being in her
presence lifted Eunice's mood. Everything that came out of
Joan's mouth was gold. Joan's mouth on hers was even better.

Eunice loved the way Joan walked. The way she looked at Eunice, like she really was the most beautiful girl in the world.

It wasn't how Joan looked at her now.

"Kenneth is an easy option to stop Mum going on about boys. If I actually had a boyfriend, I wouldn't be able to spend nearly so much time with you. I thought that would be something you could get behind."

A hint of a smile tugged at Joan's lips and she blew out a long raspberry. "You know it is." She stared at Eunice. "I just hate the way it is for us."

"I know." Getting to know Joan, her opinions and her life had been a crash course in feminism. Eunice thought she was opinionated, but Joan had unlocked a whole other realm. Now, Eunice wanted so much more, too, and she wanted it all with Joan by her side. She would do everything she could to make it possible. She didn't want to think about the alternative.

Right now, she just wanted to make Joan smile, to take away all the doubts etched onto her pristine face, her tempting lips. There was one sure-fire way she could do that.

She reached up a hand and stroked a finger down Joan's cheek. "You know, whenever I'm not with you, I think about you all the time. I wake up dreaming about you. Sometimes I wake up in my own bed and can almost feel your fingers inside me."

Joan groaned, moved her head and kissed Eunice's fingers. "Then come home with me." Joan's gaze dropped to Eunice's lips. In the blink of an eye, Joan's arms were around her, and all reason and rationale crashed to the floor as Joan pressed her lips to hers.

Eunice came alive as Joan's lips slipped across her, telegraphing her longing. Joan's lips spoke to her in ways no words ever could. They ushered her into a world where she was the only other guest, a VIP. Eunice could get used to the VIP treatment.

They came up for air to undo their coats. Joan's fingers fumbled as she bent to release Eunice's buttons. Then Joan's hands roamed over the top of her dress, before skating down to her breasts. Joan's hungry lips moved to her neck, as her fingers squeezed Eunice's nipples.

They were no longer on a draughty stairwell in the White City. Now, as Eunice clung to Joan, she could have been anywhere. On a sunny balcony in Paris. On a moonlit train in Milan. Her mind was awash with possibilities when Joan's lips were on hers, her fingers playing Eunice's tune.

When they broke apart, Eunice wanted more. Once the line had been crossed, they could never look back. Kissing Joan was one thing. Feeling Joan inside her was a whole different level. She took Joan's hand and placed it between her legs, then pressed down. She held Joan's gaze the whole time.

"We can't do this here," Joan growled.

"I want to." Eunice almost didn't recognise her own voice, it was so low, so *someone else*. Someone who knew exactly what she wanted and wasn't afraid to ask. Yes, this was risky, but Eunice didn't care. Nothing but Joan would do. "I want you." Her words left marks in the air around them. "If we can't go back to yours, we have to make do." She stared into Joan's eyes. "I want you to touch me."

Joan took a deep breath in. Then, without taking her eyes from Eunice's face, she slipped her hand under her dress, inside her underwear, and gasped when she hit Eunice's slick centre.

"You're so wet," Joan whispered.

Eunice spread her legs, then reached down and pushed Joan into her. She closed her eyes as Joan crushed her lips to hers once more. Eunice clung to her, and let out a guttural moan. Then, as Joan moved into her, she took Eunice somewhere she'd never been before. Every time she was with Joan, it happened. Eunice never wanted it to stop. She moved her hips in time with Joan's fingers, and within minutes, she came, stifling her cries as she knew she must.

She wanted to shout it from the rooftops that she loved Joan Hart. Should she tell her?

"You're so amazing." Eunice was breathless as Joan withdrew. She missed her immediately. She shimmied her dress down.

Joan quirked her lips and pressed them to Eunice once more. "You're not so bad yourself."

She could stand like this all night long. All she wanted was Joan to be close. "Joan, I—"

"Eunice?"

A male voice intruded on their very personal moment.

Eunice almost stumbled as she fell backwards, a cool wind now whipping up where Joan's hands and lips had been. Her cheeks flared red as her eyes took in the situation. Saw whose voice had uttered her name.

David.

Bloody hell. The euphoria that had been coursing through her now froze. The blood in her veins turned to ice.

David frowned. "What the hell?" His eyebrows knitted

together. "You and Joan?" He took the Woodbine he was smoking from his lips. His arm hung loosely by his side.

Eunice took a step towards him. Outside, the ground was steady. Inside, tectonic plates began to shift, as a tsunami of fear bowled through her. "It's not what it looks like."

Behind her, Joan gasped.

Eunice turned. Shit. She hadn't meant to say that. Because this was exactly what it looked like. But what else was she meant to say? She couldn't tell David anything else. He was her friend, but she knew how this worked. Word got around. Eunice wasn't ready for that.

When she turned around, Joan's face lurched from crumpled to devastated.

Her eyes narrowed. "I have to go. I'll see you at work on Monday." Joan's cold stare felt like a punch.

Eunice jolted. "Don't go!" How had this unravelled so quickly? What could she say to save it? Five minutes ago, Joan had been inside her. Now, she was headed towards the top of the stone steps. Eunice inhaled Joan's scent as she swept by her, then disappeared.

She and David listened to Joan's footsteps descending the stairs, then focused on them running across the courtyard and out of earshot.

Finally, Eunice collapsed onto the top step, head in hands. She counted to ten, then blew out a long breath. It was only then she risked a glance at David. "Don't look at me like that."

David said nothing, just sat down next to her.

Eunice reached out a hand, took the cigarette from David's mouth, inhaled, then handed it back. This time, she didn't even choke. Perhaps this was what it meant to be an adult. Learning how to smoke. Learning how to break a heart.

Eunice wasn't sure she wanted either.

"What the hell, Eunice?"

Eunice shivered, then pulled her coat around her. "You can't say anything." She glanced at him. "Promise me you won't say anything."

In all the times she'd been with Joan, Eunice hadn't had to confront the reality of them together in public. To contemplate what it might feel like to be seen as a couple. But she'd seen the reality in David's eyes. The shock and disbelief. The horror. Is that what being with Joan every day would be like? Eunice had ridden around on a wave of optimism for the past few weeks, thinking it could work.

Now, she saw that was folly.

Men and women worked. Women and women did not. Not in the real world.

She dropped her head. How could what she and Joan had be wrong?

"I won't. I'm your friend, Eunice. Of course I won't." David drew in a deep breath. "But it was what it looked like, right? You were kissing her?"

Eunice's stomach flexed. She glanced at David. Then she nodded.

He held her with his stare. "And it wasn't the first time?"

She pressed her tongue into the roof of her mouth, then shook her head.

David let out a low whistle. "Wow."

Eunice shivered. David was her friend, and he was shocked. What if someone else had walked up those stairs tonight?

Her mum? Her brother? Mrs Higgins? She shook her head. Was she going out of her mind? It sort of felt like it.

"When you've been staying at her house over the past few weekends, you've been staying... together?" He said the last word more quietly, as if scared of her answer.

Eunice glanced down at her feet. She'd never imagined being asked this question. Never imagined how it might feel to answer it. She thought she'd be punching the air. That she'd be smiling, full of joy as she answered. Just like she was when she was with Joan.

But outside Joan's flat, outside the safety of those four walls, reality made her doubt everything. Even with David. But she couldn't lie to him. Having just witnessed Joan's tongue in Eunice's mouth, he already knew the answer.

Eunice nodded again. She couldn't quite get the words out of her mouth. But her silence gave him the answer.

David let out another low whistle.

Empty space stretched before them. She could almost hear David's brain recalibrating their relationship. Everything he knew about her. She wanted to shake him and tell him she was still the same person. But no words emerged.

"Is this a recent thing?"

Another nod.

"I take it nobody else knows?"

"God, no." Finally, some words.

"And is it..." He paused, floundering for words. "Serious?" He turned to her. "I mean, is this for now, or is this something you might continue?"

Eunice flashed forward through her life with Joan. The one she'd imagined for weeks. Them in Paris. With a flat in

London. Strolling along the Thames on a hot summer's day. But now David was looking at it with the facts as he saw them, those images dissolved into nothing. He was asking her about a relationship that meant everything to her. And yet he was talking about it in terms of it being disposable. He had control over his destiny. She did not. What it must be like to be a man, and to know you had the final say.

"I don't know. Maybe. But it's not so easy. I just... I really like her." Words weren't enough. They never would be. She saw that more clearly than ever. "She makes me happy." *She's the reason I want to live. She's the moon, the sun, and everything in between.* But she couldn't say that.

David ground out his Woodbine under his foot. "You know nobody will understand. Your mum and dad will go spare. You'll lose your job. You have to be careful. You can't kiss on stairwells. What if it hadn't been me?"

Eunice hung her head, her heart heavy. "I know." She paused. "It's just that, kissing her makes sense of everything."

David put a hand on her knee. "You can't say that to anyone else." He gulped, then looked her in the eye. "I'm on your side, always. But this is not an easy thing to do. Think about it carefully, okay? But you have my word. I won't tell a soul."

Chapter Twenty-One

"There's my gorgeous honorary daughter!" Uncle Derek squeezed her tight like always. Even though Joan was 5ft 9, she still fell short of Derek's 6ft-plus stature. It was something Derek never let his third son Thomas ever forget, as he'd stopped growing and was shorter than Joan. Derek always blamed Aunt Maggie's gene pool for that. Joan got her height from her mum.

"How are you, Joanie? Any news on the romance front? Any lucky boys trying to win your hand?"

Joan winced, but tried to keep it from taking up her whole face. Why were families obsessed with this question? "Lots have tried, Uncle, but there's nobody special yet."

"You and your brother are both waiting for the right one. Good for you. Get out there and experience life before you settle down and have children, right?"

"Or just don't get married and lead a charmed life."

Uncle Derek stroked his stubbled chin, then pointed a finger her way. "Maybe you're onto something there. You'd certainly have more money."

Her cousin Stanley came into the kitchen and gave Joan a shy wave.

"I have to keep working so this one can keep eating food."

Derek gave his son a light punch on the arm. "Isn't that right, Stanley?"

Stanley rolled his eyes. "You should come into the parlour." His face lit up. "Dad won a television in a raffle. We can watch it anytime!"

It was quite the coup. Nobody else Joan knew had their own TV. "I'll come in after."

Derek and Stanley left the kitchen.

"Between you and me, there's not much on it, but the boys never turn it off." Maggie rolled her eyes, then swept her hair behind her ears. "Anyway, what brings you here on a Wednesday night? Not that it's not lovely to see you, but it's a little out of the ordinary. You've normally got your head in a book." Her aunt motioned her to sit down, then shut the kitchen door. "If they see that, they'll know that emotions are being processed and it might stop them crashing in." Maggie gave her a grin. "What's making that gorgeous face of yours so gaunt?" She sat opposite Joan at the table, then glanced at her stomach. "You're not pregnant, are you?"

Joan clutched it, looking down. "Not last time I checked, no." She paused. "Do I look pregnant?"

"No. It's just, you're giving off a weird vibe and I'm still responsible for you, even though you're 18." Maggie breathed out. "Okay, no pregnancy is good. So why the long face?"

How to put it? Joan still wasn't sure she was ready to tell her aunt fully. She was sure Maggie would love her, no matter what. But could she be 100 per cent sure? No. But she had to talk to someone. Jimmy would have been her first port of call, but he was away for the foreseeable future. So the field was narrowed down to her aunt. Her pillar of support since day one. Two weeks after her mum died, a button had popped on Joan's favourite blouse. Her aunt had found Joan slumped on the kitchen floor sobbing, a needle and thread in hand, and no idea what to do with it. "Mum would have normally done it." Maggie had picked Joan up and sewn the button back on. Then she'd taught her how to do it herself. She was always on hand for any life emergency. Joan had to take a chance.

"I've got involved with someone and I'm not sure what to do." Right. She'd practised what she might say the whole way along the corridor to her aunt's flat. It hadn't been that.

"But you're not pregnant."

"I already told you I'm not."

"So, what's the problem? You shouldn't be involved with this boy? He already has a girlfriend?" Maggie's face fell. "Tell me he's not married."

Joan spluttered. "He's not married." She paused. This week had been no fun at all. She desperately needed to speak to someone. She'd had to go to work. Being so close to Eunice had been a mix of heaven and hell. They'd shared some bathroom kisses, but something had changed. They'd been caught. Their affair was out there now, not just between the two of them. Somehow, their secret being discovered had put an indelible stain on their relationship.

"So what's the problem?"

Stanley walked into the kitchen again, took one look at his mother's face and disappeared sharpish.

Joan took a deep breath. "He's not a man." The words came out low, but it felt like Joan had announced them via megaphone.

Maggie's face got more serious. She stared at Joan. "Not a man?"

Joan shook her head.

Maggie exhaled. "Right." She got up and got two crystal sherry glasses from the cabinet under the wireless. Then she produced a bottle of Harvey's Bristol Cream, poured two glasses and sat down again. Maggie took a large slug from hers before she eyed Joan again. "Not a man. A woman." She paused. "Is it Eunice?"

Joan's eyes widened and her stomach lurched. "How did you know?"

Maggie smiled. "Because you reacted very strangely to Kenneth and her at the CND rally. I couldn't quite work out why. Plus, I've seen her around here at weekends."

Joan's cheeks hissed red.

"I've got eyes," Maggie continued. "But now perhaps I see a bit more clearly. You're not involved with a married man or a taken man. But you are involved with a taken woman."

Joan gulped. "She's not taken." Her aunt was wrong. "They've only had a couple of dates. He doesn't even live in London."

Maggie crossed her right leg over her left and sighed. "Dearest Joan." Her face radiated compassion. "My precious niece. I only want the best for you. I want you to be happy. But trust me when I say, Kenneth certainly thinks he's in a relationship with Eunice. Even if she doesn't agree."

Joan met her aunt's gaze. She wasn't going to let the truth win out. "But Eunice is in a relationship with me."

Maggie didn't flinch. "Has something happened?"

Joan chewed the side of her cheek, then nodded.

Maggie's chest rose up, then down. "Has she been staying at yours when Jimmy's not there?"

Why was this all so hard? Joan dropped Maggie's gaze. She and Eunice had something special. She wasn't taking Joan for a ride, was she?

"I'll take that as a yes." Maggie reached out and put a hand over Joan's. Her hand was freezing, but Joan didn't flinch. It reminded her of her mum. She'd always had cold hands, too. She said they were great for making pastry because the butter didn't melt. It'd always made Joan laugh, as her mum hadn't been a baker. "But if I chose to be," she'd always said.

"I'm not going to lecture you on whether or not she should be staying. You're old enough to know your own mind. I know that's what your mother would say. But she'd also say the path you've chosen — if this is truly what you want — is not an easy one. People won't understand. You'll lose friends. Jobs. Face." She paused. "This isn't a phase?"

Joan shook her head. "It's not. I've known I was different for a while. Mum knew, too."

Maggie nodded. "I know. She spoke to me about it before she died. But nothing's happened since, so I wondered if she was right. Turns out, she knew her daughter."

"What did she say to you?"

"That you were headstrong. That you knew what you wanted. And that your path to love might not be as smooth as she'd have wanted."

Joan's heart soared. Those were all things her mum would say. "But she would have understood."

"Of course she would. She worked in theatre and cabaret.

She knew queer people. She knew their lives. But she also knew it would be a hard road."

"It doesn't have to be like that." Joan put her hand over her heart. "What I'm feeling for Eunice is real. It's not fake."

"I'm not saying it is."

"The world's changing every day," Joan added. She took a sip of her sherry, then winced. Its acrid taste stayed in her throat. "Women don't have to belong to men anymore. We can have jobs, and we don't have to always get married, have children, do what they say. I could live by myself, live with my chosen partner." She paused. "I don't want to be with a man, ever."

Maggie poured more sherry. "You're sure?"

"Absolutely positive." She couldn't imagine anything worse. Especially after the last few weeks with Eunice.

"But you're so young. What if things change? What if you like Eunice that way now, but not forever?"

Joan sucked in the deepest breath of her life. Deeper than the one she'd taken on that fateful day three years ago, holding her mum's hand as she took her last.

"You don't get it." She shook her head. "If I was saying this about a boy, you wouldn't be trying to talk me out of it for the same reason. I feel it here." Joan thumped her chest with her fist. Maggie simply *had* to understand.

Her aunt nodded. "I'm your stand-in mum, Joan. It's an honour, but I have a duty to ask these questions. If you tell me this is it, of course I'll support you. I'll always support you."

That was enough to make the swirl of emotions Joan had pressed down surge to the surface. Tears swelled from her eyes and rolled down her face. She hadn't known she was fearful of her aunt's rejection until now.

Chair legs scraped along the ground and then strong arms surrounded her, holding her close. "I'll always be here for you, Joanie."

Joanie. It'd been her dad's nickname for her. Her mum's too. Now her aunt's. It always made her feel loved.

After a few moments and some nose blowing, Joan recovered. She took a sip of her sherry and gave her aunt a weak smile. Maggie couldn't fix this problem with a needle and thread. "This is me. It's who I am."

Maggie smiled. "Then I'm all for it." She paused. "But what I can't predict is what's going to happen with Eunice. Kenneth is still in the picture, whether you like it or not."

"But we've talked about a future together. She wants it, too."

Maggie stared at her. "Does she want it as much as you?"

Joan dropped her head. It was the question that had kept her awake at night. The one she longed for clarity on. The one she simply dare not ask.

Before the weekend, or whenever Eunice was in Joan's bed, she'd say it was definite. But after she saw how Eunice reacted when David discovered them kissing? Joan wasn't so sure.

Her bottom lip wobbled. "I don't know," she replied.

That was the biggest kicker of all.

Chapter Twenty-Two

"How's your week been? What have you been making?" Kenneth's breath misted in front of him as he asked. Eunice pulled her new winter scarf tighter around her neck and shivered as they approached the river from the South Bank. The Royal Festival Hall stood proud to her right, its lights dancing on the surface of the Thames.

"The usual. Dresses. Nothing out of the ordinary." That part was true. What was out of the ordinary was her relationship with Joan. The past weeks since they'd been caught had been torture. Now, they stole kisses with each other at work, but Eunice hadn't stayed at Joan's again. She daren't. However, she'd gone round a few Saturdays and evenings when Jimmy was at work, and they'd spent glorious, almost endless hours in bed, memorising every part of each other's body. It was never enough. She'd replayed them all in her mind many times since.

But this Saturday, Eunice was with Kenneth.

She shook her head. She wasn't going to dwell. She shivered again.

"Are you cold?" Kenneth pointed towards the 141 at the bus stop in front of them. He grabbed her hand and pulled her towards the open lower deck of the Routemaster. "Walking across the bridge will only make you colder."

They jumped on board, then headed upstairs, settling into a middle seat.

"I took your advice, you know."

Eunice glanced Kenneth's way as she smoothed out the back of her coat. He'd had his hair cut, and it made him look like he'd just got out of the army all over again. He was also wearing what looked like a new suit. She hadn't seen the royal-blue tie before, either.

"My advice?"

"To be good to my workers. Make them feel valued. Give them treats. I've started a Friday singalong with the wireless, and installed a regular biscuit plate to go with the 10.30 tea round."

A flutter of satisfaction danced through Eunice. She'd told him, and he'd listened. "That's how to get on the good side of your employees."

"Just listening to the person in the know." He took hold of Eunice's hand and gave her a warm smile. "I value your opinion, Eunice. You're smart as well as beautiful."

Eunice gave him a tight smile as her stomach churned. Joan had told her she was beautiful last weekend, too, when they'd spoken about their future together. She'd also gone very quiet when Eunice had told her she was seeing Kenneth today. Eunice didn't blame her.

As the bus rumbled across the river, Eunice gulped. They were on a date, and Kenneth was her boyfriend. She couldn't drag her hand back without making a scene, even though she wanted to. But her spirit screamed. She hated being disloyal to Joan, and even more so to herself.

It also wasn't lost on Eunice the way other people looked

at the two of them, either. They gave their silent approval with a smile or a nod. In society's eyes, she and Kenneth made sense. Whereas when she and Joan were in public, they had to police themselves. Eunice couldn't imagine walking across Waterloo Bridge with her, hand in hand. That people would perceive them as not just friends, but as lovers. It could never happen. Not in her lifetime.

If Kenneth was an ogre, perhaps it would have been easier to cast him aside. But he wasn't. He was kind, and he clearly cared for her. Building a life with Kenneth would be easy. This was only her third outing, and already they were rubber-stamped.

Eunice wanted to rail at society. Why couldn't the love she and Joan shared be enough?

The grand dolphin lamp posts along the Thames glowed bright in the December low evening fog. Fairy lights were strung from one to the other, and someone had wiped the windows of the bus before them, so they could see out. The air was thick with chill and Saturday night anticipation. They climbed down the bus's back stairs, Kenneth waiting at the bottom and offering a hand, before escorting Eunice down a passageway and into the foyer of The Savoy.

Eunice blinked. Kenneth was making her dreams come true.

It was so bright when they got inside, Eunice almost felt the urge to cover her eyes. A massive Christmas tree reached the ceiling, with all manner of ornaments festooned on its branches. The smell of cinnamon and cloves scented the air, and to her right, a life-size statue of Santa and Rudolph grinned at her.

"Why are we at The Savoy? Isn't it a bit posh?" These were just the sort of hotels she'd walked past before with Joan, but she'd never worked up the nerve to go inside, even though Joan had promised her they would one day. "Before we go to Paris. Me, you, and an afternoon tea that costs an arm and a leg."

Eunice pushed that thought to the back of her mind.

"Only the best for you." Kenneth gave her his warm smile, then spoke to someone in a suit, who escorted them up some stairs to a restaurant. Once there, Kenneth pulled out her chair for her, then took a seat opposite.

She hadn't been wrong. This place was posh. Her skin prickled. She felt at once out of her depth, but also excited that this possibility was open to her. Kenneth was giving her a chance to experience something for the very first time. She couldn't deny she was interested. She ran her fingertips over the starched cotton tablecloths. When she picked up the cutlery, she could see her face in it.

A waiter arrived and Kenneth ordered a pink lemonade for Eunice, and a glass of sherry for himself. "Or would you prefer a sherry?"

Eunice shook her head. She'd tried it with her nan, and it wasn't her favourite. "Lemonade is fine."

Kenneth sat up, straightening his lapels. Did he have any casual clothes? Eunice couldn't imagine him in them. Kenneth suited a shirt and tie. He probably slept in them.

"I brought you here because I wanted to tell you something. I hope I've made it clear in my letters, too." He sat forward. "Meeting you has been the highlight of the past few years. The army and me weren't suited. Thankfully, I seem to be getting the hang of working for my uncle. Factory life is quite interesting. Plus, I'm learning about business, so I see a future." He paused, reached across the table and took Eunice's hand in his. "But I hope I'm not jumping the gun when I say I see a future with you, too, Eunice. I know you're younger than me. But if I don't tell you now, someone else will come along and tell you before me."

He stared at her: his blue eyes sparkled. His voice was clear, but there was a hint of trepidation. He wasn't certain how Eunice might react. Somehow, that endeared him to her more. Most men would just bluster in and expect Eunice to fall in with their plans. It's what her dad did to her mum all the time. Not Kenneth. He was interested in what Eunice wanted, what she thought. She wished with all her heart that she liked him as she liked Joan.

She stared at his hand on hers. It felt all wrong.

"I really like you, Eunice. I want to get to know you better. So I wanted to ask: do you see me in your future, too?"

Eunice's throat went dry. She narrowed her eyes. The room pulsed in her external vision as she blinked.

Life with Kenneth would involve experiences like this.

But life without Joan was unthinkable.

Kenneth looked at her, his face faltering at her silence.

She had to say something. Eunice heard her mum's voice in her head. "He could be your ticket out of here. To a better life."

So she nodded. She couldn't do anything else. She was polite, well mannered. Kenneth had brought her to a posh restaurant. She didn't want to disappoint him.

"Of course." Eunice painted on a smile to match her breezy tone.

Kenneth sat back, hand over his heart, a smile creasing

his face. "You had me worried then!" He laughed. "But you do see me in your future?"

She flashed forward, trying to imagine it. She drew a blank. She nodded anyway. "I do. I mean, we'd need to discuss it."

He nodded vigorously. "Of course. It's not straightforward because you live here and I live in Birmingham. Plus, my job's in Birmingham. But we could work it out, I'm sure. Get you a better job with me, get married, and then a house of our own." He held up a hand. "I know I'm rushing forward here, but I might not see you until the New Year, and after that my uncle is still talking about me going to Scotland for a while. I wanted to make my intentions clear. That I could see myself falling for you, Eunice Humphries. That it might have already happened."

Eunice stared.

Kenneth grinned her way, then offered her a menu. "Let's order some food and celebrate. The most expensive thing on the menu if you like! This is a meal to toast our new future. This year you're in London for Christmas. Next year, we might be together."

She took the menu and stared. The words swam in front of her, a soup of English and French.

Sparks of fear burst in the corner of her vision. She pressed her heels into the floor and hoped she didn't pass out. How she wished it was Joan sat opposite.

Joan would know she was acting. Putting on a show.

Kenneth had no idea.

She'd promised Joan it would all work out, but now she wasn't so sure. How could she navigate the world when it only gave her one option?

Eunice was out of her depth.

* * *

Eunice spent the whole of the next week numb. Nothing was in writing, but it wasn't what her heart said. Seeing Joan all week at work had only made things worse, and she'd avoided being close to her because she knew she'd betrayed her. It had never been her intention. Somehow, she'd fallen into a betrothal of sorts because she'd been wowed by shiny cutlery and fancy menus. Also, because she hadn't wanted to offend Kenneth. He'd kissed her again. Pressed himself against her. Promised he'd be in touch, and that he was thrilled with how this weekend had turned out.

Thursday evening, she walked back up the stone steps, then walked further just so she could be back in the place where she and Joan had kissed. Yes, David had caught them, but it had still been magical while it lasted.

She and Joan had been civil to each other this week. Dancing around the elephant in the room. There was so much bubbling under the surface, and she had no idea how to move forward or how to fix it. She knew why Tommy Steele wanted to sing the blues now. She did, too.

Eunice heard someone wheezing up the stairs. When Mrs Higgins rounded the stairwell, she stopped to catch her breath. Her face glowed with exertion as she looked up to Eunice. "I thought I saw you, I just wanted to let you know that Kenneth's mother called earlier. There's been a change of plan with his job."

Kenneth had a mother. Of course he did. Who Kenneth wanted to be her mother-in-law. Eunice's stomach wobbled. She shut her brain down. She couldn't deal with that at the moment.

She walked down to where Mrs Higgins stood, then took her arm and guided her back to their floor. "What do you mean?"

Mrs Higgins patted Eunice's arm as they arrived at her front door. "Something about going to Edinburgh earlier than planned? He's going to be there for a few months, possibly longer."

Had he said something about that over dinner last weekend? It rang a bell, but Eunice had only been half-listening. "I think he mentioned something when he was here."

Mrs Higgins fished out her keys from her bag, then nodded. "He's sent you a letter." She stared at Eunice. "I hope it doesn't put you off. He's a good boy, Eunice."

She made him sound like a dog. "I know."

"You haven't been over for a while, either," Mrs Higgins added. "My spare room misses you and your designs."

Eunice gave her a tight smile. Her design ambitions had suffered since her love life had blown up. Mrs Higgins flat wasn't her number one destination anymore.

She let herself into her flat and picked up the letter on the hallway table. She took herself to her room and read it. What Mrs Higgins had said was true. Kenneth was going to Edinburgh for a nine-month stint. He was going to learn about new ways of doing business and bring them back to Birmingham. It would mean that he wouldn't be in London as much. But when his time was up, he intended to come to London and ask her to marry him. Would she wait for him? He hoped with all his heart she would say yes.

Eunice lay down on her bed, the letter beside her on her grey blanket. She had nine months to let him down gently.

Nine months longer to save up for Paris. Nine months more to plan her escape.

"Don't mess this up, Eunice. Women don't have the opportunity that men have."

But her mum didn't know her.

She and Joan were going to build a life together forever.

Chapter Twenty-Three

Joan had hated everything about this week. The tension between her and Eunice was so thick, you could insulate your house with it. She'd messed up more dresses than she cared to mention, and her fingers looked like they'd been into battle and lost. On one particular occasion, Eunice had sprung up in response to her pained cry and swearing. She'd stood beside Joan, but then retreated, not knowing what to say. They'd even met in the toilet one day, but simply stared at each other and walked away.

Joan wasn't sure what to do next.

What she did know was she couldn't go another day with things as they were.

So she'd hatched a plan. She'd heard about a place for women like her. *Like them.*

When they were together, things were perfect. When she didn't factor in Eunice's family. Mrs Higgins. Kenneth.

Joan wasn't going to think about them. This was about her and Eunice. Nobody else.

She'd taken the tube to White City, and now she walked along the courtyard of Eunice's flats in the evening gloom. When she reached the bottom of the stone steps, her bravado wobbled. But she *had* to do this. She held her breath as she took the stairs. If she ran into David, she'd say hello and be polite. Like nothing had ever happened.

She knocked on Eunice's front door and held her breath.

Please let Eunice answer.

Please let Eunice answer.

She heard footsteps, and then the door opened. Eunice.

She had on a black pencil skirt and a lemon blouse. Her cleavage winked at Joan. Damn, she was beautiful.

She stared at Joan, then her face softened into a smile. "What are you doing here?"

Eunice's words were whispered, so Joan followed suit. "I came to see if you wanted to come out tonight. To a place in Notting Hill. We could walk there."

"I haven't had my dinner yet."

"We could get some chips on the way." It wasn't fancy, but it was the best she could do.

"Where were you thinking?"

"Just a pub. It's meant to be good."

Eunice held her gaze, then looked down at herself. "Am I okay for going out?"

"You look great. Gorgeous." She dazzled, as always. Heat hit Joan's cheeks. Her hands were clammy. She stared at Eunice with what she hoped were pleading eyes. It worked.

"I can be ready in ten minutes."

Joan grinned. "Don't wear too high heels, though. We're walking all the way to Notting Hill."

True to her word, Eunice appeared ten minutes later. She'd applied lipstick and eye liner, along with her winter coat. Eunice glanced left, then put an arm through Joan's and they hurried down the stairs.

"Why are you being so secretive?"

"Because where we're going is a secret." Joan eyed Eunice and gave her a smile. The one she saved for her.

Eunice smiled right back. "Are you leading me into mischief, Joan Hart?"

"That was the plan."

* * *

They walked along the main road from Eunice's home, past White City station with its art deco styling that was a favourite of Joan's. They zigzagged past the Shepherd's Bush Empire, then across the busy green. The sharp winter air drilled into Joan's exposed neck, chilling the bits her scarf didn't cover. They went left up towards Holland Park. When they hit the main road with its grand sweeping crescent of tall, white stucco-fronted houses, Joan let out a whistle.

"It's a different world here, isn't it?" They walked up the wider tree-lined streets, and Joan marvelled at the grandeur. "How much would it cost to live here?"

Eunice shook her head. "More than we could ever afford."

"Not if you become a famous fashion designer. Think big!"

Eunice gave her a shy smile.

Joan wanted to join in, but nerves spilled from her every pore. With every step, they got closer to their destination. Joan still didn't know if she could step over the entrance. She breathed out, trying to push down her nerves.

She'd heard about this pub from her brother. She'd heard about The Gateways in Chelsea, of course, but that seemed far more out of reach. That was a proper lesbian club with dancing. Joan wasn't that brave yet. She wanted to go somewhere more low-key, more local. But it was still a risk. Homosexuality was still illegal. She balled her hand into a fist. Her ears popped as she walked. The pavements were busy with couples dressed to impress, and they paid no heed to Joan and Eunice. They weren't a couple in their eyes. Just two friends, right?

"Are you going to tell me where we're going? You've been almost running since we hit Holland Park tube, and we're nearly at Notting Hill. If we're walking all the way to Soho, I need to mentally prepare."

Joan shook her head. "It's just past Notting Hill. A pub called The Champion. Not far now, I promise." She tried to give her a full smile, but it was tight. Joan couldn't do anything about that. This might have been the most nervous she'd been in her entire life.

When the dimmed lights of the pub came into view, she ground her teeth together.

It looked like a normal pub, albeit a little rundown. The 'C' of 'Champion' was a little wonky. The paintwork could do with a touch-up. Its windows were frosted, so nobody could see in.

Joan wasn't sure what she'd expected. She'd been into loads of pubs with her mum, of course, but this was still a big step. For a start, women didn't generally go into pubs on their own. Her mum had taught her that. They'd been lucky, because her mum had always been the entertainment, the one with the power. Nobody hassled Liz Hart.

However, tonight was completely new territory.

This was Joan's first pub for people like her, with her first proper girlfriend. Was Eunice her girlfriend? She wasn't going to ask that question now.

She crossed the side road and walked up to the main door with its large brass handle. Joan's heart hammered in her chest, and she took a deep breath. Jimmy had told her the password for entry was 'Dorothy'. It was only then her nerve failed her, she stepped back and carried on walking. When she glanced left, Eunice wore a frown.

"Didn't we just walk all this way to go there?" She inclined her head towards the pub.

Joan stopped. She had to force herself. "Yes." She grabbed Eunice's hand, turned and marched up to the door, pushing it open with her shoulder. Her brain blared as she entered, then her heart tripped and fell in her chest. Smoky air greeted her, along with a roar of laughter from two men sat straight ahead.

Joan glanced left, then right.

A bald man appeared in front of them, wearing a ripped denim jacket and a toothy grin. He bowed his head. "Ladies." He looked them up and down. "Do you know whose party this is?"

Joan's eyes went wide. "Dorothy's?" *Please let it be right.*

The man smiled and waved them in. "Have a good night."

Joan clutched Eunice's hand, then dragged her to a table near the door with two chipped bar stools. A trickle of sweat dripped down her back. But they were in. Now what? She hadn't dared to think much further than this. She had to move, but took a few moments to catch her breath. A sense of euphoria washed through her.

"Shall I get us both ciders?"

Eunice nodded.

"I'll be right back."

The pub was already busy, and silver tinsel hung limply on the back-wall shelves, its one nod to Christmas. At the bar, two young men chatted, one in a glittery silver jumper. Thankfully, Joan and Eunice weren't the only women. On the far side, a table of four were having drinks. Another couple sat at the table to their right. Joan tried not to stare as she collected their drinks and made it back to Eunice. But it was hard. Being here was equal parts thrilling and terrifying.

"I've never been in a pub before." Eunice sipped her drink as she took it all in.

Joan blinked. "Not once?"

Eunice shook her head. "My mum says they're not places for young ladies."

"She's probably right in normal circumstances. But I was brought up in pubs." Joan smiled, her shoulders still stiff. "We've had very different lives until now, haven't we? Plus, this is not a normal bar."

Eunice sat up. "It's not?"

Joan shook her head. "Look around." She did just that. "There are no boy-girl couples, are there? It's for people like us who are fond of each other."

A few moments went by before the penny dropped. Then Eunice whispered: "This is a pub for homosexuals?" She whispered the final word. Her cheeks flushed tomato-red. "Isn't it illegal?"

"Yes, but it's fine for us to have a drink as friends. Plus, the police mainly turn a blind eye."

"How did you find out about it?"

"Jimmy." She smiled. "There's another in Chelsea with dancing. This one has a piano, and it welcomes everyone: people like us, blacks, Irish, whatever. Anyone who's not welcome in the outside world."

Eunice's eyes scanned the room. "So most people in here are... *you know*?" Her tone was incredulous. "Even that woman over there with the long hair?"

Joan made a face. "*You've* got long hair." Long blond hair that currently flowed around her shoulders. Joan thought about reaching over and touching it, but she was still too conditioned not to.

Instead, Eunice put a hand up to check it was still there. "I do, but I'm not... Well, I don't know what I am." She paused, then crinkled her face. "Am I *that way*?"

"Only you can answer that." Joan tried not to let the rising tide of doom overwhelm her. It was easily done when it came to Eunice. She so wanted tonight to be a turning point. To show Eunice that life could be normal if she chose Joan. Chose *them*.

Eunice still stared. "My heart is going bananas," she whispered.

"Mine, too, if it helps," Joan told her. Then she put a hand on her knee.

Eunice froze, holding Joan in an eye lock.

"We can do this in here. It's okay. You can relax, be yourself." If she told Eunice enough times, maybe she'd be convinced, too.

"I can't believe you brought me to a pub like this."

"To tell you the truth, I can't either. But after this week, I thought, why not?" She stared at Eunice. "I missed you. I hated you being out with Kenneth. I hated this whole week at work."

Eunice hung her head. "I did, too." She looked up. "But if it helps, I have semi-good news."

"Kenneth has met the love of his life, his name is Derek and they're moving to Spain?"

Eunice burst out laughing. "Imagine. What a pair we'd make."

"I believe it happens all the time."

"No, he's not moving to Spain, and as far as I know, there's no Derek on the horizon. However, he is moving to Edinburgh for nine months. Which means he's not coming back to London for a while. It gives me more time to think about what to do about him. How to ease myself out of the situation."

"You want to ease yourself out?"

"You know I do, but it's complicated. My mum thinks the deal is done. Mrs Higgins is already treating me like her long-lost daughter. And then there's Kenneth."

"Maybe he'll meet Derek in Edinburgh. Or meet a lovely young Scottish lass named Heather."

"Maybe he will." Eunice paused. "What I know is it gives us time to breathe."

Breathing was good. "Nine months is a long time in someone's life. You could have a baby."

Eunice let out a loud laugh. So much so, the two women at the next table looked over at them. Was Joan imagining it, or did they just give both her and Eunice a look? She'd never met any other lesbians before. Was this what happened in these bars? If it was, she wanted more.

"If I'm pregnant, it's the immaculate conception."

That made Joan smile wide. "You know what else you can do in nine months?"

Eunice shook her head. "Tell me."

"You can fall madly in love with no way out."

Eunice looked at her like she'd hung the moon. "I'm already some way there."

Maybe all her worrying was for nothing. Perhaps Eunice *would* choose them. Joan stared at her, this woman who'd walked in and shaken up her life. Despite all the obstacles, she wouldn't have it any other way. At this moment, it felt like Eunice was the meaning of life, the reason Joan was put on this earth. To love her, and only her.

Joan leaned over until her lips were inches from Eunice. "You're the most beautiful girl in this room. There's no competition." Then before she could talk herself out of it, she pressed her lips to Eunice's for the first time ever in a public place. Because she could. Because she felt like it. Because it was the most natural thing in the world.

Eunice kissed her back without hesitation.

Joan wanted to punch the air. Kissing Eunice in public felt like sweet freedom. All the pent-up energy inside her released, and she floated away.

When they pulled apart moments later, she stared at Eunice, then around the bar.

Nobody had taken any notice.

In fact, the two men at the bar kissed now, too. Joan stared. Maybe others had stared at them, too. She didn't care.

She'd been holding her breath her whole life.

Now, she could finally breathe.

* * *

By 9pm, the pub was full, the volume had been turned up, and there was a very large man guarding the main door. Their table was full of empties, and Joan's head kept getting whacked by elbows all around. They were taking turns sitting in the outside seat, after Eunice got clobbered one too many times. Neither of them minded. Being in this pub was giving them both life. In the corner, a man with curls like Aunt Maggie played the piano to much excitement from the crowd. He'd just finished 'Roll Out The Barrel', and now he was on to a song Joan knew well from the wireless, 'Great Balls Of Fire'.

"Look at those two over there!" Eunice leaned forward and inclined her head to the left. "Her with the red hair. She looks just like any girl we might know. But she was just kissing that woman who's dressed like a man." Eunice couldn't stop staring. "I wonder why she does that."

"Dresses like a man?"

Eunice nodded.

"So she gets less hassle on the streets. So she can kiss her girlfriend in public and people think they're normal." Joan put the last word in finger quotes. "My mum's friend Jenny used to dress like that, and she was... like us. She always had a different woman hanging off her arm every time I saw her. She was my idol when I was seven."

"We really have led such different lives."

Joan took Eunice's fingers in hers and kissed them. "We have, but now we're here." She paused. "Do you think people look at us and think we're trying to be like a man and a woman?" She touched her hair. "I've got short hair, I wear trousers."

Eunice shook her head. "But you're still a woman. You're still enticing like a woman." Eunice put her hand to her mouth. "What am I saying?"

"That you're attracted to women?"

Eunice's face went pale. "Am I? I just know I'm attracted to you. In ways I never thought possible." She squeezed Joan's hand in hers, and locked their gazes. "What would have happened if we'd never met? Would you be here with someone else from the factory?"

Joan shook her head. Nobody could ever hold a candle to Eunice. Didn't she know that? "I don't think so. It was never about the factory. It was always about you."

The piano man passed around a hat, then shouted to the pub he was taking requests for a shilling. "Five shillings and your request gets played first!"

A woman with short, slicked-back hair wearing a shirt and braces dropped some money in his hat and whispered in his ear. The pianist nodded, then cleared his throat. He struck up a song Joan didn't know, the rhythm slower. The woman who'd asked for it walked over to the woman with longer hair she'd been chatting to at the bar, and held out a hand. The woman took it, and the pair swayed together as the love song got into its stride.

Suddenly, all around the bar, couples began to sway together. Men with men. Women with women. A wave of euphoria sailed through Joan. This was really happening, in a bar 45 minutes from Eunice's front door. Did this happen all over London? Could she find something similar near her? Her mind reclined at the thought. As Joan turned her head, taking it all in, the butch-femme couple Eunice had talked about earlier stood up, embraced and began to sway. Next to them, a young black couple did the same.

This was the pub for people who weren't welcome in

other pubs. A place that celebrated difference. Inside these doors, everyone could be who they wanted to be. Love who they wanted to love. Kiss who they wanted to kiss. Joan had always known about such spaces via her mum's friends, but she'd never realised what they meant until now. At the social club, she'd wanted to dance with Eunice the way boys did. Here, she could. Her heart ached for this slice of normality within her grasp.

She wasn't going to pass up the chance.

Joan stood up and held out a hand. Was this the most momentous moment of her life so far? It felt like it. Would Eunice feel the same?

Eunice stared at Joan's hand.

Joan's insides rippled. Her breath got tight in her throat. *Please take it.*

Eunice took a moment, stood up, then put her hand in Joan's.

Joan almost stopped breathing. She wanted to throw back her head and yell at how good this felt. Instead, she gripped Eunice's hand and pulled her towards the bar, where a crowd of slow dancers had gathered.

Somebody let out a low whistle.

The pianist segued from one slow song to another, his hat jingling as someone else added a shilling, then another.

Joan didn't blink in case this scenario vanished from sight. Instead, she kept her eyes wide open, circled a hand around Eunice's waist and pulled her close.

Eunice stiffened in her arms. Joan understood. It went against everything they'd ever been told. But it felt *so* right. She wasn't going to let go. She needed Eunice to do the opposite.

Joan put her lips next to Eunice's ear. "Nobody's looking. Just relax." She dared to leave a kiss on the top of Eunice's ear. Just that small act almost took her breath away.

The music roared in Joan's ears as Eunice slowly melted into her arms. She released a breath she didn't even realise she'd been holding. She and Eunice moved together, their bodies as one, and Joan's insides shook. Was this what it felt like for men and women? When they danced together and nobody stared? It was something so simple, and yet so hard to grasp.

She wanted to take a snapshot of this moment and frame it. Put it on her mental mantlepiece, and always remember where she was the first time she'd danced in public without a care with Eunice Humphries. The first time Eunice pulled her head back, stared into Joan's wide eyes, and before Joan knew what she was doing or could second guess herself, they kissed.

Right there on the pub floor in Notting Hill.

Nobody shouted.

Nobody cat-called.

Nobody ripped them apart from each other.

They were just two girls in love, doing what came naturally.

* * *

Later that night, they lay together in Joan's bed. She drew lazy circles on Eunice's stomach, slightly more rounded than Joan's own. She loved that about Eunice. She was still dazed and dazzled about the evening. Still stunned at what life could be like. If only she could transport the mood and glorious normality from that pub and sketch it onto her real life. But she didn't want to think about that right now. Eunice had just made her come like she never had in her life before. Right now, she wanted to focus on that.

"I still can't believe the pub earlier. Other women kissing. Men kissing. Us kissing. It was like some weird dream, only I was awake."

Joan kissed Eunice's golden hair. "I know. Is that what being married is like, do you think?"

Eunice sighed before she answered. "It's nothing like my parents' marriage. Although I suppose they could have been like that before I came along and then the rest of their kids." She paused. "But I can't imagine it."

"I've seen photos of my mum and dad dancing — slow and fast. They always looked so in love." Joan eased herself out of bed.

Eunice blinked, then sat up. "Where are you going?"

Joan smiled, then grabbed the photo she was after. "I wanted to show you this." She presented Eunice with a black-and-white photo of her parents. Young, all smiles, no idea of the cruel fate that was to become them. "This is my mum and dad."

Eunice studied it. "They do look happy. I've never seen a photo like that of my parents. I don't think they were big on photos. Or smiles. Or dancing."

"Mine lived for it. They loved anything where there was a stage. It's why I want to write plays." She put the photo on her bedside table.

"And you will." Eunice leaned over and kissed her. "When we live in Paris and I'm designing for the rich and famous, you'll be writing stories that everyone will want to see."

Contentment flowed through Joan. She loved it when

Eunice spoke this way. It was usually Joan daydreaming about their future.

"Maybe I'll write a story like ours. Of two ordinary girls who meet and change each other's worlds."

Eunice stilled, then kissed Joan's hand. "I've changed your world?"

Joan climbed on top of her and pinned Eunice's wrists either side of her head. "You know you have. Since I met you, life has gone beyond anything I ever dreamed of." For the first time ever, Joan wasn't hiding. Tonight, they'd been together in public. The world was changing. Just last week, parliament had debated a relaxation in homosexuality laws. Maybe they *could* be together.

"But I'm going to write my play, whether the world is ready or not. With lesbian characters at the helm. People will flock to see it." She pressed her lips to Eunice's. She was the happiest she'd ever been, in bed with the woman she loved. Although, holding her close in The Champion came a close second.

Eunice's long lashes fluttered. "I love your optimism. Also, your lips."

"I just love you." Joan's mouth fell open after the words escaped it. Heat seared up her. What had she just said? They'd danced around it, talked about falling for each other. But Joan had never actually said it to Eunice's face before. It just slipped out, because today had been an almost perfect day. They'd danced. They'd kissed. They'd made love. Joan never wanted another minute without Eunice by her side. Did Eunice feel the same? She hoped so with everything she had. But this was no time to be timid. With Kenneth in the picture, this was the time to be bold. To play the cards she'd been dealt. Eunice was her ace in the pack. Joan was determined not to lose.

"I love you, Eunice Elizabeth Humphries," Joan repeated. She tasted every word. They were warm, syrupy and delicious. She hoped they stayed that way.

Eunice stared back, her face passive. But then, just when Joan started to get worried, Eunice relaxed into a smile that wrapped itself around Joan's soul.

"I love you, too, Joan Hart." She threaded her fingers through Joan's auburn hair. "Wait, do you have a middle name?"

Joan shook her head. "My parents weren't very inventive."

"Then it's just you I love. Like I never dreamed was possible. I need you, Joan." Eunice put a hand up to her face. "I wish we could live here. In this moment. Just the two of us."

Joan's heart stuttered. "Me, too."

"I wish I could marry you."

Tears threatened, but Joan swallowed them down. "Me, too, like you wouldn't believe." Oh, how she wished that could be. But she knew it was ridiculous to even think it. It's not what happened for people like them. The best she could hope for was to be left alone to live this wonderful life.

"Will you still love me even if I don't become a famous fashion designer?"

Joan smiled, then kissed her again. "I'd love you whatever, and however. Even if you were in the gutter."

"It's not my plan, but it's good to know." Eunice reached up and kissed Joan long and slow, her teeth grazing Joan's lips. When they parted, Eunice never took her eyes away for a second. "But for now, let's pretend we live here together. For tonight. For as long as we can."

"My brother's away until after New Year, so it's us until then whenever you're here."

Eunice's eyes were shiny. "We've got nine months, and who knows how much longer after that?"

Eunice was thinking beyond nine months? A long-term future for them?

Maybe tonight was the turning point Joan had hoped for.

Chapter Twenty-Four

The first six months of 1959 slipped by quickly. In January, Eunice turned 18. Kenneth sent a card the size of her head, along with chocolates and regrets he couldn't be there. She celebrated with her family and neighbours, Mrs Higgins baking an extra-large cake for the occasion. Then at the weekend, she and Joan called into The Champion, before heading to underground lesbian club, The Gateways, the first night of many. Once there, they danced, breast to breast, locked together as one. As Eunice pressed her lips to Joan's, she couldn't recall a better birthday weekend.

They went to the Boat Race again in April, too, this time as lovers. They spent that night and so many others together in Joan's bed, and walked to work across London Bridge the next day. *Their* bridge.

Another month slipped by. More letters from Kenneth detailing all the management systems he'd learned in Edinburgh. All the systems he was going to implement in Birmingham when he got back. He also spoke about how much he missed her. It made Eunice squirm. How could he miss her so much, and she miss him so little? How could he put so much into their relationship, when they hardly knew each other? She had no answers. However, every time a letter landed on the doormat, Kenneth cemented his presence in her life.

Eunice's mother greeted each one with fanfare. Eunice was sure her mum read them when she was at work. So much so, she didn't bother to hide them. She left them on her bedside table. It was better her mum could get to them without going through Eunice's drawers. Without finding her journal. If she read that, she might never recover. That was where the real Eunice lay. That was where her love affair with Joan was told.

However, Eunice wrote back to Kenneth, because what else could she do? She didn't want to be rude. That was a cardinal sin. Especially to a boy like Kenneth. A good man. A solid man. A man who could offer her a future.

Eunice reached into her bedside drawer and stroked her Paris fund, safe in its Eiffel Tower tin. In another year she'd have enough saved for a week there with Joan. Just the two of them exploring the French capital like they always dreamed of.

On month eight, Eunice received the letter she'd been dreading. She got it on a hot August day when the sun was bright in the sky. She kept it in her bag and read it on the bus to work. Kenneth was coming back from Edinburgh. He was going to stay at his aunt's place. He was really looking forward to seeing her. Could she keep the August bank holiday weekend free? He had a question he'd like to ask her.

The tips of Eunice's fingers glowed white as she re-read the words again and again. A question he wanted to ask her. A question he was more than free to ask her. A question she wanted to slam on the floor and stamp on. But she wrote back yes. She'd keep the weekend free. Told Kenneth she'd look forward to it.

That afternoon, Eunice ran out of the factory when the horn signalled the end of the day, unable to face Joan. At Christmastime when they said they'd make the most of their time together, see how things panned out, it had seemed easy. Part of Eunice had thought she might fall a little in love with Kenneth, too, through his letters. That he might become the best pen pal ever. But Kenneth was more of a practical pen pal. He was no poet. Unlike Joan. Who wrote Eunice sonnets, who sung to her in bed in an off-key fashion, whose eyes she longed to wake up looking into for the rest of her life.

"Eunice!"

She turned. Joan ran towards her, her face flushed. How long had she been calling her name? It was a long way from the factory. Eunice had got the bus, then kept walking. Even though she had big heels on and her feet were killing her. Now she was on London Bridge. How the hell had Joan found her? Maybe she was always meant to find her. Another thought that made the letter inside her bag rip her heart in two.

She stopped until Joan caught up with her.

"What the hell are you doing? I tried to talk to you, but you almost ran out of work like you were on fire."

"I needed some space."

Joan raised an eyebrow. "All the way to London Bridge. I'd say you got it. But you're a bit far from home."

She bowed her head.

All around them, men strode by in three-piece suits. They clutched newspapers under their arms and sweated in the late-summer sun. Women moved their sunglasses up their noses, and held their sun hats against the bridge's strong breeze.

Eunice wanted to hold tight to her heart, in case it flew away. There was every chance.

"I don't know where I was going. But it seems I've ended up on our bridge." She looked up. "All roads lead to here."

Joan stepped up closer to her. "What's going on? You haven't spoken to me all day. Did I do something to upset you?"

Eunice's heart broke. Joan hadn't done a thing wrong the whole time. It was Eunice who'd fallen in love with her, and half-promised herself to someone else.

"No, you've done nothing. I'm the bad person here."

Joan's features softened. "You're not the bad person at all. You're perfect."

She didn't need to hear that from Joan. "I'm not."

Joan put her arms around Eunice and pulled her close. This part was always easy, because this was where Eunice felt safest. Like nothing could ever happen to her in Joan's arms.

"Come back to mine and tell me all about it."

* * *

"I got another letter from Kenneth today." Eunice took a deep breath, as if trying to cleanse herself. "He's coming to London next weekend. He's got something to ask me." She hadn't been sure she was going to tell Joan until that moment. But what was the use in lying?

Joan's face fell. "Next weekend? As in a week tomorrow?"

Eunice nodded.

"Shit." Joan stood up. She walked to the kitchen window and gripped the counter. "He's going to ask you to marry him."

Eunice froze. Hearing it come out of Joan's mouth was

far worse than it sounded in her head. And it sounded pretty final there. "I think so."

"Do you know what you're going to say?"

Eunice gulped. She couldn't lie to Joan. "I know what I want to say."

Joan twitched, but didn't turn around. The clock on the wall ticked.

The front door slammed, followed by somebody whistling loudly.

Jimmy.

Joan turned, but didn't look at Eunice. She disappeared into the hallway, then came back in, shutting the kitchen door. "He's going to give us an hour. He's changing, then going out to the pub for a pint." She pressed her back against the door and closed her eyes.

The hurt painted across Joan's face was almost more than Eunice could bear. She stood up and crossed the kitchen, then flung her arms around Joan's neck and buried her face in her breasts.

Eunice couldn't give this up. There was no question.

"I'm sorry, Joan. I'm sorry this is so messed up. You know what I want, but you also know it's not that easy."

Joan tensed, then slowly wrapped her arms around Eunice and kissed her hair. "I know." Her words were stilted.

Eunice looked up, meeting Joan's stare. "It's you I want. It's always been you."

Before Eunice could process her thoughts, she acted on impulse. On what felt right. She had to do what she wanted in this moment, because how many moments did they have left? In a perfect world, a whole lifetime of moments. Every day for the next 50 years or more. But she couldn't be sure.

So she kissed Joan with a ferocity and a passion like she'd never kissed her before. Searing kisses filled with rage and passion. Filled with a first love so strong, that whatever happened next, it would never leave her.

Eunice's hands travelled over Joan's top, then under it, her fingertips skating over Joan's soft, silky skin. She kneaded her bum through her trousers, then brought a hand around to the front and cupped Joan between the legs.

Joan moaned into her mouth.

Eunice couldn't imagine a time when that wouldn't happen.

"You're everything to me," Eunice whispered. She placed hot kisses on the base of Joan's neck, then across her chest. But she wasn't where she truly wanted to be.

When she unzipped Joan's trousers, Joan's eyes popped open. "Eunice," she stuttered, her eyes dark with desire.

Eunice shut her up with another kiss, then eased Joan's trousers to the floor. Then Eunice pressed Joan against the door, before sliding her fingers into her knickers until she connected with Joan's very core.

Joan opened her mouth.

Eunice closed it with her lips. Then she slid inside Joan with liquid ease and pressed her hips into Joan. If there was more to life than this moment, Eunice was yet to encounter it. When she began to move in and out of Joan, her lover spread her legs and moaned her name.

Eunice knew she was going to be replaying that sound over and over again.

"I love you doing this." Joan's eyelids were heavy as she spoke.

Eunice pinned Joan with her gaze, then moved her lips to Joan's ear. "I love you." When she introduced her other hand to the stage, circling and pressing Joan where she needed it most, Eunice grew taller. Moments later, when Joan grasped her shoulders, spat out her name and cracked her head back against the kitchen door, Eunice could have taken on the world.

Taking Joan against this door was something Eunice could never have imagined doing all those months ago, after her first time here. But together, they'd grown as a couple, grown in confidence in and out of bed. Now, they laughed freely in the street, not thinking everyone knew. *Nobody knew.* That their secret was so big and fantastic only added to its shine. That Eunice could now do this to Joan, make her this wet, still blew her mind.

Nobody could take this away from her. They'd always have the past year and they'd have each other. She and Joan were each other's first love, whatever happened next.

Joan Hart had Eunice's heart forever.

Chapter Twenty-Five

Joan had made a pact with herself. She had to let Eunice make her own decision. She couldn't influence her any more than she already had.

Rationally, she knew that. But telling her heart and accepting it was another story.

Kenneth arrived on the midday train from Scotland today. He was due to take Eunice out for the night, with a question to ask her. Even the thought made Joan's chest burn. She paced the kitchen. Lit a Woodbine. Stood on the balcony and waved at Mr Harridge opposite. It just reminded her of Eunice. She had to get out of the flat and get some air. Should she go and see her aunt? No, Maggie would just ask her how things were going. The answer wouldn't be good.

Eunice was on the verge of disappearing. Just like Frances. Just like her mum. Joan couldn't share this with anyone else. Not even Jimmy. She had to ride this one out on her own.

She so missed her mum. She would have known what to do. She'd exuded calm. Whereas Maggie, even though her heart was in the right place, always wanted to make things right. Sometimes, Joan just needed someone to listen.

She stubbed out her cigarette, but left it on a plate for later. Waste not, want not. Outside, the sun was a bright yellow button in the sky. She pulled on navy dress shorts, pop socks, white lace-ups and a lemon shirt, then checked her appearance. Good enough to win the day? She'd soon find out.

Joan strode along her balcony, waving at her cousin Stanley, who was kicking a football against the wall. The wall with the sign on that said 'No Ball Games'.

"Where you off to?" he shouted.

Where was she off to? She'd claimed in her mind she didn't know. But she did. She was going to the only possible place she could go this morning. She checked her watch — 10.23. She still had time if she hurried.

Was it a bad idea? Probably.

Was it going to stop Joan? Not a chance.

"Just going for a walk," she shouted back, before disappearing round the corner, up the main road to the tube. However, at the top of the escalator, she paused. Jimmy said he'd waited 40 minutes for a tube the other day. She didn't have 40 minutes to play with. She reached into her pocket and pulled out all the money she'd brought. It might be enough to get her within spitting distance of the White City if she took a taxi. It would definitely be quicker than the tube. She hesitated for a millisecond, then turned and flagged down a passing black cab. The door creaked as she hauled it open and jumped into the back.

"White City Estate, please," she told the driver. "The fastest route possible."

Whichever way he took, it was set to be the longest journey of Joan's life.

She lounged on the black leather seat, her bare legs sticking in the August heat. They slid across London Bridge and the

Thames, and Joan thought of meeting Eunice on this bridge and taking her home. Eunice had looked so broken when she was trying to figure out what to do. Joan knew the reality, even if she wasn't prepared to face it. She couldn't lose Eunice after the time they'd spent together, after everything they'd shared. However, she also knew the odds were stacked against her.

She kept her eye firmly on the meter, as the cab weaved in and out of traffic and headed west. They passed Trafalgar Square, and Joan thought of the failed CND rally. They rattled past Hyde Park and she recalled planning their future by the Peter Pan statue. She turned her head to gaze at The Champion, the site of their first kiss in public. The hairs on her arms prickled as she remembered every precious moment. When Holland Park tube station came into view, with its wide tree-lined streets, the meter hit 15 shillings. It was close enough, and it was all the money she could spend, unless she wanted to walk home later. She let the cab get to the end of the road before she intervened.

"I'll jump out here, thanks," she told the driver. She paid and watched the cab speed off, then get flagged down almost immediately. Was his next fare chasing the love of their life, too?

Joan jogged along the pavement, dodging in and out of the pedestrian traffic. She stopped at a watchmakers to check the time — 10.57. She was still a 20-minute jog from Eunice's flat. She'd be sweaty by the time she got there. She couldn't worry about that now. She imagined Kenneth on the train, with his overcoat, his neat hair. Perhaps some chocolates and flowers for Eunice. Should she stop and buy flowers, too? She couldn't. She'd spent her money on the taxi fare.

All she had to offer Eunice was herself. She hoped it was enough.

Joan's brain was reeling as she sped along the main roads. Past the Shepherd's Bush Empire and Loftus Road stadium, before eventually turning into Eunice's block of flats. She skidded around the courtyard, then took the stone steps two at a time. At the top, she paused, eyeing Eunice's front door. A hunk of wood between her and her dreams. She pulled back her shoulders and ran a hand through her hair.

Just at that moment, David came down the stairs. When he saw her, he stopped.

"What are you doing here?" His voice held an edge.

"I've come to see Eunice." She wasn't going to be intimidated by David.

"Does she know you're coming? She's got a big day today. She doesn't need any trouble from you."

Joan dropped his gaze. Was this a mistake? Bothering Eunice when they'd already said all they had to say? However, when it came to Eunice, there would always be more to say. But it wasn't up to Joan. It was Eunice who'd have the final word.

"I just wanted a quick word. I won't be long." She gulped.

Something flashed across David's face. "Check the laundry room before you go to the flat. She was about to put it out when I saw her five minutes ago. Second door on your right." He didn't move. "I mean it, though. Don't cause her more pain than she's already in."

She wanted to promise, but she knew she'd be lying. "We both want what's best for her." It was all Joan could offer.

David let her pass.

Joan pushed open the door to the laundry room. This time,

only Eunice was in there. Joan could see her feet, her dainty ankles, but not her face. She walked around the washing and cleared her throat. She didn't want to give Eunice a fright.

Eunice looked up and clutched her chest anyway. "Joan? I thought we agreed about this weekend." She looked around, then sucked on her top lip, panic settling on her features. "You can't be here. Kenneth's turning up soon."

Joan advanced towards her, shaking her head. Her stomach dropped at Eunice's words. Maybe she shouldn't have come. But she couldn't help herself.

"I know. I'm sorry. But I was going mad at home thinking about you meeting him. I just…" She held up her hands. "I don't know what I was thinking. I just had to see you."

Eunice dropped the blouse she held into the white plastic washing basket at her feet. She winced, but held Joan's gaze. "I know this is hard, but it's hard for me, too. You have to know that."

Joan took another step towards her. "I do." One more step. "But I couldn't let this happen without giving it one more try." She knew how pathetic she sounded. Just like Maggie had said it would be. Women always chose the man in the end, didn't they? Joan could think Eunice turned on the sun every day, but it wouldn't make any difference.

Then Eunice took a step towards Joan. In moments, they were in each other's arms, holding each other up.

"It's going to be okay," Eunice whispered. Her breath tickled Joan's ear.

"Is it?" Joan eased back and brought their heads level.

Eunice gazed into her eyes as she nodded. "Everything will work out exactly as it was meant to. You'll see."

Joan's vision misted. "But that's not true, is it? We're meant to be together." She prodded her chest with her index finger. "I love you, Eunice. You said you loved me, too, or did you forget that? We're the ones who've talked about a future together. We're the ones who love each other."

"I know." Eunice's voice was scorched.

"Then why are you meeting him when you know what he's going to ask you? I don't get it. You don't need a man. You don't need Kenneth." Joan had to get it through to her. Didn't Eunice feel what she was feeling? Had the past year meant nothing?

Eunice's face crumpled. She shook her head, looking everywhere but Joan. Her fingers gripped Joan's elbows for dear life.

Joan stared at the floor, willing her tears to stay away. She gulped once, twice, then focused on the dead fly at her feet. Outside, she could hear the sound of children laughing. Would she ever laugh again if Eunice left? Just the thought of it made her want to vomit.

If it was going to happen, she was glad she'd told Eunice how she felt. Now, she was going to show her.

Joan closed the gap between them and kissed Eunice. That's all she'd wanted to do since she woke up that morning. To show Eunice how much she cared. She hoped this achieved it.

She was pretty sure it had when Eunice threw her arms around Joan's neck, pressed herself against her, then slid her tongue into Joan's mouth. Then, it was like they were together in The Champion, where they were invincible. This morning, in the drying room, the same vibe pulsed in the air. It lasted the length of their kiss, which could have been five minutes or five days for all Joan knew. Like always when she was with Eunice, time became elastic. Possibilities burst in her mind. So long as they were physically connected, everything was on the table.

Their lips were still locked together, their eyelids closed, when someone called out Eunice's name.

Neither moved. She was vaguely aware of footsteps, then Eunice's name being called again.

It was only when the washing moved that they jumped apart.

Joan's blood whizzed around her veins as she looked left to see Mrs Humphries.

Joan didn't dare look right to see Eunice's face. She already knew all the blood had drained from her own.

"What the hell is going on? Were you two kissing?" She looked from Eunice to Joan, then back, trying to make sense of it.

"We were just saying goodbye," Eunice began. "Joan was upset about something. I was just trying to comfort her."

"By sticking your tongue down her throat?" Mrs Humphries' tone began to scale upwards with every word. "I honestly can't believe what I'm seeing." She shook her head, her cheeks colouring with anger. She pointed a finger at Joan. "I knew there was something off about you, but I couldn't put my finger on it. Now I can." She took a few moments, and Joan could almost see the penny drop. "Oh my god." She covered her mouth with her hand. "You've been staying at her flat together at weekends. Has something been going on all this time?"

Neither Joan nor Eunice said a word in reply.

Mrs Humphries gasped, then pointed towards the door.

"Get out, you harlot! Corrupting my daughter like that. Get out of our flats, and get out of our lives!"

Joan flinched as if she'd been slapped. Her ears rang. Her limbs were numb. The room seemed to tilt.

"Get out!" Mrs Humphries roared once more.

"I'm sorry, I never meant any harm," Joan said, glancing at Eunice.

"Well you didn't succeed. I've no idea how you managed to cajole Eunice, but it stops here. She's met a lovely boy who's very fond of her. He's coming today and he can offer her a great life. A job, a home, a family. Normality. What can you offer? Nothing!"

Joan threw Eunice a final look, but her head was turned, her body shaking. All Joan wanted to do was comfort her. But she'd have to get past Mrs Humphries first, and that wasn't happening today. She had no choice but to leave.

This had not worked out as she hoped.

"I'm really sorry, Eunice." Joan took a few steps, then turned back. When she did, Eunice stared at her, her face wet with tears.

But Joan could do nothing but walk away.

Chapter Twenty-Six

Once Joan had left, Eunice stood, staring at her mum. She had no idea what to say. She trembled, her blood hot with fear. This was new territory. Her mum had just found out she'd been sleeping with Joan. That she might be a lesbian.

Her mum had no idea it was way more than that. That Eunice was in love with Joan.

Maybe Eunice could reason with her. Make her see what she wanted. That this wasn't pretend. It was the realest thing Eunice had ever felt.

"You do your best by your children. It's all you can do. I thought things were going well for you." Her tone was full of nails. "But this? What on earth is *this*?"

Eunice bowed her head. "I didn't mean for it to happen."

That's not what you should be saying! Fight for her!

Eunice swayed on her feet.

"How can it happen by accident?" her mum hissed. "You kissed a girl, and goodness knows what else you've done." She glowered. "I've no idea how she convinced you, but it stops *here*. It's vile, unnatural, sick. While you're living under my roof, you abide by my rules. No more staying out at night." Her mum took a step closer to her. As close as she dared.

Almost like if she stepped any closer, she might get infected with the sickness, too. "Do you understand?"

Eunice nodded. What else could she do? She'd never seen her mum so angry. She was normally on her side. Not this time.

"This on the day you're meeting Kenneth. What if he'd walked in here? Nobody wants sloppy seconds, Eunice. Especially a man. What if someone else had seen you and told him? What if it had been Mrs Higgins?" Her mum shuddered. "After everything that woman has done for us. Fed us, opened up a door for you with Kenneth. Do you realise what that kind of perverted behaviour brings? Shame, that's what. On us, on you. You'd lose your job, lose your friends, and for what? Where was it ever going to go?" Her mum threw up her hands and shook her head. "I can't believe I'm even having this conversation with you." She walked up to face Eunice. "You're my good girl. My reliable girl." She peered closer. "Where's she gone? What happened, Eunice?"

Eunice shook her head, then wiped tears from her face. She didn't know what to say, how to describe it to her mum. She didn't know what had happened. Only that Joan had walked into her life, turned on the lights and shown her what love was. Simple as that. But it wasn't what her mum wanted to hear.

"I just… I like her." Eunice closed her eyes.

"Well you can just unlike her. Rewind the clock. Pretend this never happened." She paused. "Does anybody else know?"

Eunice blinked. David. Jimmy. Maggie. The crowd at The Champion and The Gateways. She shook her head. "Nobody."

Her mum sighed. "At least there's that. Let's keep it that way. Right now, you know what you're going to do?"

Eunice stared at her mum. Collapse on the ground? Wail at how unfair life was? She shook her head.

"You're going to pull yourself together, shake these strange ideas from your head and get ready. Put on a nice dress, a bit of lipstick, and try to present yourself as a respectable option for Kenneth." She grabbed hold of Eunice's shoulders. "You can get over this. One day you'll look back and see how right I was. How you just needed a guiding hand to put you back on the right path. The acceptable path. Okay? Now, go and get ready. I'll bring the washing. And Eunice?"

She met her mum's gaze.

"Never breathe a word of this to your father, it would kill him. Never tell another soul. It's better that way."

* * *

Kenneth turned up an hour later carrying red roses for Eunice, and a bunch of sunflowers for her mum. Eunice put on her brightest smile and accepted them with grace, her mum's gaze policing her every move. Despite that, Eunice didn't want to move from this kitchen. Didn't want to leave the flat. Because once she did that, the day was only going to get worse. She'd spent the past hour touching her lips, reliving the kiss Joan had laid on them. When she glanced at Kenneth, she was certain he was going to erase it later on, pressing his lips to hers.

She closed her eyes briefly. She couldn't think about it. She had to focus on getting through the next hour. If she tried to do any more than that, she'd break down and cry.

"You look lovely, Kenneth. Is that a new suit?" her mum asked.

Eunice glanced at it. It was ordinary, plain. Joan would never wear anything plain. She had style, grace, passion.

Kenneth tugged on his jacket lapel. "It is, thank you. Bought for the special occasion of coming here." He gulped and looked around the kitchen. "Actually, I was wondering if Mr Humphries was around? I'd love to take him to the local for a pint if he is."

Eunice's mum's eyes widened, then a slow smile spread across her face. "I'll just get him, I'm sure he'd love to." She scampered out of the room.

Which left Kenneth with Eunice.

She focused on the roses.

He focused on her. "I won't be long. A pint, a question, and then I'm coming back to take you on the date of your life."

Eunice tried to conjure up some sort of happiness, but she'd forgotten the shape of it. The feel of it. Happiness was elusive, and could slide away in the blink of an eye.

Her dad walked in, shrugged on his coat and slapped Kenneth on the back. They disappeared. Eunice wanted to as well.

She stood, twisting the strap of her handbag in her fingers, as her mum stood beside her.

"He's taking him out to ask the question."

"I know." Lead filled her stomach.

She cupped Eunice's elbow. "This is not a bad thing, Eunice. This is good. Kenneth is a lovely man. You can be happy with him if you give him a chance. You'll be able to live a normal life, but with an upgrade. Kenneth is an upgrade. Just remember that."

* * *

Seven hours later, Eunice sat in a secluded Italian restaurant overlooking the Thames. A stiff white tablecloth came down almost to her lap. The only other time she'd encountered a tablecloth was at their flat at Easter and Christmas, and at The Savoy. Tablecloths were for best, for an occasion. She fingered the thick material. She was at an occasion. She knew that now.

"They're called olives. Try one." Kenneth held out a small bowl of round green things to her.

Eunice furrowed her brow, but took one anyway. She put it in her mouth and chewed. She tried not to screw up her face, but she wasn't sure she managed it.

Kenneth did the same. "They're a little on the tart side, aren't they? My uncle told me that Italian food was going to be the next big thing, and he recommended this place to me. Met a big client here. When we move to Birmingham, I'll still have business meetings in London. You could travel with me and see your family while I'm having meetings, then we could eat out at restaurants like these." He paused, gauging her reaction.

He was talking about moving away from London. Why would she ever do that? Her brain couldn't compute. Instead, she tried to match a flavour to the olives. It wasn't like anything she'd tasted before.

Kenneth wiped his mouth with his white cloth napkin, then stood up. "But I'm getting ahead of myself."

A waiter arrived bearing a silver tray. He put two tall glasses of champagne on the table, gave Eunice a bow like she was the Queen, and left.

She glanced up at Kenneth. His face was flushed deep red. He took a long breath. Then he stood beside Eunice's chair, and got down on one knee.

First a bow. Now Kenneth was on one knee.

Perhaps she *was* royalty for a few moments.

Kenneth reached into his pocket and took out a small black box. He flipped the lid. Everything around Eunice stilled. It was like it was happening to someone else. Eunice watched, fascinated to see what happened next. Light flashed off the surface of the ring. The diamond was bigger than anything she'd seen before, its gold band winking, too.

Eunice stiffened. She tried to keep her face neutral. Tears danced behind her eyes. Would it be the worst thing to cry? Could she pass them off as happy tears? Why had she agreed to go out with Kenneth in the first place? How had her life come to this moment? She didn't love Kenneth, she didn't even know him. Despite that, he was about to ask her a question that might change the course of her life.

But only if she said yes.

It didn't help that Kenneth looked the most stressed she'd ever seen him. He took another deep breath, and his fingers shook as he held up the ring to her. Was he worried she might say no? He was doing all he could to avoid that outcome with this shiny bribe.

"Eunice Humphries."

He didn't know her middle name.

Joan did. Joan knew everything about her. Eunice loved Joan with everything she had.

She couldn't say yes. It would ruin everything. It would ruin Joan, her, *and* Kenneth.

But Kenneth couldn't hear what she was thinking.

"I've only known you for a short while, but you've made the biggest impression on me in that time. Now, all I want to do is get to know you better. For the rest of my life." He paused, making sure he had her gaze.

Eunice had read about this moment, and seen it in films. She'd heard her peers talk about it. Her friend Grace was engaged, the first of their group to be so. Was Eunice about to be the second? Her stomach caved at the thought, and her blood stilled. Up until this moment, it hadn't been real. Kenneth had been an abstract part of her life. A far-off boyfriend, busy doing his own thing, and letting her do hers. Now, he was right in front of her and looking into her eyes.

"Eunice Humphries, will you marry me?"

She'd known it was coming, but she still wasn't prepared. His words punched her in the gut, and Eunice sucked in an aching, jagged breath. Kenneth had done it. Sweet, gentle, kind Kenneth. On one knee, gazing at her nervously.

He didn't deserve her. He deserved someone who loved him. Someone he could hang his dreams on. Someone who didn't struggle to breathe at the thought of what came next.

She recalled being in Joan's bed, talking about getting married. She'd say yes to her in a heartbeat. No hesitation. She didn't need a posh restaurant, a flashy diamond ring, olives or champagne. All she really needed was Joan. Oh god, she wanted to scream, but she couldn't. Was this why men proposed in public? So women said yes?

Her whole body shook as she fought to keep a grip on her emotions. She could still feel Joan's lips on hers this morning, the thrill of being truly loved for who she genuinely was. Could she give that up?

Eunice licked her lips and tasted despair. What choice did she have?

"It's vile, unnatural, sick," her mum had said. But she didn't know what Eunice and Joan had, and her mum would *never* understand. She could never know the feeling of being totally laid bare, undone, and trusting the other person with everything she had.

Eunice was about to betray that. She had no choice.

Maybe it wouldn't be so bad? But even as she thought that, Eunice baulked. She knew how married people lived. She knew what women gave up for a 'normal' life. Even the thought of sex with Kenneth left her cold. How could it compare to Joan, to the pure pleasure she'd experienced?

As the net closed around her, and Kenneth's face wrinkled with concern, she knew she could only do one thing. It was her duty. She couldn't live the life she wanted. Her mum was right. Deep down, she'd always known. But how she wished it weren't true.

Eunice took a gulp of air and gathered all her courage. Then, with a leaden heart, she nodded and squeezed out the smallest smile.

It was enough to send relief flooding through Kenneth's face. "Is that a yes?"

Her body wasn't her own. Neither was her voice. She'd been taken over by somebody else who knew the part she had to play. She was the woman. The fiancée. The bride-to-be. The woman who her mother would never speak to again if she didn't say yes.

So Eunice nodded again, this time with slightly more conviction. "Yes," she whispered. Just one syllable, but it sealed her fate.

Kenneth grinned, rose to his feet, pulled her up and enveloped her in his arms. "We're going to be so happy. You're going to love Birmingham. My parents are going to love everything about you, too. I'm going to make sure you never regret this decision." He eased her back and held her at arm's length. "I'm going to make you the happiest Mrs Starling the world has ever seen."

Then he leaned forward and pressed his lips to hers, claiming her as his own.

But all that swirled through Eunice's mind was Joan. Her soft lips. Her pleading face this morning.

"I just had to see your face." *Darling, gorgeous Joan.*

"It's going to be okay," Eunice had told her. But she'd lied. She wasn't strong enough. She couldn't go against her family, against society, against the world. She loved Joan with everything she had. Maybe, in time, she could love Kenneth, too.

She just had to take the first step down the garden path, like her mum said.

Chapter Twenty-Seven

The rest of Saturday and all day Sunday had been almost unbearable. The amount of times Joan had gathered her keys, got to her front door, then stopped, were too many to count. It hadn't worked well the first time, had it? She had to wait to see Eunice today. To find out her fate. Although the weight in her body suggested she already knew.

The past eight months of Monday mornings had always been some of her favourites. After spending 24 hours with Eunice before she had to go back for Sunday lunch with her family, Monday morning was when Joan got to see Eunice again. Got to spend another eight hours with her. While they weren't as intimate as the weekend had been, it was always enough. Watching her as she sewed. Meeting in the toilets for secret kisses. She'd never enjoyed her job so much and Joan knew why. The reason was already at her machine when she walked in.

This Monday, though, Joan didn't bounce up to Eunice, tap her on the shoulder and give her their special smile. Today, it was difficult to even walk towards her. Did her hair look different? Did she look different? Joan couldn't fathom it. So instead, Joan got to her machine, hung her coat, then ran to the bathroom. She got into a cubicle, then put the lid down and sat on the cold cistern. She put her head in her hands. She thought she was prepared. But it wasn't that easy.

She took a barrage of deep breaths, but none made a difference. If anything, she found it harder to breathe. What on earth was going on with her? Her aunt had spoken about her maternal grandmother having breathing difficulties when she suffered with 'nerves'. Did it run in the family? If so, this was a very bad time to find out.

The door to the toilet swung open and Joan lifted her head. A few seconds went by before the silence was disturbed.

"Joan? Are you in here?"

Joan's heart wheezed in her chest. She stood up and unlocked the door. Eunice stood by the sinks, her hair pulled back with a clip as it always was. She wore her overall, like normal.

Everything was as it should be.

Nothing was as it should be.

Her right hand fiddled with her overall buttons.

Her left hand was wedged behind her back.

That's when Joan knew. She twitched as the impact hit her. "You said yes?" Her words were like bullets.

Eunice dropped her head. "I wanted to talk to you first, to explain."

Joan walked over and grabbed Eunice's left arm. She pulled it to the front and glanced down at her finger. It was adorned with a large ring that sparkled under the toilet lights.

Eunice's sparkle belonged to Kenneth now. He'd seen to that with this ring.

Joan's stomach lurched, and she almost fell to the floor. Somehow, she held herself up. She remembered what her mum had said after her dad was killed. "Sometimes, even if you play the best hand you can, the deck is stacked against you." That's what had happened here. Joan could never win in a straight shoot-out between her and Kenneth. It wasn't how the world worked.

She moved her gaze up to meet Eunice. "After everything we said?" She paused. "Congratulations." She spat the word onto the floor.

Eunice shook her head. "You've got to understand, it was so difficult…"

Rage rose inside Joan, until her whole brain caught on fire. "What about *our* plans? *Our* future? Was that all made up? Did you think of us when he got down on one knee? Think of anything apart from yourself?"

"Of course I did! You know I did." Eunice's words were strangled with emotion. "But I had to think of my family. My mum would never talk to me again. I can't take that."

Joan ground her teeth together. "I get it. I was only ever temporary until the right man came along." She stared at her hard. Suddenly, Eunice's face wasn't so vibrant. Everything about her wasn't so thrilling. The colour had gone from their relationship, and now Eunice appeared in black and white. If Joan stared long enough, she was sure her mind would start scrubbing Eunice from her memory completely.

"So this is it? Now I just get to wait for the wedding, throw my confetti?"

Eunice threw up her hands. "I don't know. This isn't what I want either, you know that."

She shook her head. "You say that, but actions speak louder than words. You said yes."

"But I still love you." Eunice's eyes sparkled like her ring.

But Joan couldn't comfort her. People left, she knew that. It hadn't stopped her hoping this time would be different. However, the outcome was the same as ever. After everything, *this* was where they ended.

"You say this isn't what you want, but it *is*. I'll be the brave one, because you can't be. We're over, Eunice." Every word burned her throat. Life meant nothing without her.

Joan gazed at the woman she loved, gathered up every last ounce of courage and walked out of the bathroom, straight into Kitty.

She blinked. Kitty existed in a different universe to the one she just left.

"Hey! Where's the fire?" Kitty held up both palms, then stared at Joan closer. "You okay? You're very red."

Joan just shook her head and walked back onto the main factory floor. Once inside, she glanced around. It wasn't yet 8.30. People were still arriving at work. She hadn't done a single stitch, and yet this day was already over. She sought out Mrs Armstrong and feigned illness.

As she strode back to her machine to get her coat and bag, the sound of the radio filled the air, and then it was tuned to their favourite station. A song crackled to life. Julie Andrews. Joan collected her bag, took a final deep breath and walked across the floor. She already knew that every time she heard this tune, she'd remember this. The moment her life changed forever.

Eunice was nowhere to be seen.

Chapter Twenty-Eight

December 7th, 1959

My dearest H,

I think about you most days. Okay, that's a lie. I think about you every day. So I decided to write it down, and perhaps that might make me feel better. It's worth a try. Writing this letter at least lets me get the feelings out onto the page, something I know you'd approve of. But I'm never going to send it, and you're never going to read it. It's just to stop me going mad.

Life in Birmingham isn't terrible. Kenneth is a good husband. He's even got me a job at the factory. He wants me to put together some designs and perhaps they can start making my lines. It's sort of unbelievable, but he's being true to his word. That's exciting. Some day, you might be able to buy some clothes I've designed. I'm always thinking of you when I design them. How they might look on your body. Even though I might never know, just the thought makes me smile.

I hope you're doing well. I hope the factory is still singing. I miss it. I miss getting pie and mash with Kitty and Mari.

I miss walking along the river with you. I miss our evenings at shows. But mostly, I miss you.

I know you probably think terribly of me. Some days, I don't know if I understand, or if I ever will. They say that time heals all wounds, and I suppose it might be true. I'm still waiting for the magic potion to flow through me. Maybe it never will. Maybe I'll always be wondering what if.

It's 5.30pm on a Wednesday. I got in half an hour ago. Kenneth gets home around 6.30pm, so I always have a little time to myself. I treasure it. It's then I can sit and daydream about my other life, about what might have been. I know it's not healthy, but it's the only thing that's getting me through. Just imagining and remembering our time together.

I'll never be sorry.

You told me once that all you ever wanted was to be loved and treated well. No, I think you said equally. We both know life's not like that.

Could it have worked? It's a thought that keeps me awake at night. Should I have been braver? I made the sensible decision. The one where my family still speaks to me. Where I have a place to live, a good job, and a good life.

But we were better than good. You were too good for me. What is it they say? You get what you deserve? Maybe that's why I'm here. Staring out the window of a three-bedroom semi-detached in Edgbaston. Facing up to a life as a wife, and one day probably, a mother. We haven't talked about having children, but I know Kenneth is keen. He has mentioned it, but every time he does, I shut down the conversation. He hasn't pressed it further.

I wasn't one of those little girls who liked dolls. I suspect you weren't, either. I haven't picked out my children's names. I'm scared witless about having them, to tell you the truth. Because right now, I can still feel you. Still remember you pressed up against me, the utter thrill of your skin on mine. You inside me. It wasn't just because it was forbidden. How could anyone consider that wrong? I've never known such rightness in my life.

But if I have children, it means I have to commit in a whole new way. That Kenneth and I are tethered together forever. And while that's not terrible — plenty of women have it worse than me — every time I think of it, there's a lump in my throat. If I have children, it's another step away from you. I know none of this makes sense. I know you'll never read this letter. I know the choice I made.

But it's all still fresh, still new. It feels like there's still a glimpse of you in my rear-view mirror. That I could just turn around and erase the past few months. Tell him it's all been a huge mistake and that I need to go back to London to be with my one true love. Kenneth liked you. I imagine he might even smile and wish me luck. Or maybe that's painting him fairer than he deserves. I did only marry him three weeks ago, after all.

But when I drift off to sleep at night, it's you I'm thinking of. It was always you.

I want you to know that if it was allowed and if you asked me, I would have said yes to you in a heartbeat. I wish we lived in a different world, one where we could be married. But that's never going to happen. We're more likely to be locked up in a mental asylum.

I wish we could have worked. I imagine setting up house with you every day. What I'd give for one more night.

Just know, it was never an easy decision. It was the hardest of my life, and it's one that still makes me catch my breath on a regular basis. I think Kenneth sometimes thinks he's married a mad woman, I'm so often lost in daydreams of you. I wish it could have been different. I wish it with every fibre of my being.

I'm going to finish now, before I wet the paper with my tears. Also, the pen's almost out of ink. I must bring some home from the factory tomorrow.

I'll never be sorry for loving you.

With all my love, darling H.
Eunice xxx

March 14th, 1960

My dearest H,

As spring bears down on us, I find myself thinking more and more about you. About us. About last summer and the time we shared together. The heat of your stare. The shimmer of your smile. How my breath was never steady when I was around you. I miss that. My birthday this year was nothing compared to last.

Kenneth took me out for dinner, and I couldn't help but compare everything he did with everything you did. He wanted it to be special and romantic, and he insisted on choosing everything we ate. It wasn't what I would have chosen, but I didn't tell him that. What was it mother told me before I left? "The man doesn't have to do romantic gestures, because they're paying for everything. But when they do, you must be grateful." I nodded and smiled, and it was a perfectly fine evening.

But it wasn't you and I, dancing together at The Gateways. Pressed together like nothing could ever tear us apart. Our evenings were never perfectly fine, were they? They were exquisite. You were exquisite.

I remember the look on your face, your eyes on my heart. I recall the casual way you skimmed your fingers across the top of my arm as you spoke. But most of all, I remember how effortless it all was. I never had to try with you, H. It was as natural as breathing.

As nice as Kenneth is, sometimes I feel like I'm underwater and nobody can hear me. Our conversations are muffled, the connection patchy. He doesn't understand me like you, and I'm starting to wonder if anybody ever will.

Is this what my life's destined to be? A series of events that all pale when put side by side with you? Sometimes, it feels as if I'll never be able to take a full breath in, and then out again. They're always rushed, and I'm always flustered. What if I'm not cut out to be a wife?

If you ever read this, I know what you'd say. You'd shake your head, and give me that look. You always said that life dealt people hands, and you have to play the one you have well, because you only get one chance. I'm terrified I might have blown it already.

What are you doing today, my darling? Are you lying in bed, windows open, listening to the sound of Southwark traffic? It's not just you I miss — although it's you primarily. I also miss London. I miss my family. I miss my mother, and who would ever have thought I'd say that? There are questions I need to ask that only she would have the answers to. I feel like I should have paid more attention to what she was doing as a wife when I was growing up, but I always had my head in the clouds, dreaming of something else. At least, that's what she always said.

The reality I'm living now is a world away from where I imagined I might end up. It's so quiet here for a start. I'm not used to quiet. Kenneth says it's preferable to London, and he's already settled. He has three pairs of slippers and a pipe, and he's only 22. He doesn't need much to be happy. In marrying me, it seems all his wishes have come true. I don't want to let him down and show him the real me.

The other day, I was walking back from the bus stop after work and there was a woman walking ahead. From the back, she looked just like you. When I looked up and saw her, it was like an out-of-body experience. My heart stalled, and all the breath rushed out of me. In my mind, I shouted, and you turned, and the smile that crossed your face? It was the one you always had when you saw me first thing in the morning at the factory.

In reality, I didn't shout. Because I knew it couldn't be you. Why would you be here, apart from if you'd come looking for me? Why would you do that, when I was the one who ended it, who chose a life of stability and duty over a life with you? That thought still wakes me up in the middle of the night.

Life is just not right without you. Even on my best days, when things at work go right, there's something in me that's off-kilter.

But when I saw this woman, there was a shred of me that believed it was you. That so wanted it to be you. I quickened my footsteps, felt the blood rush to my cheeks. When I got close to her, I was just about to reach out a hand and turn her around when she did it herself. Seeing her and realising it wasn't you was like a slap in the face. I stumbled, almost fell. My bones felt as if they might crack one by one. I so wanted it to be you, and yet, I didn't.

Because even if it was, what could we do? I'm still married. Nothing's changed. I played my hand and now I have to live with the consequences. For the record, the woman gave me a stare that told me not to walk so close to her. I stood still while she walked on, not wanting to make her feel strange.

I miss you, H. I thought the last letter would make me feel better, getting it all out on paper, but I'm not sure it did. If anything, it crystalised everything that's wrong in my life. You were the only thing that ever felt right. After I met you and we talked about a possible future, I began to see that perhaps there was a reason why I never paid any heed to anything my mum said to me. I always thought I was on a different path to everyone else. I was popular enough at school, but always disengaged. I was good at work, I fulfilled my tasks, but I always wondered what more there was to this life. There had to be something more, right?

I played the wrong card, didn't I? I listened to my mother. Why did I falter at the last? It's still a mystery. But getting away from your upbringing is so hard to do.

I know the road with you would have been so much harder. I just never accounted for my feelings being this strong. It doesn't matter if the ship you're in is stable when you realise it's the wrong ship altogether. Perhaps if I was on the right ship but the water was choppy, I could have learned to live with it? I don't know. And now, I never will.

Just know, I think of you every day. You're in every radio show I listen to. Every book I read. Every step I take.

With all my love, my darling H,
Eunice xxx

April 29th, 1960

My dearest H,

I'm sorry it's been a few weeks since the last letter. Life has been busy, and the factory is doing well. Kenneth has had to hire more staff as our lines have taken off. The company got a contract with Debenhams, which was a real coup. Kenneth brought home a bottle of wine to toast the success. It went straight to my head and I was a little squiffy when I was preparing dessert. I don't know how my dad used to drink so much. Apparently you get used to it, but I can never see that happening for me.

I should tell you also that I came to London to visit. It was Boat Race weekend, but we didn't go. I was glad of that. I felt bad not looking you up, but what would I have done? Shown you my wedding ring? I hope you understand. So instead, we visited with my family, and it felt all wrong. I saw David, too. That was the one bright spot. He told me he's got a job in Dagenham. Good for him. He's engaged, too. I can't imagine David a married man, but I suppose it comes to us all. Maybe even you. But if I think of you with a man, my stomach gets tight. If I think of you with anyone else, I have to distract myself. You've no idea the amount of stress baking I do at the weekends to keep myself busy.

My family were thrilled to see us. Mainly because we brought clothing samples from the factory, so everyone got new clobber for free. My mother told me it looked like I was settling into marriage just fine. That I suited the new hat, bag and shoes I'd bought for the occasion. Apparently, we're in a good place, now I have a husband, a house and a television. Possessions and money are how she measures the world. I only measure it in love. You once said to me you never wanted to live anywhere but London. I always wanted my own house with a garden. But it comes with a price.

Coming back to London was such a wrench. Everywhere I went, everywhere I looked, I saw you. I took the twins to the shops to buy sweets, and there was a woman in there buying bread and milk. She wore the cologne you wore. She had short hair, and wore similar clothes. We caught each other's stare, and I swear there was an unspoken language, something that passed between us. She looked nothing like you, but she smelled like you. I wanted to wrap my arms around her, but I made sure I kept them by my side.

Why weren't you there, H? Being in London without you made no sense at all. The streets sagged. The sky glowered. Everything tasted sour. It was as if someone had sucked the life from the London I knew.

Kenneth was all smiles, but I knew he'd rather be back in Birmingham. But he's polite and he does family well. It's another reason my mother was keen that I married him. "Men who tolerate your family are as rare as the Crown Jewels."

Kenneth's parents moved back to Birmingham, too, did I tell you? They live a ten-minute walk from us, and his mother has started dropping round on a Saturday. She enjoys my baking, and she knows there will be something fresh to eat. I think they're ready for grandchildren. They'd like a son to carry on the family name. It's all they talk about when we go there for Sunday lunch. After we left my family and Mrs Higgins, we called in on Kenneth's aunt and uncle before the drive home. They live in Battersea, so it was out of the way, but he insisted.

It was absolute torture driving across London Bridge, and being so close to Southwark, where I know you are. I could feel myself sweating under my Sunday dress. I shut my eyes as Kenneth drove the car. He asked if I was feeling car sick, and I told him yes. That way, he kept quiet, and I could be alone with my thoughts. The world you and I existed in has no place for anybody else. Especially not my husband. The world of us is just that. For us, and us alone. Even if it only exists now in my head.

I wish I could bake something for you, remembering how much you enjoyed cakes. There's not a day goes by when I don't hope it's you who walks through the door and not Kenneth. But I know it won't happen. I know I'm destined to visit London a couple of times a year and find it a foreign place without you. Even David will be gone next time I go back. He's moving nearer to his new job. He seems a little sad about it. I wish happiness for you, and I wish happiness for David. But perhaps happiness isn't as common as songs lead us to believe. I heard Tommy Steele on the radio the other day, and it reminded me of that day we saw him in Soho. I'm smiling just thinking about it. About us.

I love you, H. I know I told you before I left. I know we promised so much. I wish I could have followed through.

I hope you're having a lovely weekend by the river. I hope your aunt has dropped off some pie. I hope you're thinking of me, wherever you are. And if that's true, I hope you can cut out the bad thoughts and replace them with only the good. I know we had some good times. Some great times. Some incredible times.

With all my love, darling H.
Eunice xxx

June 17th, 1960

My dearest H,

The previous letters have all been about my sadness that you'll never see these letters. That you'll never know how much I think about you every day. That you'll never know how much I miss you.

This letter is different. I think I'm happy now that you'll never read them. Because this one delivers some news. News that I don't want you to hear. News that means I've betrayed you all over again.

I'm pregnant.

I told Kenneth last night, and he's over the moon. It's all he's ever dreamed of. Continuing the family name is important for Kenneth. I hope I can deliver a son. Otherwise, who knows how many more times this might have to happen. I knew it was going to happen, but knowing and then being told by the doctor are two very different things.

I feel numb. I know I should feel more, but I don't. I hope I begin to, because this baby doesn't deserve a mother who doesn't care. It's not their fault.

I don't want to tell another soul. Not my family. It will only become even more real when that happens. I've told Kenneth I'm not feeling well this morning, and he told me to take a week off. To put my feet up. That it's not just me I have to consider anymore. I absolutely hated those words. The only other person I've been considering is you. That's all about to stop, isn't it?

Is this the end of our time together? I know we haven't seen each other for months, but in my heart, I keep hoping we'll meet again. I suppose this means it might never happen. You're not going to run down the street and chase after a woman with a baby in a pram, are you? Not that you were likely to run down any street anywhere near me soon.

I've got something growing inside me now. Another human being. I've always been scared about it happening, and now it has. I remember talking to you about it, and you telling me that it can't be that bad, that women do it all the time. I wish you were here now, to put your arm around me, to console me, to tell me everything is going to be okay. I really need that. Kenneth is just so happy about it. He promised me he was going to skip home from work tonight, and that he was going to bring me flowers and chocolates. He also promised me fish and chips so I didn't have to worry about getting dinner. But it's not a kiss on the lips, or your strong arm around me. It's not what we had.

Right now, it feels as if Kenneth and me are leading two separate lives.

But this truly glues me to this life, and rips me from you. My stomach will balloon and I won't be recognisable. I'll start to walk with a wince, supporting my back with my right hand. I'll start to talk to other mothers, and I'll always be wondering if they're feeling out of their depth. If they're hankering after a former lover they can never see again. How many things are left unsaid, unspoken in our lives? How many of the women I see pulling toddlers and pushing prams are living the way they want to? We never ask, do we? So we'll never know.

Kenneth's uncle has a book of poems that he gave us as a wedding gift. He's a professor at Birmingham University, and very well thought of. I did wonder why he gave us such a gift, because Kenneth is not literary. He studied bookkeeping before his national service. Now he's in operations in the family business. For pleasure, he plays cricket and supports rugby. He thinks the poetry book would make a grand doorstop.

But I've found solace in that book today. I spent the morning reading it, while staring at the outside through the net curtains. The poets involved appear to have experienced love and loss, so they're now my new best friends. One of them describes himself as 'pierced with regret' for leaving his lover. I know exactly how he feels, and I don't think I could have ever described it better if I'd sat here for a week.

Our love has left me pierced with regret, H. It filled me so much at first, that it energised me, made me fit to burst. But as another of the poems says, falling in love is surprisingly easy. You slide into it. I know I did with you. But now, I'm trying to clamber out of it, and it's an uphill task. As if the fall was into a well, and getting out is impossible. The sides of the well are greased, and every time I think I might be close to getting out, a new memory hits me, or a smell takes me back. Then I lose my grip, and I fall back to the bottom.

I keep reading the 'pierced with regret' line. If I had to do it all again, would I change the outcome, knowing what I know now? I would love to say yes, but I know the world hasn't changed. Women like us are cast out, ostracised. I know you're loved at work and in your family, but what would have happened when everyone found out about us? As the years slipped by and we still weren't married? I don't have the answer to that question, or my original one. *Perhaps I would have stayed a coward. Perhaps I will to my dying day.*

The poetry, though, has also shown me that happy endings aren't the norm. Romance withers if you make the wrong choice.

Now it's not just me to think about, perhaps I need to focus on the life I'm living, not the imaginary one I crave.

I will never stop thinking about you and what we might have been. But my life has taken a different direction now, one I must live with. Writing these letters, far from getting my feelings down on paper, is now making me sad, so I'm going to stop. I hate that I'm going to stop. But it's the right thing to do. I'm going to focus on this pregnancy, as weird as it is. I will probably destroy these letters in time. Not right now. I can't face that as they're my only link to you.

I will always love you, and I will never forget you. Wherever I go, and wherever life leads me, I will forever have left a chunk of my heart in Southwark with you. I know you will look after it.

Take care of yourself, and find love when you can.

Yours forever and always, darling H.
Eunice xxx

Chapter Twenty-Nine

Present Day

"I behaved dreadfully, but I was so young. So green."

"We both were," Joan replied. "You broke my heart, but I think you broke your own, too. I tried to hate you, but it's hard to turn love to hate overnight."

"I couldn't do it, I know that much." Eunice stared at Joan, then shook her head. "I never stopped wondering where you were, how you were. If you were still alive. My greatest hope was to see you again, to tell you I was sorry. And here we are."

India sat forward in her chair, then glanced at Heidi behind the camera. "You're getting all this, right?"

"Of course."

"Good." India smiled at them. "Like I said at the beginning, if you don't want anything included in the final cut, it doesn't have to be. You've been remarkably candid and I so appreciate that. It's going to make your story resonate so much more. It's also going to turn you into superstars, I hope you know."

Eunice smiled. "I highly doubt that. Although my granddaughter will let me know if it comes true, I'm sure." She glanced at Joan. "I might be a little busy catching up with this one."

India tapped her pen on the white table they were sat at. "So that was it? You haven't seen each other since that day at the factory in 1959?"

Eunice shook her head. "Not quite. It was meant to be. I handed in my notice the next day to make it easy on Joan. I was moving anyway. She tried to do the same, but when she heard I'd gone, she changed her mind."

"It was never the same without you there."

Eunice covered Joan's hand with hers. Her heart thudded as she stared at Joan's fingers. She remembered what they'd done to her in the past. They still held power today. Every hair on Eunice's body stood on end. She was 79 going on 17 again. She still recalled crying in the toilet when Joan had left. How Kitty had comforted her, not knowing what was wrong so early on a Monday. Eunice wouldn't cry now. She'd had decades of experience in bolting down her emotions. It was going to take some time to unlearn that.

She glanced up at the camera, then at India. "It wasn't quite the last time we saw each other. The wedding wasn't until November, which meant two final months living in London without Kenneth. I tried so hard to be good, like my mother wanted me to. God love her, her heart was in the right place. She just wanted a better life for me than she'd had, like any parent. I understood when I became one myself." Eunice sighed. "I stayed away from Joan until one night a month before my wedding. Kenneth had come down to see me that weekend. Everything he wasn't, Joan was. I was going out of my mind wanting to see her. He went back to Birmingham, and that

Sunday, I got the tube to London Bridge. I hung around outside her flat, and amazingly, she appeared fairly quickly."

"I was on my way to get milk and bread from the shop."

"She never got it." Eunice smiled at Joan and squeezed her hand.

Joan squeezed right back. "We had a day together," she told India. "Jimmy was at work. We had the place to ourselves. A last hurrah."

India's mouth dropped open. "But that must have made it all the harder to say goodbye again."

Eunice nodded. "There were tears, I remember that. We got slightly tipsy, too. Drunk on some liqueur that Joan's mum had been gifted by an admirer at a show."

Joan let out a bark of laughter. "Did we? That memory eludes me. I just recall being thrilled to see you. To have a final time with you. But after that, we never saw each other again until today." She shook her head. "I can still barely believe you're here."

"Flesh and blood," Eunice said. "We had eighteen months together, and they taught me about love. They taught me so much. They also taught me about heartache, and they toughened me up. I never forgot you, not for a second. Nothing ever compared."

A tear worked its way down Joan's cheek, followed by another.

"Oh, my love," Eunice said. She still remembered the emotions like it was yesterday. She'd learned to bury them. Joan clearly had not. Good for her. Eunice leaned across and kissed Joan's cheek.

Joan stilled under her touch, then held her gaze.

In a flash, Eunice was back in those factory toilets, pressed up against the cubicle wall. Back in Joan's bed, lying knotted in her sheets. She already knew that would happen again later. But they'd have to take it slowly. Otherwise, Eunice might be overwhelmed.

"You were my first love." Joan wiped her tears with the tissue India offered her. "The one I measured everyone against. Reading those letters that you never sent was so heartbreaking. I wondered, though, why was I referred to as 'H'?"

Eunice sucked in a long breath. "It was my code, just in case anyone found them. I didn't want to put J. It seemed too obvious." She laughed. "It made sense in my young mind."

Joan gave her such a sad smile. "The thought of you away from home, so young, so alone. I'm glad I didn't read them at the time. I'd have come to Birmingham and kidnapped you."

"I wrote them over the first nine months of my marriage, until I got pregnant. When I still thought you might turn up, that I might get my fairy-tale ending. But it didn't happen. Then, once I was pregnant, I didn't see the point of writing anymore. The die was cast. There was no going back. It was me, Kenneth, and our future family. I had to try to forget you. I did the best I possibly could."

"You did the only thing you could have done in the circumstances. You were young, it was 1959, nobody would have blamed you for the decision you made." Joan paused. "Was Kenneth good to you?"

Eunice nodded. "He was the very best husband. Kind, considerate, and probably a little baffled by his wife who never seemed to settle. I was always looking out the window, waiting for you to come."

Joan raised Eunice's hand to her mouth and kissed it. "I wish I'd known."

"It's probably best you didn't." Eunice gave a wry smile. "We went on to have four children: two boys, two girls. And I have plenty of grandchildren and great-grandchildren, too. You met Cordy earlier. She's queer, too."

Joan's face lit up. "How wonderful!"

"The most wonderful thing is that she gets to be who she wants to be. How the world has changed in 60 years. In ways I could never have dreamed of." Eunice sat up and shook her head. "But anyway, enough about me." She fixed Joan with her gaze. "I forgot how gorgeously grey your eyes are." She could still drown in them. She looked forward to doing so later. "Tell me what happened to you."

Chapter Thirty

Joan glanced up at India, then back to Eunice. This was still so surreal. Some of the details might elude her, but she recalled the heartache like it was yesterday. Nobody else had ever had such an impact on her. Yet, even though Eunice had crushed her, that she was beside her now was a miracle. Joan was so nervous this morning, but now, she was so glad she'd taken a chance and come.

"When you left, it was awful. I kept on at the factory for another year. Someone else replaced you in your chair."

"You didn't fall in love with them, too?"

Joan snorted. "It was hard, but I didn't." She sighed. "Nobody could replace you."

Eunice gave her a sad smile.

"After you left, life was a constant rollercoaster. I just about managed to get myself back on my feet when you came back the month before you got married and we slept together again. I couldn't resist, but that pushed me back further."

Eunice dropped her gaze. "I'm sorry. It wasn't kind of me."

Joan gave her a slow smile. "I agreed to it. We were young and in love. You do things you shouldn't."

"That's the understatement of the century."

Joan shook her head. "Don't be so down on yourself. I'm

266

sure you had a good life. If nothing else, you have a family. You wouldn't forsake them, would you?"

"Gosh, no," Eunice replied. "My family are all a blessing. Life could have been so much worse." She glanced up at Joan. "But every step I took into my new life always had an echo of you. Whenever I saw lesbians on the TV. Pride parades. Gay pubs. It would always take me back to The Champion. To our fabulous nights dancing at The Gateways. Mine was a story well hidden. Nobody knew but you and me. How many others are there?"

"Maybe we'll inspire more to come forward."

"That would be very special." Eunice blinked. "But we're still talking about me. I want to know about your life now."

India sat forward, rapt. "You're not the only one."

Joan took a deep breath. "We still went for lunch at Rayner's, I even went to the Boat Race with Kitty and Mari the following year. But everything about my life reminded me of you. When I realised you weren't coming back, and that being a seamstress wasn't my destiny, I got a job in the theatre. Jimmy helped, of course."

Eunice's face softened. "You said he died?"

"Ten years ago. I still miss him dreadfully. He was so there for me when Sandra passed, too. But Vincent, his son, is a gem."

"Gay family! I still love that you have some," India said. "I'd love to get a quote from him for the documentary if possible. My company, Stable Foods, is sponsoring the biggest bus for this year's London Pride. If your nephew would like to come on it — with his partner or friends — he'd be very welcome. You two are our guests of honour, after you've led the Pride parade in your lesbian-pulled love chariot, of course."

Joan smiled. When she'd told Vincent they'd been asked to lead the Pride parade this year, now their story was big news, he'd been amazed. "I'll let him know, but he normally volunteers as a steward. Perhaps he can pop by later, though."

"Does he look like Jimmy?"

Joan nodded. "He's the spitting image. Sometimes when I see him, I have to do a double-take. He's married to a lovely man called Gary and living in the flat where we fell in love." She paused. "He really wants to meet you."

"I can't wait to meet him, too."

"But I digress." Joan sat up straight. "I got a job in the theatre, and when I wasn't working and seeing as many plays and films as I possibly could, I wrote. What is it they say? A broken heart is the perfect moment to get creative. It turned out that was true. I produced a few plays, and Jimmy had connections that got them in front of people who mattered. But obviously, I was a woman, and that counted against me.

"But I never gave up. Neither did my future wife, Sandra. She worked at the National Theatre as the director of productions. It was a prestigious role, and very unusual for a woman to hold it. But Sandra was tenacious and smart and she didn't take no for an answer. We met when I was 25 and she was 40. She helped me get noticed, we fell in love, and we were together for a very happy 32 years, until she died when she was in her early 70s."

"Did you get married?" Eunice asked.

"We did, but it wasn't legal. We had a ceremony with close family and friends in 1975. We were trailblazers."

"You certainly were." India shook her head. "This story is something else. You two were both so successful despite

268

the odds. Joan becoming a playwright, and Eunice a fashion designer."

Joan's eyes widened. "You did?"

Her former lover nodded. "For Kenneth's factory, but then the ranges I designed were picked up and produced around the UK. I never did a Paris fashion show, but in my own small way, I made my dreams come true."

Joan clasped Eunice's hand again. "I'm so thrilled for you. I always took more than a passing interest in the fashion world after we parted. Just in case your name ever came up. But I never saw it." She stared into her eyes, and suddenly they were back in her bed in Southwark, Joan stroking Eunice's golden hair from her hot face.

It was half a lifetime ago, and yet Joan could still remember how Eunice's lips tasted. Would they taste the same now?

"And you were a successful playwright?"

Joan nodded. "I was. TV writer, too. Plus, I lectured in scriptwriting at Goldsmiths and City universities."

"Wow." Eunice shook her head, smiling. "We both did what we set out to do. I'm so proud of you." She squeezed her fingers once more.

"And I of you."

India cleared her throat. "You two are making me well up. I'm also feeling like I'm intruding on a very private moment, so apologies."

Joan laughed. "One thing you find as you hit your 80s is that you care less about what people think, and also that you want to tell the truth, and you don't mind who hears it." She looked back to Eunice. "This woman here was my first love. I never loved anybody like I did her. But I had a happy life with

Sandra. I just loved her in a different way, that's all. When I explained it all to my nephew the other day, he asked me who was the love of my life. I told him you both were. Eunice set the ball rolling. Sandra kept it going. I thought that was my lot. Two great loves makes me pretty lucky." She sucked in a breath. "Meeting Eunice again is the icing on the cake."

* * *

Eunice was amazed at Joan's ability to forgive and forget. She'd hoped she might say something lovely about their time together, but now it had happened, she was overwhelmed. Eunice had led a charmed life, she knew that. Kenneth had provided well, she'd worked, her children were all a credit to her. But none of it made up for her erasing a part of who she really was. Stamping on her real identity and pushing it down so far, she'd almost never found it again.

As the years slipped by, she'd often thought that if she'd been born a decade or two later, perhaps she'd have had more courage to live the life she wanted. To be with a woman. She'd still have wanted children, just like Cordy, but her granddaughter could have it all. Eunice never thought this much change would happen in her lifetime, and she was thrilled it had. She'd thought it was too late for her. But maybe, just maybe, her final years were about to take a very queer twist.

She blew her nose, then pressed herself into her seat. She was fed up of the cameras now, but India had promised it would be just another 15 minutes, and then they'd be done. Then, they could go back to one of their rooms, and finally, she could kiss Joan Hart again. They'd both been a little shy of each other during their initial meeting. Now, she kept having to remind herself not to focus on Joan's lips. If she did, she'd lose her train of thought. It had already happened a couple of times today.

"What about your family and friends." Joan sat forward. "You've told me about your children and grandchildren. Are you still in touch with David?"

Eunice shook her head. "Golly, no. I saw him when I came back to the White City to visit my family, which we did a couple of times every year. But then he moved away with his wife and family, and we lost touch." She shrugged. "There was no social media back then, no smartphones. I hope he had a good life." David had been her touchstone throughout her childhood. "Remember when he caught us kissing on the stairs?"

Joan threw her head back when she laughed. "Like it was yesterday." She paused. "So I know you got married, had children, became a designer. But the big question: did you go to Paris?" Joan glanced at India. "It's all she talked about when we first met. She had a metal tin with a photo of the Eiffel Tower on the front of it. It was her savings box, and I never doubted she'd get there. Tell me I wasn't wrong."

"I haven't thought about that tin in years." Eunice remembered filling it with notes, counting them, then putting it back. "I took it with me to Birmingham when I moved, I remember that," she replied. "But I've no idea what happened to it. It got lost, subsumed into my life." So many things did, especially after you had children. "But I did get there. Kenneth took me for Paris Fashion Week. We left the children with his parents and had a glorious three days there." It had lived up to all her dreams, and more. But she'd thought about Joan while she was there. Joan had been like a shadow throughout her whole life.

She rolled her shoulders. The weight was gone. The weight of her shadow. Suddenly, Eunice was free. She let out a laugh.

Joan narrowed her eyes. "What's funny?"

Eunice laughed some more. "This is. We are. Sixty years. Wow."

Joan laughed, too. "You can say that again." She stared at Eunice. "Your letters, though. I know they were found down the back of a cabinet. Why did you put them there?"

"They weren't in the cabinet until right at the end. I kept them in my closet at first. How ironic is that? But while they were still in my house, we were still alive. Does that make sense? Then, once I had a child, then another, I wondered if thoughts of you, of who I really was, would recede. If anything, they got bigger. The letters were always there, a living monument to you.

"So one day, when Kenneth was getting rid of an old drinks cabinet, I decided to put them in the back of it. Stuff them way down, and off it went to the tip. I thought that would be the end of it. Only, it wasn't. Somebody rescued the cabinet, and then years later, the letters were found. I spoke to the woman who found them. She was lovely." They should send her a gift. After all, she'd brought them back together.

"The whole story blows my mind," India said. "It also makes me so in awe of you both. What rich lives you led, and what successes you were with so much stacked against you."

Joan glanced at Eunice. "You could have just burned them, though. We all had open fires in those days. Did a part of you want them to be found?"

Eunice stared at Joan. Her one true love. "Maybe. Who

knows? I didn't want them anymore, but burning them was too final. Those letters were part of our story, however painful. Even though I accepted it was over, I couldn't put a match to them."

"I'm eternally grateful you didn't."

Chapter Thirty-One

They walked back into Eunice's room so much wiser than when they'd left. The formalities of the initial meeting were gone, replaced by a strange familiarity. Even though they'd lived their whole lives apart, there was still something pulsing beneath the surface. Something Joan couldn't quite believe.

Her feelings for Eunice were still there.

"That was… emotional." Eunice sat in one of the gold velvet wingback chairs by the floor-to-ceiling window in The Savoy suite. She gave Joan a smile.

"It was." Joan sat in the chair opposite.

"You know, Kenneth used to bring me to The Savoy for dinner when we visited London, but somehow, it always reminded me of you. Central London was always flavoured with you. And now, here we are." Eunice fluttered her lashes. They were still long.

"I'm glad, and sad, all at the same time." Joan paused. "Can you believe we're going to be poster girls for long-lost lesbian love?"

"I can't. I'm not sure my family can, either."

"They're not supportive?" Eunice had said they were in the interview.

"They are. That's what they tell me to my face. But I'm

not stupid." Eunice's shoulders went up, then down. "I know it's a stretch to rethink what your mother is after all this time. My son, Tom, is having the hardest time. He's Cordy's dad, and he took a while to come around to her when she came out. But I think telling him this, it was almost like he thought I never wanted him and the life I had. He questioned his whole existence. We've had some big chats, but I hope with time, he'll be okay. His wife is great, as are all the rest of my children. They understand I loved them and Kenneth, and the life I had. That's all true. But I also want a chance at *this* life, too. The one I wanted all those years ago. Tom will get there, he just needs a little time. But I of all people can't push him to understand. I took 60 years to get there."

"I'm glad you did eventually."

Eunice licked her lips. "I never thought it would happen, but I am, too." She paused. "I'm so pleased you were happy, though. That you found Sandra. That I didn't ruin your life."

Joan gave her a wry smile. "You ruined it for a while, but everyone has the one that got away, right? But I found happiness, so it worked out how it was meant to."

"I guess that's what we have to believe, isn't it?"

"Otherwise, you'd go mad chasing a bunch of 'what ifs'."

She locked eyes with Joan. "You were always my 'what if'. I never stopped asking the question." She paused. "Did you ever go back to The Champion? I often thought of our nights there with great fondness."

Joan nodded. She'd gone back on her own and pulled a few times. She'd kissed numerous women in the bar, in the toilets, got her fingers tangled in their hair. But none of them had been Eunice. Once she realised she was only going back to find her, she'd stopped. "I did. It's still there, although it's not a gay pub anymore, so Vincent tells me. We should go back."

Eunice laughed. "Two old codgers, they'd never believe we used to have sex in the loo."

Joan's vision misted. "Some things are best kept to ourselves. But we can definitely do a tour of our youth. The Champion, my old flat, the factory. That's luxury flats now. Someone's sleeping where we used to sew."

"The old factory." Eunice shook her head. "It was great grounding for my future career. I'll always have a special place in my heart for Prestwick's because it's where I met you. I loved working with you." She fixed Joan with her velvety stare. "I loved you."

Joan trembled, then took a breath. She'd forgotten the power of those words, it'd been so long since a woman had said them to her. Eunice still had the capacity to leave her breathless. "I still love you. After all these years. Isn't that something?"

The air sparked with electricity.

"And I still love you, Calamity Jane. My secret love."

Joan's grin was the width of the Thames. "You remembered?" Her heart boomed.

A knock at the door interrupted their chat.

Joan blinked. She'd almost forgotten there was an outside world. She got up, floated to the door and opened it on autopilot.

A waiter in full suit and black bow tie came in with a shiny gold trolley. "Compliments of India. She thought you might like an afternoon tea." He whipped two chrome domed lids off two plates to reveal dainty, crust-free sandwiches, scones, clotted cream, jam and shiny cutlery. A pot of tea and coffee accompanied it, along with two glasses of fizz.

"That's so thoughtful." Joan closed the door. When she turned and walked back to the trolley, Eunice met her there, her focus intense. Joan's pulse quickened. Eunice had crow's feet round her eyes. Her face, though older, was still heart-shaped and beautiful. It was a face that had laughed, and had loved. One she could fall for all over again.

"Your hair's darker these days."

"I stopped dying it."

Joan blinked. "You weren't a natural blond?"

Eunice laughed. "Until I was about 12. Then I needed the help of a bottle." She smiled. "Afternoon tea is the perfect activity for two old women, isn't it? It's funny, but I don't feel old right now. I know how I look, and I'm not a teenager anymore. But being here with you, suddenly, I am."

"Me, too. Maybe we should start an Instagram account, really shock our families."

Eunice let out a hoot of laughter. "I'm game. Now we just need to work out how Instagram works."

Joan glanced at the tray. "Afternoon tea is great, but I was wondering if we could order room service." She raised her eyes to Eunice. "Say, fish fingers, chips and peas, and maybe some peaches for dessert?"

Eunice's smile lit up her face. "You remembered, too."

"One other thing. I took a chance that we'd be happy to see each other. Tomorrow, I bought us matinee tickets for the show that's on at the theatre next door. Would you believe it's *My Fair Lady*? Not with Julie Andrews, sadly, but it's had good reviews all the same. I thought we could do a West End show one more time. Like the old days. Only this time, I got us the best seats in the house. The posh seats. Remember we made a pact we'd sit in them one day?"

Eunice nodded, then entwined their fingers together. "That's so thoughtful. I'd love to sit in the posh seats with you." She sighed. "Oh Joan. So many wasted years."

Joan shook her head. "Don't dwell on the past. Like we said, 'what ifs' are no good. We have now, that's what matters."

Eunice gave her a defiant nod. "I want to make the most of now. I'm not eating a morsel of scone before I've kissed you again. The entire time in that interview, I tried not to look at your lips. I'm sure I failed, because they're as inviting as ever." She squeezed Joan's hand and pulled her close. "What do you say, Joan Hart? You always had *my* heart. Even in my darkest times." She brought Joan's fingers to her lips.

Joan focused on staying upright. A shiver ran through her. "That means everything to me." She stepped closer to Eunice. "I've dreamed of kissing you so many times." She ran a hand down Eunice's cheek. Then Joan leaned forward and pressed her lips to Eunice.

It was like she'd never left. Eunice felt the same, her delicious, soft lips the perfect place for Joan to land. She slid across them as Eunice's arm tightened around her waist.

In the blink of an eye, 60 years fell away, and it was just the two of them. Two teenagers in love. All they ever wanted was to be together. For the world to accept them for who they were.

Finally, they had their wish.

Chapter Thirty-Two

"Careful, Cordy!" Joan stepped back up her stairs as Cordy and her brother Elliott carried in Eunice's sideboard. "She wants it in one piece."

"Don't worry, it'll be in one piece." Eunice followed them through the front door. "They know how much that piece means to me. Any scratches, and they're out of the will."

That brought a laugh from Joan.

Eunice walked up to her and took her hand. "This is really happening, isn't it?"

"Looks like it."

After heading up London's Gay Pride parade and becoming two of the most famous lesbians in the country, Eunice had moved in with Joan for a month at her house in Greenwich. "Just so we can spend some time together, get to know each other again," she'd told her family. But she'd known if it was successful, she'd want to stay. She'd never lost her hankering for London, and now Joan was back in her life, there didn't seem much point not putting her two great loves together.

Now, three months later, Eunice was moving her sideboard and her favourite armchair in, along with her clothes and herself for good. Joan had told her they could buy a new house together if she wanted. However, Eunice loved Joan's

279

house. She loved where it was. Who wouldn't want to live by the river in Greenwich? If her teenage self could see her now, she'd never believe it. Eunice was getting her dream: a house with a garden in London, with the person she loved.

"Where's the armchair going, Mum?"

Eunice turned to her son, Tom, his face shielded by her favourite chair. "In the lounge. First door on the right."

She'd put her house on the market, and she'd already accepted an offer. She'd put most of her stuff in storage until she decided what to do with it. She'd never felt so light and so confident about a decision in her life. Her family probably thought she was mad doing all this at 79, but as Eunice had told them, she could have a good ten years in her yet. She wanted to live them to the full. She couldn't imagine doing it with anyone else, or anywhere else. London had always been her home. Now, Joan was, too. It was as simple as that.

Tom returned from carrying the armchair, smiling at the pair of them. They were still holding hands. Eunice fought the urge to drop it for Tom's sake. Her children weren't used to her being so tactile. She'd never been so with Kenneth, but with Joan, there was so much time to make up for. Her family would have to get used to it.

She and Tom had talked some more, and he'd insisted on driving her to London today. Like his father, he wasn't one for huge displays of emotion, but that was as good as him giving Eunice his blessing. She didn't need it, but it was lovely to have. Eunice suspected she had her daughter-in-law, Brianna, to thank for talking him around, along with Cordy and Elliott.

"It's a lovely place, Joan," Tom said. "I can see why Mum wants to live here." He flicked his head towards the lounge.

"I even saw some Julie Andrews records in there. Mum's always loved her, too."

Joan glanced at Eunice with a broad smile and a twinkle in her eye.

Eunice returned it with interest. Tom didn't know why his mum always had a soft spot for Julie Andrews. But they both did.

"Gran's not the only one who wants to live here," Cordy said, walking back into the hallway. "She might have made me homeless in Birmingham by selling her house, but I'm hoping I can stay in the spare room when I come to London. To visit you both, of course. But also, the queer bars and clubs. I might even trade on your fame, tell everyone you're my gran. Might score me a kiss from some hot woman."

Tom's forehead creased. "These are conversations a father never wants to hear."

Cordy gave him a grin. "Suck it up, Dad."

"You're always welcome, you know that," Eunice said. "But give us a few months before you crash our newly-wedded bliss."

Tom's face fell. "You got married?"

Eunice dropped Joan's hand and took her eldest son's. "A turn of phrase, darling. Don't worry, we'll invite you if it happens."

"I could carry you over the threshold later," Joan chipped in.

Eunice gave her a look. "You're 80, and you've had both hips replaced! I'll walk, thank you."

Cordy burst out laughing, then punched her dad on the arm. "Look at Dad's face. He's led such a sheltered life."

"I'm beginning to think I might have," Tom agreed.

Brianna walked out from the kitchen. "I love your kitchen tiles, Joan. I need to consult with you where you got them. I thought Eunice had great interior style. Looks like she met her match."

Eunice's heart swelled as she looked around the hallway. To her son and his wife. Her grandchildren. And finally to Joan. She never thought she'd get to be herself, never mind that when she did, all the people who mattered most in her life would meet and get on. Yet here it was, happening in real time.

"You're not wrong," Eunice told Brianna. "When I met Joan all those years ago, I knew I'd met someone special. My ideal match. But life had other plans. I'll never regret anything. I had a wonderful, full life. However, meeting her again is the sweetest ending of all." She glanced at Cordy. "When you eventually meet a woman you love, hold on to her, okay? Never let her go."

Cordy gave Eunice a salute. "Promise, Gran. I want exactly what you two have. Minus the 60 years apart."

Joan put an arm around Eunice's shoulders. "Making up for lost time starts here, right?"

* * *

They waved her family off, then walked back into Joan's hallway. Her hallway too, now. How life could change in the blink of an eye. Six months ago, she was pottering around her house in Birmingham, living with Cordy, enjoying her later years as much as she could. Now, she had a whole new chapter ahead.

Joan kissed her cheek as they sat on the sofa together, hand in hand. Eunice loved how physical they were. She'd convinced herself in her marriage that she wasn't that kind of person. It turned out, with the right person by her side, she was.

She nodded to Joan's marble coffee table, adorned with a huge seasonal bouquet, a housewarming gift from India and Gina. India had been in constant contact since she got them back together, and they'd even been for dinner at India's flash new pad. Eunice had been wowed by the deck, but she still preferred being here. She had no head for heights. Plus, her hot tub days were long gone.

"So sweet of India and Gina to send us those."

"It really was. She drove over to say hi while you were back in Birmingham sorting your house, which was lovely of her, too. Having worked in TV and met some questionable characters, India isn't one of them."

"She's not doing TV so much anymore, she told me. Focusing on her company. Good for her."

Joan nodded. "How was today, anyway? Your family, moving here for good. It's a big move."

Eunice smiled. "The right move."

"I hope so."

"I know so." She did. Her heart was full. She didn't need to know any more.

"No regrets?"

"I think we've both said they're pointless. So no, just excitement about the future with you."

"Me, too." Joan turned. "One thing, though. Your newlyweds comment. I know it shocked Tom, but it jolted me, too."

Eunice tilted her head. "It did?"

Joan nodded. "It's something that's crossed my mind. Because we can get married now. Whoever thought that all those years ago, kissing you in The Champion?"

"Not me." She paused. "I never thought it would happen in my lifetime."

"But it has." Joan held her stare.

Eunice took a deep breath. "Are you asking me to marry you, Joan Hart?"

A smile spread across Joan's face. "I don't know, Eunice Starling. If I asked, would you say yes?"

"Try me." Eunice quickly raised a finger. "But please, no getting down on one knee. Act your age."

Joan took her hand in hers. She trembled.

Eunice's heart swelled.

They locked gazes. Then Joan leaned forward and pressed a kiss to Eunice's lips.

Eunice's stomach swooped. How she'd missed it. "Yes," she whispered into Joan's mouth.

Joan pulled back. "I haven't asked you yet." She laughed. "You always were impatient." She kissed her once more, then sat forward. "Eunice Elizabeth Starling, the love of my life. Will you marry me?"

Eunice flung her arms around Joan's neck and kissed her ear.

"There's nothing I want more," she whispered.

THE END

Want more from me? Sign up to join my VIP Readers'
Group and get a FREE lesbian romance,
It Had To Be You! *Claim your free book here:*
www.clarelydon.co.uk/it-had-to-be-you

Did You Enjoy This Book?

If the answer's yes, I wonder if you'd consider leaving me a review wherever you bought it. Just a line or two is fine, and could really make the difference for someone else when they're wondering whether or not to take a chance on me and my writing. If you enjoyed the book and tell them why, it's possible your words will make them click the buy button, too! Just hop on over to wherever you bought this book — Amazon, Apple Books, Kobo, Bella Books, Barnes & Noble or any of the other digital outlets — and say what's in your heart. I always appreciate honest reviews.

Thank you, you're the best.

Love,
Clare x

Also by Clare Lydon

London Romance Series

London Calling (Book One)

This London Love (Book Two)

A Girl Called London (Book Three)

The London Of Us (Book Four)

London, Actually (Book Five)

Made In London (Book Six)

Hot London Nights (Book Seven)

Other Novels

A Taste Of Love

Before You Say I Do

Christmas In Mistletoe

Nothing To Lose: A Lesbian Romance

Once Upon A Princess

One Golden Summer

The Long Weekend

Twice In A Lifetime

You're My Kind

All I Want Series

All I Want For Christmas (Book One)

All I Want For Valentine's (Book Two)

All I Want For Spring (Book Three)

All I Want For Summer (Book Four)

All I Want For Autumn (Book Five)

All I Want Forever (Book Six)